Diamonds for Death

DIAMONDS
FOR
DEATH

Gregory C. Randall

Windsor Hill Publishing, Inc.
Walnut Creek, California 94596

ISBN: 978-0-9656510-6-6

DEDICATIONS

This book is dedicated to those young men and women athletes who strive everyday to be the best competitor and person they can be.

ACKNOWLEDGEMENTS

I have been a baseball fan for my whole life, first the Chicago White Sox and then the San Francisco Giants. I sat through frigid night games at Candlestick Park, a World Series earthquake, and two World Series victories during the past forty years. I saw Willie Mays, Willie McCovey, Bobby Bonds, Juan Marichal, Gaylord Perry, and Cuban Tito Fuentes, play the game in my early days in San Francisco. The new Giants' ballpark, AT&T in San Francisco, is a wonder and a spectacular venue to watch the new greats: Buster Posey, Pablo Sandoval, Matt Cain, and Madison Bumgarner. Sports books can be notoriously lame and boring. I have tried not to present the sport itself: the hits, the outs, the grinds, and the inevitable injuries; while interesting, they tend to be all too familiar to sports fans. It is still a simple kid's game of throwing, hitting, and catching the ball.

Every player who plays professional baseball has a story about their journey, Toro Rodriquez's is just one. With the recent increase in the number of outstanding Cuban players in professional baseball, I thought that this one journey—fictitious as it is—might give the reader a sense of what these men and their families go through to achieve their dreams. I am indebted to sports books by Jon Miller, George Will and others. I also need to thank the play-by-play announcers for the Giants, Mike Krukow, Duane Kuiper, Dave Flemming, and the afore mentioned Jon Miller. Their broadcasts are like going to baseball school; they not only describe the action, they teach the game. They are, by far, the best in the business.

As an independent publisher it is normal not to have the legions of people associated with a book's production. There are only two people who helped with the development of the manuscript. My companion, friend, and wife for more than forty years, and a new friend, Laurel Leigh, who was the editor for the final manuscript. Without either the story and the final product would be poorer. Many years ago when I told my father that his soon to be daughter-in-law was a baseball nut, he tested her. "Tell me what the infield fly rule is," he asked. Her description was better than the one in the rulebook. In most ways she is a bigger baseball fan than I am. She is also the sounding board and muse for all my books and stories. Many breakfasts and dinners become extended discussions of storylines and "what ifs?" Laurel is a new editor to me and has brought a fine pen to the story. Hopefully the typos, punctuation, and spelling errors are at a minimum. As always, any errors are the responsibility of yours truly.

"Play ball!" No greater words are ever spoken.

Fall, 2014 (2022)

The Night Before the All-Star Game

It wasn't surprising to find Jorge Guadalupe Cortez dead. It wasn't; he deserved it, really. What was surprising was that how the manager of the Cuban national baseball team died was a mystery—his body found sprawled over second base with no visible wounds on the infield of AT&T Park in San Francisco in the early morning hours before the All-Star game. His were the only footsteps in the vicinity on the manicured infield. The head grounds superintendent on hand when the body was discovered was extremely annoyed. To confuse matters even more, two days earlier in Amsterdam, he had been seen in the company of a lovely, tall blonde woman. His wife, at home in Cienfuegos, Cuba, stood four foot ten and was definitely not blonde. Since where Cortez's body was found was a potential crime scene with bizarre international ramifications, there was serious concern that the All-Star game would have to be delayed.

Chapter 1

Cienfuegos, Cuba, July 2000

In the shadow of the Cinco de Septiembre Stadium in Cienfuegos, Cuba rests a baseball field broiled by the tropical afternoon sun. The grass has long since dried to gray straw due to the lack of rain. Home plate anchors the ball diamond and is a square of splitting plywood spiked into the ground with rusted rebar. Each base is a top of a buried cinderblock, and the pimple of the pitcher's mound is marked with a wooden board nailed into the sand. The backstop is mostly missing; built originally from a tangle of iron pipes that predate the revolution, much of the chain link fencing is now rotted away. The baseballs match the color of the dirt, and are worn beyond recognition and might be mistaken for stones. Gloves are old, tattered, and often shared. The bats are dented Japanese aluminum. But in the world of Castro's Revolutionary Cuba, baseball is a religion with each base a Station of the Cross, each pitch a prayer, and each hit a sacrament. The ballplayers, teenagers really, stand along the rangy field's sidelines shuffling dirt, some with bare feet and others with spiked baseball shoes—now with their fourth or fifth owner—who mock each other and call the other team names.

"He's a good shortstop, but a *ganso*," one of the players yelled. And everyone laughed.

"That pitcher is damn good," said another.

"Yeah, but a *ganso*," laughed the pitcher's teammates.

Nobody joked or called the seventeen year old Toribio Rodriquez *ganso* when he stood in at the plate.

"*Primer strike!*" the umpire roared.

The tall youth in the batter's box turned to the umpire.

"*Si. Deberia haber oscilado,*" he said, smiling.

"*Si.* It was a good pitch."

"*No, hay problema.*"

The pitcher studied the catcher, reset his faded cap and nodded at the receiver's hand-sign. He glanced to second base and slowly began his windup, briefly stopping as he brought the ball past his waist. His eyes burrowed into the chest protector of the receiver; nothing else mattered in the whole universe except the center of that chest protector. He let the ball fly.

Toribio Rodriquez, bent at the waist, bat high, watched the ball fly from the fingertips of the pitcher and rip across the battered plywood home plate—and heard it thud into the catcher's mitt.

"*Strike dos.*"

"*Bajo!*" Toribio objected.

"*No! Strike,*" the umpire said loudly, talking over the head of the catcher. "And it was not low."

His hero, Barry Bonds, would have been proud of Toribio for staying inside the batter's box. He looked out at the mound and smiled. The pitcher ignored Toribio; he only looked at his catcher.

The next pitch was high and inside, just missing the batter's chin. He still hadn't left the box and continued to grin.

"Hey, Toro, he's trying to hit you. You gonna stand there and take it?" someone yelled from the bench.

Toribio winced as he dug his cleats into the earth, throwing dirt onto the plate. Finding size fifteen shoes in Cuba, especially cleated baseball shoes was difficult. The ones he was wearing hurt his feet. He was known to kick them off when he ran the bases after hitting a homerun.

Again, the pitcher looked in, paused, and then took a slow peek at the player standing eight feet off second. All he had to do was strike out Rodriquez and tally a win.

"Time," the catcher called and jogged out to the mound, which was no more than a dirty pimple in the coarse infield of Bermuda grass and weeds. "He's yours, keep it low outside, down. The most he can do is hit it to first. My guess the *ganso* will strike out."

He waved his threadbare mitt at the kid.

"Chico, look at my glove. Hit my glove."

When the catcher was set, the pitcher again wound up and threw. The pitch, a sharp, fall-off-the-earth's-edge, breaking ball mistake, bore in low on the hands of the right-handed batter. The stained and battered ball tumbled as if featured in a slow-motion movie and then with a sound like that of a single firecracker it impacted Toro's scarred bat, dead center. The ball rose like a rocket, high and arcing toward left field—all that was missing was a contrail of smoke.

When Rodriquez was three strides out of the box, he kicked off his too-small shoes and sprinted toward first. A gang of neighborhood kids, standing behind the low, ancient board fence that ran alongside left field, chased after the ball as it cleared not only the fence but the dirt street beyond and then bounced one great hop after another toward the great Cinco de Septiembre Stadium two blocks away. As Toro tapped second with his bare foot, his thoughts were of that magnificent stadium and a summer day when he would hit home runs to its cavernous left field. Watching all of this, the pitcher was pissed; it was his favorite ball and now it was gone, stolen by the street kids.

Toro's team met him at home plate—there were backslaps and bullshit, all aimed at him, celebrating their victory. The other team, until moments ago one strike away from a win, dejectedly headed to their bench to gather their equipment. Their coach, a small, wiry man, gathered them in like a goose gathers her goslings when there's trouble. He pointed to the other team and proudly watched as his young men walked over to shake the hands of the victors. Within minutes, there were jokes and more backslaps among the teams, especially for Rodriquez.

"That was the greatest home run I've ever seen, Toro," one

fellow said.

"Huge, maybe it rolled all the way to the stadium," said another.

Toribio *was* happy. It was a good hit; it was a huge home run. He took in a deep breath of the warm air coming off the sea and looked up at the rich, azure blue sky. It was filled with bulbous clouds that saluted their win by being exceptionally fluffy.

Then he noticed the strangers.

There were three of them, obviously government officials, standing alongside a formidable-looking sedan, its black exterior shimmering in the heat rising from the cracked asphalt. Behind the limousine idled an army truck flanked by three soldiers, none of them looking happy in the heat.

Toro and his teammates took furtive glances as they stowed their gear in thick canvas bags they slung over their shoulders and started to cut across the infield to head home. Looking at government people meant they would look back—and you never wanted that.

The two men standing by the limousine were dark. One had a pockmarked face and a mustache that resembled a jumbled mess of black wires. Swarthy would be a word used to describe him. The other man was narrow but not skinny, and looked as though he had been purposefully stretched to his height. Even his face and skinny-brimmed Panama hat looked extruded. Both men wore traditional white linen guayabera shirts over loose, wrinkled grey linen slacks. Pock Face smoked a cigar.

In contrast, on the left, stood a woman. Her green slacks and grey military shirt with red appliqués at the collar were in disturbing contrast to the men and their indigenous wear. Her hair was black and hung to her shoulders. What caught the boys' attention, besides the obvious fact that she filled the military blouse exceedingly well, was the pistol strapped to her hip. She and the others all watched the coach of the team that had lost.

Rodriquez and his teammates stopped and put down their bags, their curiosity expectant.

The losing coach hadn't yet noticed the agents. His back was to them as he talked to his young team, trying to raise their spirits. The loss had been tough. It was their third in a row and the trip home would be a long, hot bus ride.

As Toro and his friends watched, one of the boys said something to the coach, who turned and noticed his observers. He blanched.

The two men and the woman walked toward the coach; he bent down, said something to the boys and rubbed the head of one of the players. Then he bolted toward the lagoon across the street. The three officials followed and barely changed their pace, but the diesel engine of the truck roared as it lunged down the road after the coach. It was obvious to Rodriquez and his friends that the soldiers would intercept the man impossibly trying to escape. And within seconds, the truck had caught up to the manager and was pacing him. He slowed to a stumbling walk, unable to catch his breath, he heaved in and out; and finally stopped, his hands on his thighs, chest heaving. One of the soldiers jumped from the back of the truck, walked up to the coach and with an easy swing, hit him across the back with an old baseball bat. The blow dropped him to the street.

The three officials stopped in the shade of a large tree and watched as two of the soldiers took hold of the now limp coach by his armpits and tossed him into the back of the truck.

Toribio and his teammates picked up their gear and, not saying anything, resumed their walk home. When they reached the next corner, the government car passed them, the two men seated in front, and the woman in the back. Right behind came the truck, a tarp flapped across the rear opening briefly showing the shoes of the coach on its bed.

The boys watched the vehicles disappear down the road that passed in front of the Septembre 5th Stadium.

"He should have run faster," one of them said.

Toro agreed; they would never have caught him.

1b

Rotterdam, 2005

Toro Rodriquez—only his wife and mother called the twenty-two year old Toribio now—stepped outside the dugout and looked up into the packed stands of Rotterdam's Neptune Stadium. It was his second trip to the World Port Tournament playing for the Cuban national team. His All-Star team had won the last international series and was now leading in the final against the same opposing team, their hosts, Netherland's national team. Toro ran a pine tar rag above the handle of the bat; he was in the hole.

The stadium and surrounding countryside were even more beautiful than he remembered; it all sat in contrast to the hard, weed-infested playfields back home. Here it was like playing in an elegant church, almost like the great baseball cathedrals in America that Toro barely allowed himself to dream of. Barely age twenty, his life had changed for the better—everyone wanted his autograph and when he traveled, kids wanted to have their picture taken with him. It was all a whirl; he went where he was told, did what he was ordered to do, ate what he was given. There was only one thing the officials who now organized his life couldn't, or rather, didn't need to make him do, and that was to play baseball.

He'd heard that the tough American ballplayer Pete Rose had once said he'd "walk through hell in a gasoline suit to play baseball." Toro knew what Mr. Rose meant; it was all he thought of during the days, baseball. In the evenings spent alone in his hotel room, it was his wife waiting at home, their one-year-old son, Carlos, and baseball. For Rodriquez, life was perfect. At least it had been until a man stopped him in the hallway outside the locker room on the first morning of the tournament. The fellow had shaken Toro's hand, spoken to him in Spanish with a Caribbean accent and, after glancing up and down the corridor, passed him a small, thin envelope. *Confidencial* the outside read in stylish, handwritten script. What it contained was a simple list of questions on a single sheet of paper: Do *you* want to play in the greatest ballparks in the world? Do *you* want to play with great baseball teams that have the greatest ballplayers in the world? Do *you* want to be the greatest ballplayer in the world? And do *you* want to make millions of dollars and take your family out of the Cienfuegos concrete blockhouse they live in?

Twice since that morning, Toro had seen the man in the stands, well-dressed, huge gold ring on his right hand, Panama hat, obviously Latino, maybe Puerto Rican. But the man never stopped to talk and as far as Toro could tell, never even looked at him. But those questions on that small piece of paper nagged him. They were questions he was afraid to think of, they were forbidden—so forbidden he'd burned the paper and the envelope it came in. He was sure that someone, maybe one of the government chaperones, could read his mind. Afraid that his thoughts would betray him, he tried not to think about the questions, and instead thought of his beautiful wife and son. He had never forgotten the man who'd been clubbed in the street and never seen again—the affable coach who had only wanted to help the neighborhood kids living in their shit hole of a small village twenty miles outside of Cienfuegos. And the woman, he always thought about the woman, her sharp eyes and beauty, even if wrapped in a Cuban military uniform. He thought about her often on this trip. He had to because she sat directly behind him on the chartered plane from Havana.

She'd introduced herself to Toro as she passed him in the aisle of plane. Unlike on that hot day in Cienfuegos, her appearance was decidedly unmilitary: tight black skirt, blue blouse, and a black linen jacket. Her hair was pulled away from her face and wound up in a tight confection on top of her head. Gold earrings dangled and flashed in the sunlight cutting through the cabin windows like a movie projector's shaft of mechanical light. She'd looked down at Toribio.

"Good morning, Señor Rodriquez. Congratulations on the batting championship. It is a rare honor."

"Thank you. Are you with the tour people?" Toro asked,

knowing full well who the woman was, or at least who she had been five years earlier.

She told him that her name was Marta de la Vega and that she worked for the management group in Havana.

"It's a pleasure to finally meet you," she said.

"Thank you, *mucho gusto*," he'd answered carefully and watched her settle in and open a not so politically correct book on the Cold War and spies. He wondered if it was research. On the day the envelope had been passed to him, de la Vega had been absent from her usual spots in the hotel where Toro's team was housed. She always stationed herself in a corridor or a hallway or the hotel lobby, always.

Never standing still in the on-deck batter's circle was Toro's trademark. Now, like a great bull, he paced back and forth, taking loose swings as he studied the pitcher work the batter ahead of him. For a European, the blond kid could throw, fast hard-breaking pitches that broke down below the knees, a few so hard they bounced off the plate. The catcher was a kid from Aruba. Toro knew him from his younger days when they'd played other islands in the Caribbean. The catcher was hard and strong, huge hands, and not someone to take lightly if you were crashing the plate. One out, no one on; Toro slowed and scratched the ground with the club's head and watched. Baseball is a game of watching, looking for tells, looking for mistakes, looking for an inch to hit the ball a mile.

The Cuban batter popped up to the shortstop; the ball sailed like a dead pigeon tumbling through the Dutch air. The bat had been sheared off by the inside pitch—only six inches of handle remained in the hands of the batter. The kid tried not to show the pain in his fingers as he jogged past Toro to the Cuban dugout. Rodriquez touched his bat to his own helmet in salute; he knew the feeling.

To Toro, the Netherlands seemed like an entirely different world, the grass greener than anything in Cuba, a soft rich turf that he could feel through his custom-made shoes. As he waited in right field for an inning to start, he would often bend down and run his hands through the blades of grass. It felt as sensual as stroking a woman. The colors also seemed different here than in Cuba. He didn't know why. Maybe it was the sun and its angle, they were closer to the North Pole, he knew that. The colors dazzled, yet what he most appreciated was the temperature. Even on hot days, the weather was comfortable. For him, it seemed almost chilly for July.

He tapped his bat on the plate and listened to the crowd, which was more subdued than the ones in Latin America and Venezuela. There, in the dry barrios and desperate backstreet alleys, baseball was a religion, a game, a consecration; here it was a sport, a nuisance and annoyance to the real religion of Europe, soccer. Toro took his stance and looked at the lanky white kid on the mound whose long, blond hair stuck out like straw at odd angles from under his cap.

As the pitcher began his wind up, the first question popped into Toro's head. *Do you want to play in the greatest ballparks in the world?* All he could think was: *Get the hell out my head, now.*

"Strike one!" the umpire yelled.

Get out, now!

Toro raised his hand, calling time; he never left the box. He took a deep breath and raised the bat, two-handed, high over his head to stretch his back.

It flashed in his mind like a strobe light: *Do you want to play on the great baseball teams that have the greatest ballplayers in the world?*

Rodriquez concentrated on the pitcher, doing everything he could to push the questions out of his head.

"Ball," snorted the umpire.

Watch his arm, watch for the release.

The blond kid wound up and drove down the mound with his left leg, his foot sliding forward on the yellow dirt, the ball released exactly to where Toro wanted it, boring tight inside. He held up.

"Strike two."

Toro took a relaxing breath. *Got you, blondie, you're mine—do you want to take your family out of that shit hole?*

"Damn it. Time," Toro said.

"Be careful, kid, I need to keep this game moving," the umpire said in Dutch.

His authority was lost on both Toro and the catcher, who chuckled; neither of them understood what the man said.

Rodriquez tapped the thirty-five ounce bat on the plate.

Of course I want my family out, to be safe, she deserves it. She has no one but me and she's so good with my mother. Shit, concentrate.

"Ball two."

An easy one, low outside. He'll come in high, climb up on me.

Toro tapped the plate again and took a deep breath.

Do you want to be the greatest ballplayer in the world?

"*Madre di Dios, ya basta!*" Toro said aloud.

The catcher chuckled; he knew that a game was going on in Rodriquez's head and that the umpire's Spanish was limited to "taco" and "cerveza." His bare hand, snug against his crotch, flipped out one finger and pointed up.

The pitcher nodded.

Toro crowded in on the plate, tapped the dish and waited.

The greatest. Yes, I can be the greatest. I will be the greatest.

The pitch, unlike its predecessors, seemed to climb every foot on its travel from the pitcher's low-slinging fingertip release; the big Cuban stepped forward with his left leg, driving it into the ground, and spun on the rising outside fastball. *The greatest* flashed through his mind at impact; he saw the ball literally compress to half its diameter and then explode off the bat. It sailed high and kept rising. Toro turned toward first base to watch. No dead pigeon, this was a brilliant white canon ball fired at the high right field fence, six paces beyond the edge of the outfield grass. The right fielder spun and ran fast and true. He knew the park, knew what he needed to do. He timed his leap at the split second the ball and the fence were exactly the same distance from home plate. His glove just kissed the hide of the spinning ball, two inches short of an out. Cuba had won the game and the series; they owned the World Port Tournament.

Toro's new shoes felt like heaven as he stepped on third and headed home.

1c

That evening, the teams that still remained in Holland were celebrated on the lawn at the great museum Boijmans Van Beuningen by the Dutch organizers. Japan, Cuba, and Taiwan joined with their hosts in celebration; the United States left immediately after losing the consolation game. Toribio thought the American managers and coaches were poor sports. He knew that many on the team wanted to stay but the excuse given was that they needed to be back in America to rejoin their minor league teams. He was fond of and intrigued by the players he met from places he never knew existed, most especially Japan and Taipei. He respected their play and their sportsmanship, albeit a little taken aback by the Japanese habit of bowing to everyone.

Toro sipped on a Coca-Cola as more players and guests filled the lawn cluttered with great pieces of sculpture. They were lost on the poor boy from Cienfuegos. *Why would someone make a sculpture that looked like a bent screw?*

"Señor Rodriquez, have you been thinking about my message?" a voice said from behind him.

Toro turned and again confronted the man from the tunnel.

"De la Vega's not here right now," the man said, in response to Toro's nervous glance around the gardens. "She has a small problem at the hotel with some missing passports."

"Something that you may have had a part in?" Toro asked.

The man—who introduced himself as Eduardo Mendez—half smiled.

"Things can go missing," he said.

Rodriquez looked down on Mendez, easily eight inches shorter. He wore the same Panama hat as well as a crisp suit and dark tie. Toro could tell that this man had spent his life in the sun; his hands and face bore a tan that was layers deep.

Surprised, Rodriquez asked, "Are you the Mendez from Puerto Rico who played maybe pro ball twelve years ago?"

"The same, but twelve years ago I was at the end of my playing. I spent twenty-four years in baseball at short and third, four

American major league teams, a good career."

Mendez gestured for them to walk, and they moved through the crowd toward the edge of the lawn. Mendez walked with a slight limp.

"You are an excellent fielder, and congratulations on the batting title," he said to Toro. "There are a lot of excellent Cuban hitters in your squad."

"Then why didn't you give them the letter?"

"What makes you think I haven't?"

Toro looked around again for de la Vega or any of his other minders. He kept his voice low. "I have been warned about men like you, coyotes, who prey on the Cuban youth and tease them with dreams of America. You get them to America and then abandon them. They can never return home and they die, lost and forgotten."

"I know that line. De la Vega uses it a lot. Scares men like you, scares men who would be their own heroes. Yes, I am something like that. To be honest, I'm a scout, a baseball scout. I look for talent and then try to put that talent together with an opportunity."

"For money."

"Hope to God yes, kid, for money. Major league teams pay me to find players with great skills and abilities, and if these players are successful, I am successful. I make a good living. I see below the roughness of the stone, I see the diamond inside."

"*Que?*"

"Someday you will understand, I see it in your eyes. Some kids can field, like yours truly, or are special and can hit huge home runs, such as you. There are many with talent, but few are complete players. But when natural skills and talents come together, I become interested."

Toro still felt nervous, but he was too interested in what Mendez was saying in quiet tones to walk away.

"You can run the bases with speed, you can hit for power and average, and there are not many who can cover right field as gracefully and as fast as you. So of course I'm interested. There are some in this world who can be truly great playing this game. And Toribio, my boy, you are one of them. With the right people, you can be the next José Tartabull from your hometown, or a Hall of Famer like Tony Pérez. Good God, boy, all these fellows had to fight for their greatness. And they and hundreds more were all Cuban baseball players."

"Can I be as good as Señor Bonds?"

"Maybe, if you let me," Mendez said. "Not everyone gets the opportunity."

Rodriquez stood looking across the lawn of the museum; the lights from Rotterdam's high-rises and towers shimmered in the evening. He thought of his wife and son in their two-room house, his mother, their life with nothing. This man was throwing him a lifeline, and with it maybe a new life.

"I need to think about this, Señor Mendez. It is a big decision."

"I know that, kid. Tomorrow you go home to Cuba to your pretty wife and child. I understand. Yet your keepers and managers won't let you piss without help. I only have a minute more, so listen. Tomorrow morning, if you decide to go with me, I will be at the coffee shop across the street from your hotel. Stand outside the lobby of the hotel like you are waiting for the bus. If you are going with me, wear your baseball cap. A taxi will pull up in front and a man will call your name. Get in, and the new life will be yours. Very simple."

"And if I don't show up?"

"My loss, and have a good life."

"My wife?"

"I know some people who will get your wife and baby out. They are quite good at it."

"My mother, too?"

"Yes, and your mother."

After a long and sleepless night, Rodriquez stood at the hotel entryway, his bag sat next him on the terrazzo paving. Grey clouds scudded in from the North Sea, flattening the shadows and leaving a heavy mist in the air. As he looked out at the street, drizzle began to spot the pavement. The Cuban players were starting to gather in the lobby; the bus was to leave in twenty minutes. He was scared; he had never been this frightened in his whole life. He twisted the cap he held in his hands. More players arrived, filling the lobby with their bags. After ten minutes, Toribio was about to throw up.

"You okay, Señor Rodriquez? You look a little ill," Marta de la Vega said, startling him.

His stomach flipped.

"*Si*, Señorita de la Vega, I'm fine. Maybe the weather, maybe something I ate last night."

Vega studied Rodriquez. She was wise to the ways of the Americanos and knew this was the time to watch and study her players. Nervousness was always the giveaway. Once they were on the bus, she could relax. Her people were watching all the exits, making sure they were secured.

"You sure? Can I get you anything?"

"No, I will be alright after the bus comes. Just the weather, my head is all stuffed, I'll be fine."

Two ballplayers standing next to him and not seeing Vega bragged quietly about the girls they'd met the night before. Toro ignored them as he stared at de la Vega.

She smiled hearing their remarks; it was one of her jobs to make sure the girls for the players were appropriate. *Ballplayers were such fools, so easily managed, like children.*

"Tonight you will be home," Vega said. "There is nothing better—"

Yelling from deep inside the lobby interrupted her. The noise spilled out into the main room as two Cuban players bolted through the lobby and flung open the double doors to the outside, two of de la Vega's men in close pursuit. Vega sprinted after them as all four men ran down the road toward a slowing trolley, and with every stride of her long legs she gained on them. Rodriquez knew the boys; they were from Havana, a shortstop and the left fielder. As the two ballplayers neared the trolley, four white teenagers stepped out from an alley and intercepted the Cuban minders, knocking them to the pavement. In seconds a brawl began, kicks and fists thudded into soft bodies. Screaming at the men, Vega reached into her coat and drew out a pistol. Seeing the gun, the four white thugs threw up their hands and backed away, laughing and jostling each other. The trolley pulled away, the two players looking out the rear window at Vega. The shortstop waved.

Two hundred feet away, Toribio watched, shocked by the theater and the sudden appearance of Vega's pistol. When she turned back toward the hotel, she looked directly at him. He pulled his ball cap hard over his brow. The short toot of a car's horn turned his attention back to the auto-court, where a black Mercedes taxi sat idling. It's passenger side window slowly opened to reveal Mendez.

"You coming, boy?"

Rodriquez took one more look at Vega; she had her mobile phone out and was furiously yelling. She signaled to her men and they began running back toward the hotel; Vega slipped the pistol into the holster under her left arm, the gun once again hidden under her coat.

"Now, boy, you have five seconds to decide."

Rodriquez looked again at Vega and then, without a thought, walked to the taxi. The rear passenger door swung outward, and he threw his small bag onto the seat and climbed in. The door was yanked shut behind him and Toro immediately lost his balance and bounced off the back of the seat as the car briskly accelerated.

"Stay down, it's not over," Mendez warned.

Crouched on the seat, Rodriquez looked over the top of the rear headrest as another car, a BMW, suddenly appeared and slid to a stop on the damp pavement of the hotel drop off. Vega climbed in and the driver turned onto the wide street in front of the hotel. As Toro stared out the rear window, the BMW wove in and out of traffic, closing the gap.

Mendez said something to the driver that Toro didn't understand. His friends had chided him for years about learning English, claiming he would get further in America if he spoke the language.

"Why would I need to do that?" he had answered. "How do you know I will be going to America?"

"As sure as there is a God, you will play in America, Toribio Rodriquez."

And Marta de la Vega was trying her damnedest to stop it from happening. The cars continued speeding through traffic; Mendez shouted orders and their car made hard turns.

"Lot of good to someone in America if I'm dead," Toro said.

"And if she catches us, you will never play Cuban baseball again. That's the price you will pay. So pray that we can make it the tunnel."

"Tunnel?"

"The Maastunnel, under the river."

Mendez had his phone to his ear and was speaking rapidly, waving his free hand about.

A sharp crack sounded behind them, and the rear window of the Mercedes crazed from a hole halfway across its length. The bullet exited out the front windscreen.

"That's new; she's never fired a gun at us before," Mendez said, sounding much calmer than Toro felt. "That's a big gamble. The Dutch aren't too keen on firearms. She must really want you back, Toribio."

Mendez put his hand on the driver's shoulder.

"Now, Klaas, here, hard right, toward the tower."

The Euromast tower loomed above, marking the entryway to the seventy-year-old tunnel under the Mass River. The Mercedes leaned heavily into the turn but never lost speed. A massive truck trailering an orange shipping container was ahead of them. The Mercedes made a sudden move to the left lane, seeming to startle the truck driver. As the Mercedes roared past, the tractor rig began to fishtail and slide, ending perpendicular to the lanes of traffic. Smoke billowed from the skidding tires and the fifty-foot long container teetered on the outside rims of the trailer, threatening to roll off and chase the Mercedes into the tunnel.

Caught behind the sliding rig, tire smoke engulfed the BMW, whose driver had not been able to overtake Klaas's maneuvering. Good German brakes prevented the BMW from sliding under the trailer and becoming a convertible, or worse, guillotining everyone in the car.

When the Mercedes climbed out from under the Maas River on its southern bank, Mendez was again on his phone.

"Good, excellent. Yes, I'll pay the fine if there is one—don't I always?"

Mendez winked at Rodriquez, then tapped Klaas on the shoulder.

"The train station at Dordrecht."

"She will have people there," Rodriquez said, trying to help.

"Not this station. It's in a small hamlet just outside of town, no passports. The Europeans are so civilized. If anyone asks, speak Spanish, say Brussels, look confused."

"I am."

The train took them to Brussels-Central, the main station in the heart of the capital of Belgium. Señor Mendez and Rodriquez walked the two blocks from the train station to the Royal Windsor Hotel, where Mendez had reserved rooms; the hotel was just off the city's famous Grand Place. His room shocked Toribio, its elegance and style beyond anything the young ballplayer had ever seen.

"You have gone to a lot of work," he told Mendez.

"Not a problem, kid, tomorrow we are going to the American embassy here in Brussels, and you are going to ask for asylum. You are now a refugee from Castro's Cuba. Some paperwork will need to be done and hopefully within a few days we'll be heading for New York. From there, well, we will have to see what happens, but I have friends in immigration. So, my friend, you will have to trust me a few days more."

"My wife and baby?"

"I'm waiting to hear they are safe. We couldn't do anything too soon, it would have tipped off the government. So again, be patient. I'll know in a day or so."

The paperwork was complicated yet, as they headed to the airport with Mendez holding two first-class tickets, they still hadn't heard from Cuba. Rodriquez's gut turned over with every thought of his family. Finally, in the waiting area as they readied to board their flight, Mendez's phone buzzed.

Toro felt his knees go weak as Mendez spoke into the phone. "*Si, si, yo no lo entiendo?* Are you positive?"

He barely heard the older man saying, "I'm sorry, Toribio, no one knows where they are. They've vanished."

Chapter 2

Sharon O'Mara sat at her kitchen table, a stack of papers sat to one side, a brokerage firm's header visible on the top five pages, a large ashtray holding seven cigarette butts sat opposite. An unopened 750-ml bottle of Johnnie Walker Red Label sat midpoint between the papers and the ashtray. She took a deep breath, looked again at the trio, and then scratched the top of the head of her pooch, Basil.

"I never thought being rich would be this fucking hard, Baze. This girl has always liked the simple things. Now we can do anything we want, go anywhere, eat anything, and all I really want is a night's sleep."

Basil harrumphed in agreement; his mistress's late-night insomnia and wanderings about the cottage had cut into his sack time as well. He was having trouble getting used to her new schedule, such as it was.

Since the death of her friend and client, Alain Dumont, everything in Sharon's life seemed confused and off center; she hadn't had a good night's sleep in months. When she did sleep, her dreams were troubled and she awoke anxious. The two years she'd spent in Iraq began to come back in hellish nightmares of explosions and body parts. This was new; she had never had nightmares before about Iraq. Others, some close friends of hers, had gone through the PTSD shit and spent time in VA hospitals with shrinks who didn't have a clue as to what was going on in their heads. Maybe it was her attitude, maybe it was because her head was right, and maybe it was her red hair. Shit, she didn't know, she'd just counted herself lucky. Now, almost ten years later, she wasn't sure. She looked back at the stack of brokerage papers.

Taking a close friend's financial advice, Sharon adjusted the Apple stock gift she'd receive after Dumont's death and rebalanced the portfolio. She'd weathered one downturn and was very comfortable with how the stock had turned around. It'd been a smart move and one she wouldn't have made on her own. She stared at the account statement; she now had more money than she used to think she would ever see in her life. The fears of bills and living day to day were now gone. Basil would be in bones for the rest of his life.

And she also discovered that she had the abilities to handle her new professional gig well, in fact damn well. After returning from Iraq she'd taken her skills as an army cop and parlayed them into a new business, FACILITATOR it said on her business cards. She was now someone who could help those with a tough problem, a problem that might need more than, "… please and thank you." She imagined herself now as the capable character in John D. MacDonald's thrillers, Travis McGee—with tits. Yet even with all her friends and their grateful assurances, they couldn't keep away the gnawing thoughts that came late at night—thoughts that said faker, imposter, phony. In the light of day they went away and solid confidence returned, but the nights alone with her thoughts had become something she feared—hence the unopened bottle of scotch sitting between the papers and the ashtray. She stood and slipped on the *Go Army* Sweatshirt over the tank top and kaki shorts she wore and pulling her long red hair away from her face she twisted it into a makeshift bun on the back of her head and secured the pile with a large hair clip.

"Walk?"

Basil ran to the coat rack screwed to the wall near the rear door; his leash hung on the last hook. He sat and looked impatiently at the leash, then his mistress, then the leash. His broad tail slapped back and forth across the linoleum floor, throwing bits of dog food, dust balls, and God knew what under the refrigerator. Sharon pulled down the leash and secured it to the ring on Basil's wide red leather collar. It was new with big chrome diamonds, bound to make Basil look tougher and richer to the bitches in the neighborhood.

"No pulling, got it? This will be a quick walk, and then back home. I have a lunch date with your good friend, Kevin."

The dog looked at her with his brown eyes, and at the mention of Kevin became even more animated.

"Sorry, fella, not here. He's buying me lunch. Now that's a shock, especially since he doesn't have a job. But he sounded excited, so what's a girl to do? Free lunch, you know."

The stroll about the neighborhood was perfunctory. Basil never missed a bush and when they approached a neighbor, an elderly gentleman walking his standard poodle, the brief conversation about the weather allowed the German Shepherd–Rottweiler mix an opportunity, actually a mutual opportunity, to sniff all the right places.

Spring in the East Bay community of Walnut Creek was unusually warm and pleasant. But Sharon knew that her reputation in the tight collection of cottages in this small part of the village was held circumspect—three shootings inside and outside her small home during the past few years had firmly set her neighbors against her. Maybe it was time to move now that she had the filthy lucre to do it, just one more thing to add to her growing list of what-if-I and what-should-I do's.

After their walk, she dressed in comfortable jeans and a loose-fitting blouse held at the waist with a black patent leather belt. She stowed her Beretta in the small wall safe in the hallway, filled Basil's water dish, and left him a bone.

He looked at her as if asking, "That's it?"

"I'll be back in a few hours, be good."

She left Basil sitting in the hall looking at her like she had assigned him to detention and walked the six short blocks into town. Kevin Bryan sat in a back booth at one of their favorite restaurants, the Yacht Club. She watched his six-foot-six form slide out of the booth as she pushed her way through the lunch crowd at the bar—his black hair tousled Redford-like, and his face had finally acquired some spring tanning. She accepted a big hug and a kiss on the cheek and noticed the glass of whiskey on the table.

"So this won't be a dry conversation," she said.

"Not a chance, much to tell."

Kevin and Sharon's relationship was at once simple and complicated. They had known each other for more years than they openly discussed. Bryan had been recently released from his duties as one of Lafayette's better detectives due to budget cuts on the same day that Sharon O'Mara inherited millions, as if the money gods had switched off one poor soul as they clicked on another. However, the two of them supported each other as only friends could.

Sharon signaled the waiter and a glass of Johnnie Walker Red appeared.

"I have mine, you have yours, now what's so important?" she asked.

"I have a job. It's enticing and problematical at the same time; I've been offered a consulting contract for an insurance company."

"Good God, not that. Lord knows, I've been there. Those bastards steal your soul and your heart"—she waved him off with her fingers—"it's nothing but a dark road."

"It's short-term, three months. They want me to review security systems for a large client."

"What kind of client?"

"An international diamond trader. I start work next week, first New York, then London. All expenses paid."

"You dog, you know nothing about diamonds."

"Shhh, keep that to yourself. I know systems and how the bad guys work, so I look around at what they have and recommend changes and adjustments. Then a report, simple."

"I have found that nothing is simple with insurance companies, especially when big money is involved, and diamonds are big money. They are some of the most easily fenced goods in the world. Millions can fit into the palm of your hand, hundreds of millions in a size four shoe box."

"I know, I know," Kevin said. "That's what's got them spooked. Big money attracts professionals and they need to be sure their systems are as tightly controlled as the Pentagon's secret bathroom keys."

"That's not a good comparison in today's world; just remember what one man with a keyboard and thumb drive did to all those secrets hidden away on a server at the NSA."

"Yes, but secrets aren't diamonds. Gold is too heavy, a million dollars weighs forty pounds, and a million in diamonds is ounces. Scale is important."

The waiter had been standing discreetly to one side, and Bryan waved him over.

"Two fish tacos and another round."

"Make mine a chardonnay," Sharon corrected.

"I'll stick with the Jameson," Kevin said.

"How did you get the offer?" she asked him, after the waiter had departed.

"Remember the trouble with that kid and the stolen car, the one that ended up in the Lafayette Reservoir with water up to the doors?

Sharon nodded.

The driver, a bored, rich kid out for trouble, had been found passed out inside. He'd just missed plowing into a group of ladies jogging around the lake.

"Drunk as a skunk and only fifteen," she said to Kevin.

"The same. I got to know his father fairly well during the follow-up; he's an executive with a commercial insurance company. I helped the kid get probation and restitution. Dad was grateful, and the kid's done a good job of turning himself around."

"There was also something about the car's owner, a sports figure, if I remember."

"Ballplayer with the Athletics. He's now at Kansas City."

Kevin bit into one of the mahi-mahi tacos delivered by the aproned waiter.

"Took it quite well, I must say."

"It was a brand new Porsche, Kevin. It was absolutely the wrong way to treat that car."

"As the kid found out. The point is, the dad didn't forget, and when he heard about my forced retirement he offered me this opportunity. I have bills, there was a serious advance, and voila, I took it."

"I hate voila. You know how voila got us into trouble in Paris. Just don't say voila again."

"A change in perspective for me would be good right now, besides London's not so bad," he told Sharon. "You could come and visit, we could finally see the city that we spent only one hour in during our last crazy visit."

They both smiled at the memory of running from a bunch of Nazis.

"Speed *was* critical," Sharon said.

"So think about it, change is good."

"Don't talk to me about change. What I've been through, well, I wouldn't wish it on anyone."

"It's tough being rich, I get it, and I really mean it. There are responsibilities, but the past couple of years have been good for you."

"Thanks for that," Sharon said, as she finished her last bite of taco.

"You jumped in up to your cute neck and now have a good business and have some wonderful friends because of it."

"True, you never know what will happen unless you get out of your comfortable skin once in a while. London, one of my favorite cities and only two hours from Paris and . . ."

"Claudette?"

"Yes, you were good for her."

Claudette Leclair, the granddaughter of Sharon's inheritance benefactor, owned a Paris-based software company and had become a close friend to both Sharon and Kevin. It was through a mutual friend that Sharon had met Claudette's grandfather, Alain Dumont. Eventually, Sharon and Claudette and a house full of others had to be rescued by Bryan late one night, when a gang of Neo-Nazis busted through the front door of Dumont's mansion looking for the key to a horde of Nazi SS gold. Shortly thereafter, a romance had developed between Claudette and Kevin, but it was hard to keep a love affair alive with six thousand miles and an ocean between them.

"It would be nice to see her again," he said.

"Nice? I've never seen you happier. When do you go?"

"Next week. A couple of days in New York to get acclimated, meet their people. In fact, they are flying in from London. Then to England and take a look at what they have. The director of the diamond exchange believes there are holes in their systems. He thinks his staff is becoming lazy and complacent. Since that big diamond heist in Amsterdam a few months ago, he's concerned that they might be next. The insurance company agrees and"—he grinned at her—"voila, I'm off to jolly old England.""Must you? But it makes sense. I heard that heist was fifty million in stones," Sharon said, as she nursed her wine.

"That's what was told to the press, but the company director believes it was four times that amount. The fifty million number was to save face."

The company execs hadn't wanted to scare the market, nor did the insurance company want to pay out the real amounts if it happened to their client, Kevin explained.

"Didn't want to scare the market?"

"Exactly and the insurance company doesn't want to pay out the real amounts if it happens to their client. So their request for help."

"Who *would* want to pay?" Sharon agreed. "But you know my opinion of insurance companies, thieves, and villains."

"Don't start. I received a good retainer, and I need to get a few things."

"Yes, you do. Your closet looks like Wal-Mart's bargain basement. So a stop is in order at Nordstrom's. I can't have you traveling about looking like a poor Irish tourist on a cheap holiday."

"Exactly, I knew you would help."

"As if all that could help you was a new suit. I feel like Professor Higgins and you are my Eliza Doolittle."

"Cute, real cute."

2b

Walnut Creek, California, a short forty-minute commute to San Francisco (on a good day), is a nouveau riche town sandwiched between a collection of Hispanic and other minority neighborhoods to the north and the moneyed refugees from San Francisco ensconced in newly constructed gated neighborhoods strung along Interstate 680 to the south. The town is common ground for class mixing and class friction. And it is a town where some people stand out, especially those with baggy pants, exposed underwear, too much makeup and tats. Then again there are the Persian and Lebanese refugees speaking Pashtun and Arabic at the local Starbucks taking up all the chairs. There were times Sharon could close her eyes and imagine herself in a Baghdad Green Zone cafe listening to locals talk about their day and the trivialities of their lives in a war zone. The town had become the classic cultural melting pot of the San Francisco East Bay. There was a time before the towers fell that the community had been diverse but the language was Spanish, now a dozen languages could be heard.

After a less-than-successful shopping expedition to the Nordstrom department store, situated in Walnut Creek's downtown plaza, and which targeted a younger and decidedly smaller male, Kevin found meager pickings.

"That one suit would've been okay," he said, as they left the store.

"It wasn't you, and I'm sure there wasn't enough fabric left to recut it to fit your shoulders. You wouldn't have been happy."

"Me? I would have been fine, but it seemed short."

"Tall and long is what we need," Sharon said, pointing toward the southern end of the open mall to the big-and-tall store.

"Although my guess is we're going to end up in San Francisco to see what we can find."

"Probably. Maybe tomorrow?"

"That'll work."

Interspersed between international handbag shops and glitzy women's underwear boutiques with their overly ripe window mannequins were a mix of high-end jewelry stores that featured diamonds and Rolexes in teasing sidewalk displays behind thick, bulletproof windows. In the mid-afternoon sun, these look-but-don't-touch trinkets dazzled window-shoppers. On the crowded sidewalk that bisected the mall, Sharon thought the women seemed purpose-driven, whereas the men, Sherpa-like, dutifully carried bags and boxes. Weaving in and out amongst the mostly middle class crowd were women pushing babies in strollers—wheeled battering rams clearing the crowd for their attending mothers, who steered with one hand on the stroller's crossbar and used the other to press a cell phone against their cheek.

"They probably drive that way," she said to Kevin.

"What?"

He was looking in one of the lingerie windows filled with a colorful and revealing array of unmentionables.

"Never mind," Sharon said, sidestepping a four-year-old on a silver scooter. "They say there are fewer children these days; wouldn't know it by all the parading going on."

"No kidding," Kevin said.

"A joke?"

He thought for a second, then frowned.

"No, just a poor choice of words."

They stopped mid-block and waited with a small cluster of shoppers at the curb for the parade of Mercedes and Lexus SUVs to come to a stop at the crosswalk. People were jabbering with each other and talking into phones, each within their own world, oblivious to their fellow shoppers.

"Now that's something you don't see every day," Sharon said, nudging Kevin.

He looked to where she nodded with her head; her red hair flashed in the late-afternoon sunshine. Double-parked in the street was a turquoise-blue Chevrolet Impala, a beefy arm, covered in tattoos, rested on the driver's side windowsill.

"A sixty-eight, looks in great condition, seems a little out of place if you ask me," Kevin said. "Especially sitting directly in front of that jeweler."

"The tats?"

"From what I see, gang and prison work. Pretty obvious," he added, as he pulled out his cell phone.

"You thinking what I'm thinking?"

"Well, it could be a gang banger buying his girlfriend a nice broach to wear to the prom, or it could—"

A scream came from the direction of the shop, and a woman began to frantically push her stroller down the sidewalk away from the store's double doors, starting a stampede of shoppers.

"I'll take the driver," Sharon said.

As she ran toward the Chevy, Kevin was yelling into his phone.

"Robbery . . . Broadway plaza . . . now. I'm a cop, plain-clothes on scene," he said, forgetting for the moment that he wasn't, his instincts cutting in.

The sharp report of a gunshot came from inside the shop.

"Gunshot!" Kevin screamed into the phone.

Sharon quick-walked to the side of the Impala. The driver, the only occupant, and clearly panicked by what was happening in the store, hadn't looked in his mirrors. She grabbed the door handle and jerked the door open and with her free hand deftly pulled the beefy man out of the car. His momentum and her leverage quickly had him laid out on the pavement.

"Don't move or you're dead, asshole. Police," Sharon said.

Meanwhile, Kevin slipped up next to the door of the shop and took a quick look inside. He waited. In the space of three heartbeats, a thin man bolted out the door toward the Chevy, clutching a huge chrome revolver in his right hand. Kevin crashed down hammer-like with his fist on the man's forearm.

The gun flew through the air and disappeared under a parked car; the kid's scream of pain was lost in the shouting and chaos as Kevin pinned him face-first to the sidewalk.

The sound of police sirens began to fill the swank street. Black and whites rolled in from both directions and slid to a stop, flanking the Chevy. Within seconds, ten of Walnut Creek's finest, guns drawn, surrounded Sharon and Kevin and their prostrate prisoners.

"Jesus H. Christ, is that you, O'Mara?" a voice asked.

"If it's not Sergeant Glenn Stack," Sharon answered. "You want to take these guys off our hands?" — she pointed — "Kevin has one by the door."

"Kevin Bryan?"

"The same."

"Moonlighting in my town?"

The sergeant looked over toward the jeweler's door, where three of his officers had joined Kevin and one was handcuffing the suspect. Another of his men was cuffing the driver still sprawled on the pavement.

The storeowner ran out the door.

"He put them in his jacket pocket," he said, pointing at the man Kevin had taken down.

One of the officers reached into the man's coat pocket and extracted a handful of stainless steel and gold watches. Diamonds embedded in the bezels flared in the sunlight.

"At least ten watches that I know of," the owner said. "And he stuffed some diamond rings in his pants."

The officer, not too gently, rolled the man over and felt his pants pockets and extracted a small handful of rings and baubles.

"You trying to fucking feel me up, pig."

"Shut up," the cop said, applying even firmer pressure with his knee on the man's kidneys.

"Shut up? Shut up? You shut the fuck up. Hey, that hurts," the man protested, as he was bodily lifted by two of the officers. "Shit, that fucking hurts."

"Don't twist, you just might accidentally dislocate your shoulder," the smaller of the two officers said, and she gave the man another jerk upwards.

"Shit, stop that, you motherfucker," the robber yelled to the crowd that was beginning to gather. "Police brutality, these fuckers are trying to hurt me."

In another neighborhood, he might have received some vocal support, but not here. In fact, there were a couple of people beginning to clap, as if the street theater was for their benefit.

Sergeant Stack walked over to where Sharon and Kevin waited.

"Awfully stupid thing to do, don't you think?"

"The robbery or our takedown?" Sharon responded.

"Both, damn stupid."

"You think? Don't know what got into us," Kevin said. "Just knew we couldn't just stand here and not get involved. Something had to be done. And Stack, there's a revolver under the car there."

The storeowner joined them.

"You the fellow who knocked that asshole down?" he asked, looking up at Kevin. "Damn you're tall."

"Accident of birth, I didn't have much to say about it. But yes, my friend and I seemed to have stopped them."

"Thank you so much. One of my clerks recognized the kid. He was in a couple times this week, just looking around, or so he said. He knew when Jake, that's my guard, would leave on a break. Jake wasn't gone for two minutes before he walked in."

The shopkeeper noticed the car in the street, its door still open.

"The other guy was waiting?"

"Yes, amateurs if you ask me," Sharon said. "He wasn't paying attention, stupid. Anyone hurt, I heard a gunshot?"

"*No, thank God*," the storeowner said. "He walked in, went straight to the display case with the watches and busted the glass with the handle of his gun. Then pointed the gun at the ceiling and fired. Everyone hit the floor. After he shattered the diamond case and shoved the rings into his pocket he ran toward the door. I couldn't see what happened next. The sun was shining directly through the windows, then the sirens and more of his yelling. After making sure my customers and staff were alright, I came out."

Sergeant Stack turned to Sharon, "And you, O'Mara, what the hell?"

Sheepishly, Sharon raised her hands, palms up.

"As Kevin said, couldn't let it happen. Fairly easy, as fat as he is, his reactions were a bit slow. Also got a whiff of hash when I pulled the door open—he reeks of the stuff. All contributed to his poor reactions. The other guy was probably blinded when he came out; the sun was right in his face. As I said, amateurs."

After the storeowner went back inside, the three stood along the sidewalk and watched the would-be robbers as they were pushed bodily into one of the squad cars. The scrawny one was still screaming and yelling at the police, who ignored him.

"Shitty the way they treated you in Lafayette, Kevin. Damn shame," Stack said.

"Thanks, but enough time has passed and I'm over it," Kevin answered.

"You know we'll have an opening this fall. I have two retiring."

"Thanks, but I have a gig with an insurance company, at least through the summer. It'll get me out of here for a while; gives me some time to think. So don't worry, this old cop won't starve. When I get back, I may give you a call."

"Good. Budget cuts and politics—if it weren't for those two things, being a cop wouldn't be too bad."

"There is the shooting and wounding thing to think of," Sharon added.

"Yeah, but it would be fun to see ol' Kev here roll up at your house after another one of those neighborhood shootings you seem to have semiannually and haul your ass into jail. I'd buy a ticket."

"They weren't my fault; gangs and bad guys. I was the innocent victim."

"Innocent victim? They went down in my town and I haven't heard the last of it from one of the councilmen and a couple of the older people on the street. One even thinks you're with the IRA and that you're running some type of Irish mob out of your house."

"And I'm sure you didn't say anything to dissuade them. And I'll call that racial profiling, by the way."

She jerked a thumb toward Kevin.

"How about this guy? His name is Irish."

"It is often better to stay quiet and watch what happens," Stack added. "And besides, I don't have enough personnel to follow each and every person with an Irish name in this town."

"Cute. Thanks Stack, I'll remember that."

They watched the parade of police cars leave and slowly drive down and out of the narrow retail street. With the bright lights and sirens gone, the crowd dispersed quickly. Shortly, the CSI van pulled up to take photos and collect evidence, and the jeweler stuck his head out for one last look into the street.

"Well, never a dull day in suburbia, contrary to what the sociologists say," Stack said, grinning. "We'll book these two, but we'll need your statements. Can you stop by later?"

They agreed on first thing in the morning—"see Nancy at the desk," Stark said, before shaking both their hands and heading back to his command cruiser.

The sun had settled below the horizon, leaving the sky orange and changing to magenta.

"Surreal, all surreal," Sharon said.

"Time and place. Five minutes either way and they would have gotten away. So yeah, kind of surreal. Dinner?"

"I'm up for a pizza, my place. We can pick one up on the way. There's a ball game on, they're playing San Diego, and I have a great cabernet from Mendoza. Pizza and baseball, nothing better."

"After all that happened, I'm surprised you can drink that South American stuff."

Kevin meant the horrible Argentine Nazi business that had, months earlier, occupied their lives. Sharon had also just closed the case of the murder of a famous America's Cup skipper, working on behalf of the dead girl's twin brother. In the process, she'd aided the U.S. government in shutting down a plot to steal a high-tech sailboat and use it as a missile against American naval ships in the Strait of Hormuz. Then had come the inheritance from Mr. Dumont, incidentally coinciding with Kevin being fired from his job as a detective in the town next door to Walnut Creek. Although budgets and politics had been offered as the reasons, he knew it was pensions and payroll. At least he'd been able to negotiate and save something of his pension and he had received a sizeable separation bonus. But now that money was dwindling, and the insurance job had come along at the right time.

"Had no effect on the wine industry," she said. "Besides, it's a bottle from Alain's collection. Claudette made sure I got a few cases from his cellar."

Since Sharon had walked to town to meet Kevin, he drove. When Sharon opened the door to her cottage, balancing a pizza in one hand and keys in the other, Kevin was almost flattened to the porch by Basil. The big dog nuzzled and barked at the big man.

"I give, I give," Kevin said laughing. "Sharon, call this damn dog off me."

"Basil, off, sit."

In a split second, Basil ran to her side and sat and watched as Kevin straightened his frame vertical.

"These bones and joints just don't work the way they used to."

"Tell me about it. Basil, inside and get your nose away from the pizza box."

Basil froze, thinking crusts and sausage, then suddenly spun around and faced the street; a man slowly exited a large black Crown Victoria. He waited for a moment, then in a full voice, asked, "Are you Ms. O'Mara, Sharon O'Mara?"

"Who's asking?" Kevin said.

"I'm not a big fan of dogs and they sense it. May I ask you to put the fellow in the house and then I'll tell you."

"Oh, he's fine right where he is and is extremely well trained. You act quiet and all nice like, and he and us won't have a problem," Sharon said, cautiously watching the stranger.

"I've been waiting for more than an hour, so I guess that's the way it is. May I approach?"

"You can approach all you want, just nothing quick. And let's, just for the sake of fun, see your hands. I don't get many evening callers."

Under her breath, she said, "Kevin, watch him."

"Watch him with what? If he had a gun we'd both be dead; you know I don't have a gun. Should I point my finger at him, real threatening like?"

"Yes, but he doesn't, so puff yourself up and act like a big animal or something. I'll get mine."

Kevin tried inflating himself until Sharon returned, her Beretta very visible against her side in her right hand.

The man walked up to the porch and took off his Panama hat and held it in his right hand.

"Good evening, thank you," he said, with a wary glance at Basil. "My name is Eduardo Mendez. A mutual friend suggested that I talk with you, a Mr. Julius Diamond, Esquire."

Sharon thought for a moment, then his name flashed by: attorney, her benefactor's attorney.

"Yes, I know Mr. Diamond. Your name rings a bell; let me think for a minute"—she turned to Kevin—"any help?"

Kevin laughed, then squinted as he looked down at the man's face in the light from the front porch.

"Son of a bitch, you're Eddy M, damn. I saw you play a hundred times with the A's and a bunch of other teams. Nobody was sweeter moving to his right than you, and fast. Good God, you were stupid fast; I think you hit more triples one year than anyone in the franchise's history.

Kevin turned to Sharon.

"Eduardo Mendez. Played for the Athletics for two seasons maybe sixteen years ago, short stop, then the Angels. I was very glad to see you leave the American league and go National," he said, looking back at Mendez.

"Ricky Henderson was faster. He's a friend. Not sure I have the record but I did hit fourteen triples in one year, not bad," Mendez answered, before looking apologetically at Sharon. "You have a pizza, and I'm sorry to intrude, but I only have a day until I have to go home to Puerto Rico. And we need to talk to you, Ms. O'Mara."

"We, I only see you," Sharon said.

"I have a friend in the car; he would like to join us. May I?"

Kevin looked at the limousine. Now he wished he did have his pistol, baseball star or not.

"Sure, why not," he said. "I suppose you have Orlando Cepeda in that thing?"

"To be honest, he wanted to come but couldn't, although he's the man who suggested Mr. Diamond."

Mendez waved to the car.

The rear door on the passenger side opened and even from fifty feet away Sharon could see that the man, as he stood, was substantial. His broad shoulders filled his elegant bespoke suit, and as he came around the back of the car and walked across the small lawn he had the athletic swagger of a lion.

Basil stood, a low growl working its way out his clenched jowls.

"Stay; I think he's a friend, but I want to know what the hell he's doing here and not in San Diego," Sharon said.

"Ms. O'Mara, I would like to introduce you to Toribio Rodriquez," Mendez said. "And Toribio, I would also like to introduce you to her friend, Kevin Bryan."

Kevin looked at Mendez; he had not given the man his name.

"Mr. Bryan, I am very thorough with my research, yes I am," came the answer.

"Señorita O'Mara," Rodriquez said. "*Buenas noches*, thank you for taking a few minutes. May I suggest we go inside?"

Stunned, Sharon led the way into her house. Between Bryan and Rodriquez, there was little room in the hallway for Mendez and herself.

"I'll put the pizza in the oven, you three go into the living room. Anyone want a drink?"

"My usual, since this night can't get any more unusual," Kevin said, leading the guests further into the cottage and into the Mediterranean styled front living room. He pointed toward the overstuffed leather couch and matching lounge.

"Water is fine for me. I don't drink during the season," Toribio said, his English softly rounded by his Cuban accent. "I don't wish to be too forward, but may I turn the game on?"

Kevin looked at the Giants' right fielder. Until now he hadn't realized how big Toro Rodriquez was—television and even watching games from the stands just didn't tell the true story. In O'Mara's small living room, he felt as though one of them would have to leave to let Sharon in. The ballplayer was almost as tall as his own six-six height, but Toro had him by at least fifty pounds, pounds that were muscle, not the kind of pounds Kevin had earned sitting at a cop's desk. And to beat it to hell, Rodriquez was damn good looking.

"Bottled okay?" Sharon asked, as she handed Mendez and Rodriquez their drinks. "Kev, yours is on the counter with mine. Would you bring them in?"

She watched the Giants' game appear on her small flatscreen TV atop a low cabinet, studied Rodriquez as his eyes darted from Mendez to the TV and back.

Kevin took another look at the men before heading for the kitchen at the end of the hallway

"You should be in San Diego; they're already down two in the third," Kevin said from the hallway.

"Yes, but I pulled a calf muscle in St. Louis a week ago and the manager wanted me to rest it. So I was sat down for a couple of weeks—disabled list, first time in my career. I'll rejoin them when they return. It is hard getting old."

"You're having a good season."

Like Kevin, Sharon couldn't not stare at the two men.

"I can't believe you're here, in my house," she went on. "Why? Diamond is a good attorney, as far as they go, but he doesn't know me that well."

"He said your friends are loyal to you, and you have helped them, often at great risk. They admire you and what you do for them. Señorita O'Mara, all we really have are our close friends and family. Without them we are nothing," Rodriquez said.

"Ms. O'Mara," Mendez added, "We have come here for your help."

Kevin handed Sharon a tumbler. She looked up at him and smiled.

"What kind of help?" Kevin asked.

"I would like to tell you a brief story, if I may," Mendez said, and seeing Sharon nod yes, began. Ten minutes later they understood how Toribio became a San Francisco Giant. "But his heart is heavy."

Kevin said, speaking mainly to Sharon. "He has over four hundred home runs in less than ten years, two MVPs, God knows how many stolen bases."

"Two hundred and thirty four," Mendez said.

"And he's arguably the best right fielder in the game."

"His career has been a dream. Wherever he goes, Cuban exiles want his autograph and he has spoken a hundred times about their homeland to civic groups. His reputation is impeccable, but it is a heaviness I put there."

"That's okay, Eddy, that's okay," Toribio said.

"No, it's not. I promised you that I would take care of them and I didn't. This is on me, all on me. And now that we finally know, it is even heavier."

Sharon had been listening intently as she studied the two men. Mendez had the proud look of a father with a son, a son that was troubled or in trouble. Her army career had put her in amongst the warrior class and they often developed the same relationships with senior officers. More than once her role as a commanding officer placed her in the same role as Mendez, mentor and parent.

"What is it? Sure as hell isn't money," she said to Mendez.

"When I convinced Toribio to go to America, I promised him that I would also protect his family and get them out. I failed. Within hours they disappeared from his home in Cienfuegos. There have been messages passed from someone in the Cuban government to Toribio, asking him to come back to Cuba to show his respect and support for the government."

"I can't, I won't. I know what they do to those that don't like their rules; I've seen it myself. If I give in, they win, but they have my wife and son and my mother. It's all I think about when I'm not playing ball. Baseball has kept me sane; without it I would die. And my son is now eleven and I have not seen him for ten years."

"Just tell them what they want," Kevin said. "You don't have to believe it."

"They would know. When I was a boy, I was sure they could read my thoughts and I still believe it. I know they are safe but prisoners, like the millions of others on the island, a prison without walls, only an ocean to keep them in."

"You couldn't buy them out?" Sharon asked, half-guessing what was coming, but she waited to hear Mendez out.

"We tried, but for some in the regime money is not important. So we are here to ask for your help."

"I don't know anyone in Cuba, and outside of a good restaurant in San Francisco no one here that could help."

Mendez looked at Toribio and spoke softly.

"Ms. O'Mara, we want to hire you to go to Cuba and rescue his wife and son and bring his family back to him."

2c

The conversation between O'Mara and Bryan and Rodriquez

and Mendez went well into the night. The pizza, rewarmed, was split four ways. Sharon wasn't sure what to do; every job was different and required different skills. But then, at one time or another, much was beyond her skills; she learned and adapted. She absorbed everything; her youth as a foster teenager in Colorado, her months at officer training school, and her two tours in Iraq and Baghdad had yielded an education she would stack against anyone's. She trained her mind and her body to skill levels most professional soldiers would be proud to own, yet there was always a nagging voice in her head, one that said she wasn't good enough. Sometimes she literally had to tell the voice to shut the fuck up.

The Giants won the game in the eleventh, on a crazy suicide squeeze by Toro's stand-in. The announcers said that without Rodriquez it had been a good call. For years the San Francisco team had played small baseball, hits and bunts and moving batters around the bases. With Toribio they became a home run club again, like during the Bonds years, feared and appreciated for their pitching and power hitting. The word dynasty was being thrown about by sports writers and bloggers; it was rumored that the reporters from New York were hoping to find a way to break up the team. Only Mendez, Toro's agent, and his attorney knew about Toro's family, imprisoned on the communist island just ninety miles south of Key West.

"I need to think this through," Sharon said at one point. "This isn't just a simple issue of knocking on a door and helping them pack. There's a lot to pull together and a hundred things I haven't even thought of."

"With Cuba, there are a lot of things the American government doesn't want talked about," Mendez replied, when she asked him why the U.S. government hadn't helped Toro's family.

"Like these great ballplayers. They arrive or, more truthfully, defect and produce a lot of money for the teams and the owners; even the cities where they play want to show them off. Some are given passports when they arrive since theirs, such as they were, were confiscated by the Cuban government. Passports are acquired or in fact stolen in more ways than I want to remember. I was told that one agent, a fellow like me, dressed as a Cuban and faked his position as a baseball coach to a maid. She let him into the Cuban official's room, where he took the player's passport. There's no simple way to make it happen. You offer, you hope, and sometimes, like Toribio here, they come along for the ride. I've discovered Cuban players in Japan, Mexico, and even the Netherlands. That's where Toribio left the team."

"Kind of strange, a lot of these kids are innocent, only want to play the game, don't know about the glamor and the money," Kevin said.

"True, Mr. Bryan, very true. But it's up to them and some don't make it. Not every Cuban ballplayer has the talent or even the cojones to make the big leagues. That's my job—to find those with the skills and the desire. And I make sure they get to a good team, one that understands what they're going through. For some it's the loneliest place in the world, a nice hotel room, a big bank account, and no family, no wife, no father, no mother."

Mendez patted the huge thigh of Toribio, like a father would that of his boy.

"This man is my son now. I have done all I can to make him a big league ballplayer, but it's his God-given talent that has made him a star."

"He's given the Bay Area a lot to be proud of over the past seven or eight years," Sharon added. "And he swings a bat that would scare Sandy Koufax, if he still pitched."

"Señor Koufax was very nice to me when I met him a few years ago," Toro said.

"You met Sandy Koufax? My God, what I would have done to have seen that," Kevin added.

"And you call yourself a Giant fan," Sharon said, looking at Kevin.

"Señor Koufax told me that he had never seen a man turn on a fastball as fast as me. I was very humbled, even if the remark was from a Dodger."

The sparkle in Toribio's eye could not be missed.

"We have heard that Toro's wife, Elena, and his son, Carlos, are somewhere in the southeast part of the country, far from their home of Cienfuegos," Mendez explained. "They are rumored to be on a farm with others held there for their own safety; some are family of other players. The Cuban authorities say that the Cuban people might harm them if they find out they are Toro's wife and son. They tell our contacts that they will be reunited with Rodriquez when he comes home to Cuba to stay."

"Bastards," Sharon said. "It's just their way of controlling through fear. I saw it in Iraq, even by our supposed friends. It's all about control and pressure. With enough of each, you can make children into walking bombs."

"Toribio has been to the State Department, and they tell him to be patient—his patience is gone. The Giants have a great chance to make the playoffs, even though the All-Star game is a month away. It's a sure bet Toro will start in right field, and they are already talking about the Home Run Derby. And you know the game will be here in San Francisco. He rejoins the team when they arrive back in San Francisco this Friday. He hopes that you can help and will take the job."

Sharon turned to Kevin with a "What should I do?" look on her face.

"Your call. I can't help. I'll be out of the country. There are people who can help if you need them, good friends and good people."

Sharon thought for a moment.

"Bobby Gillis, and you don't mean Inspector Detective Xavier Immanuel Lopez?"

"My guess, Lopez has connections to Cuba through his police contacts. Hell, for all I know he's on a first name basis with the head Cuban cop," Bryan said. "And besides, he has a crush on you."

"Bobby might play, but I don't know about Xavier."

"Xavier now? Wasn't that way after you took down the Chinese slavers."

"It was as much your help as Xavier's."

The two ballplayers watched like they were seeing two married people argue in public.

"Señorita O'Mara, are you interested?" Mendez at last asked, sounding a little exasperated.

"Señors Mendez and Rodriquez, yes, I may be interested but I will need help, people I know and trust, so it will take a few days for me to get the logistics together and to see what can be done. I will give you an answer this Friday. You can call me or we can meet."

She paused and with her right hand released the clip that had been holding the bundle of her red hair, it tumbled to her shoulders, then added, "Maybe we can meet before the game, if that's permitted."

"Thank you Señorita, I will be forever grateful," Toro said, extending his hand.

"Don't be too grateful yet, I haven't said yes or no. If I say yes, the costs will not be cheap and I will have a contract ready for both of you to sign."

Mendez gave her a questioning look.

"You said he's like your son, well, now you can prove it. The contract will be a per diem for three people, plus all expenses. I will give you an itemized list when we're successful. If you don't get the list, it will be because, after our arrest, they wouldn't let me mail it from the shit-hole Cuban prison where we'll be thrown. So Friday at noon at Momo's, okay? I'll reserve the back room."

They stood and began to walk toward the front door. Basil stood at the end of the hall in front of the door, staring at two men.

"Is he okay?" Toribio asked. "Me and dogs just barely get along."

"Señor Rodriquez, it's my experience that dogs know more about people than people. They seem to cut through the crap and see into your soul. Basil, come."

The dog looked at his mistress and slowly walked toward

them. When he reached Toribio, he pushed his big head into the space between the man's legs.

"Scratch the top of his head," Sharon said.

Toro did as told; the big dog purred in response.

"He likes you. Good, you've got half the answer."

Chapter 3

3a

Jorge Guadalupe Cortez leaned full face into the gale that blew in from the Caribbean. The hurricane's eye was somewhere north, carving itself into Florida.

At least it missed Cuba—this time.

Massive waves, one after the other, broke over the seawall that extended along the length of Havana's waterfront throwing sea foam across the small plaza. The sky was an angry grey-green that blended seamlessly with the churning surf to the point where he couldn't see the edge of the ocean to the north, yet the lighthouse at Castillo el Morro stood implacably at the eastern end of the harbor, as if old Fidel was giving the storm the finger. The late-afternoon gloom had forced the *castillo* to turn on the beacon light; now Fidel's "digit" could be seen for thirty miles out to sea, almost a third of the way to Key West.

The salt spray stung his old eyes, and Jorge held his Panama hat tight in his left hand, his right hand painful from worsening arthritis. Even the larger-than-life bronze monument to Francisco de Miranda behind him seemed to shake from the onslaught of wind and surf. Cortez smiled to himself thinking that Cuba's revolution had come almost full about. Miranda had been a revolutionary hero to his Venezuelan people more than two hundred years ago, and the late Hugo Chávez saw himself in the same vein; this statue of Miranda on the Havana waterfront was a match to one in Caracas. But the old Cuban guard was just that, old. Cortez had tasted the world and liked what he found. Now, even in the worst neighborhoods of Miami and Mexico

City, the food was better than Cuba. The fine wines of Europe could barely be bought in Cuba, and the cheap rum from home-made Cuban distilleries was just that, cheap. The only thing that wasn't better anywhere in the civilized world was *beisbol*, Cuban *beisbol*.

"Excuse me sir, are you soon going back to the hotel?" a voice asked from behind Cortez.

"Are you getting wet, my boy? Doesn't this storm just shake you to the bone, make you feel alive?"

A slash of lightning cut through the grey, followed by a rumble that rebounded off the pre-revolutionary stone and stucco buildings that faced the ocean on the Malecón, Cuba's highway Route 1a. The buildings flanking its deteriorating pavement needed more than paint to return them to their splendor. Behind and above them stood a mix of Soviet-style high-rise apartments and hotels, all in stark contrast to the half century of neglect that had settled in on this once vibrant jewel in the Caribbean. If the writer Ernest Hemingway, who lived and loved in Havana were alive, he would be perhaps crying.

"Yes sir, if you say so. Me, I like to be dry."

Cortez looked at the man. He was no more than thirty; all he knew was the revolution.

"Yes, Miguel, we can go back. You take the car, I'll walk. I'll meet you in the bar at the Nacional in an hour with our visitor. I can use a shower and it will give you time to change into some dry clothes. But isn't this storm spectacular?"

"Yes, sir. In one hour, in the bar."

Cortez watched Miguel sprint to the rental car, a Japanese car of some make, he wasn't sure what kind. Cars were something he was interested in growing up in the hills to the south of Havana. But the cars in Cuba had been frozen in time, each a reminder of the past. These new rental cars had no stories, no personalities; they were like the tourists, cheap and foreign. As a boy all he was interested in were cars, and girls, and *beisbol*, and not necessarily in that order.

The wind began to die down as he reached the hotel. The

Nacional was one of the few hotels in his Cuba that still carried herself as well as could be expected in the austere world of a communist state. This hotel, designed early in the last century by the famous New York architectural firm, McKim, Mead, and White, had over its eighty years hosted hundreds of the world's politicians, industrialists, as well as the criminal elite. During the heady days of the Great Depression, stars Errol Flynn and Marlene Dietrich had stayed at the Nacional, and later Hemingway and even Winston Churchill prowled its halls. American mobsters met for summits in its rooms and Russian diplomats smoked cigars while trying to find ways to undermine the American dream. Aging from neglect, benign and intended, she struggled. Yet if her walls and hallways could talk, much would be too pornographic for holy ears.

Cortez stood at the window of his eighth-floor room overlooking the auto courtyard and smiled. The scene below was like an image from a time machine; all the cars were at least fifty years old, some much older. The men in guayaberas were leathery and dark, most younger by half than the Detroit steel they drove. He knew the old Chryslers, Fords, and Studebakers that lined the entry drive, all held together with a mechanic's skill and prayer. The roar of a modern tour bus, all shiny with dark windows, shattered the illusion. The bus pulled into the turn-around and began to spill pasty, white-skinned Europeans into the porte cochere and hotel lobby; the last man out of the bus stopped and looked up the face of the hotel until he spotted the window he wanted, put two fingertips to the brim of his Panama hat, smiled, then disappeared into the hotel.

At least he's on time.

Cortez resumed his dressing, his pale blue guayabera, dark blue slacks, and chocolate espadrilles would identify him as Cuban and separate him from the tourists and their overly tight Izod polo shirts with huge numbers and team logos and too-short, short pants. His only jewelry was the gold Rolex he'd acquired in Zürich the season his team won the World Port Tournament. As manager of the team, he'd told the handlers that he would be taking a few days—if they wanted to they could follow him, if not, he would see them back in Cuba. He'd arrived two weeks later at the Cuban team training center rested, sporting a new watch, and the nascent beginnings of a new life as an international diamond smuggler.

Even communists want more, and filling that want with paper currency has its problems. Worldwide almost every dollar earned, printed, or even stolen can be traced; many travelers and thieves try inventive ways to game or subvert the system but are seldom successful. A few hundred dollars or euros may slip through, but for the rich and those aspiring to be rich, big money has tails. Driven by disparate governments and their need of tax money, their fear of terrorists (internal and external), and even the demands of social leveling by playing Robin Hood of sorts—taking from the rich and then keeping it—these political leaders try desperately to follow the world's billions of daily financial transactions, all in an attempt to make sure they get their slice. Currency has too many strings attached to it, too many ways of following the money, too many interested parties.

So what's a smuggler or money launderer to do? Gold's too heavy when ten million dollars weighs almost five hundred pounds, depending on the spot price. To be a gold-backed billionaire like the legendary King Midas, one would have to store more than twenty tons of the yellow metal. It is not something easily loaded on a Gulfstream and taken on vacation or when trying to skip town. Platinum and other metals are worse; paintings are easy to track and hard to convert to ready cash. Drugs? Ask any cartel member what they do with their shipping containers full of hundred dollar bills. Having money and using money are two different things. Jewels and diamonds are all that's left to the stressed international player or felon.

A one-carat diamond of fine quality is worth about four thousand dollars, less for a poorer stone, more for a finer stone. Two hundred and fifty stones are worth a million dollars and weigh about one and three-quarter pounds; a billion dollars weighs one thousand times that amount. And this is when each stone is just one carat. The ratio of value to weight in diamonds is almost exponential; a ten-carat diamond in almost flawless condition could be worth as much as one million dollars. A billion dollar bag of these diamonds, while rarer, would weigh less than ten pounds. These bright baubles are significantly more mobile and even more marketable. Laser identifications will be polished off and larger stones can be recut or broken, they are indestructible, won't rot or rust when wet, won't burn—a cool million-dollars can fit in your pocket. Diamonds are not only a girl's best friend but a smuggler's too.

Miguel stood off to one side of the bar nursing a glass of pineapple juice, watching the two men sitting in the corner. His job was simple yet very dangerous. First, he was to ensure that no one came to the table of Señor Cortez and his guest. The other was to look as uninterested as one could while he carried a Glock 17 hidden under his shirt in the band of his pants. If caught with the weapon, he would spend the next ten years in prison. Señor Cortez paid well enough to take the risk.

"Was your trip comfortable?" Cortez asked the man, who was now similarly dressed to himself. The new arrival's shirt was an off yellow; between the two men it looked like a planning meeting for the Easter Parade. Neither would have seen the humor.

"It was not. We were held at the Cancún airport until we could be assured of a safe landing through this fucking storm," the pasty man said, with a German accent. "In addition, the stewardess looked like an old whore I once knew in Budapest, and the food was barely edible. But, I am here and alive and well. It is good to see you, my old friend. It has been too long."

"Two years, two long years," Cortez said. "Not since I visited you in Zürich. Much has happened and much has passed."

"So true. You remember Gerald Altheimer? He had dinner with us one night."

"Certainly, a fine man."

"For a thief and liar. Yes, he was a good man and had a wonderful cellar, many fine bottles from France, very fine. I remember that Petrus like it was yesterday."

"Yes," Cortez said, nodding his head in agreement. "I assume he's dead?"

"Yes, last spring in the driveway to his house, his wife found him. Very dead; it is rumored that it was the Albanians."

"It's always the Albanians."

"True, true, that is until you find out that it's not."

"Who do you think it was?"

"Most probably the Israelis. Seems that Mr. Altheimer kept some of the product, a few here and a few there. With so many, he thought they wouldn't count them."

"I take it they did."

"Every one. And his answers were not sufficient, so he died. I think it was a lesson."

"It is a very good one, I'm sure."

"Yes it was, very good."

"And the Israelis?"

"They too are dead. Seems they couldn't count either and they missed the most important part of the whole transaction."

"That Mr. Gerald Altheimer is, or sadly was, your brother?"

"Yes."

"I'm very sorry to hear that my friend. I liked him," Cortez said.

"Thank you. Our mother is heartbroken, but she was still strong enough to give the order to remove the Israelis. She is very strong."

"May I toast your mother, Heinz?"

"Certainly."

"To Mrs. Altheimer, a very fine woman and a most protective mother."

Miguel watched the two men engaged in intense conversation and wondered what two old men like these could be talking about. His own circle of friends was very small; the number of people Señor Cortez knew impressed him.

"Thank you, Jorge, I will tell her of your devotion. I don't wish to be rude or forward, but I am very tired. The trip from

Zürich to Madrid, then Cancún, and now sitting here in such great company has been already too long and I need to sleep. So if I may."

"Most certainly, my friend, I understand," Cortez answered, and reached for a small teddy bear he'd earlier placed on the seat next to him. "This is for your granddaughter; she is now seven?"

"Yes, she is my daughter's jewel and mine as well. I will be sure that this is properly restitched before it is presented."

"Excellent, I wouldn't want her to think I was not careful in selecting her toys."

"I'm sure she will be glad to see you when you visit again. Do you know when?"

"Later this summer. First are the games in Amsterdam, then maybe Italy for an exhibition, and then some work with some interesting prospects. Some might make it to the American League," Cortez answered.

"You and your baseball; I sometimes think it means more than this present for my granddaughter."

"Sometimes it is, my friend, sometimes it is. I have been told that there might be a package arriving soon from Johannesburg, a package that may have your interest."

"Yes, wonderful things do arrive in small packages. In a few weeks, I will get in touch. As always your sources of information astound me."

"My friend, not as much as your resources astonish me," Jordy added. "No, let me rephrase that. Not as much as your resources impress me. I am pleased to call you friend."

"And I too, Señor Cortez, am pleased to call you *compadre*."

Miguel, at the bar, watched as the men raised their glasses. He could just make out, over the din, the sharp ring of the crystal as they touched.

3b

The next morning, in the early humidity and sun's glare, Cortez stood behind home plate at the *Estadia Latinoamericano*. Three young men, squinting hard, looked into the face of the man who would make their fortune or make them take the next bus home. Each prayed silently to whatever baseball God they believed in. One had an old chicken bone in his back pocket, a gift from his neighborhood Santera priestess intended to assure him of success.

"So you want to be ballplayers? You want to play on this holy ground and make your country proud? Remember our dear leader played this game, and if it weren't for the revolution and his belief in his people he would have been one of Cuba's greatest pitchers," Jordy lectured.

Cortez had given this speech so many times it took everything in his heart to try and make it sound new and exciting, even though he had personal doubts about Castro's real playing abilities. Cortez had been too young at the time of the revolution to remember anything about the civil war other than some of his uncles and one aunt were never heard from again after the shooting had stopped.

"For the rest of this day you will be playing with the others who arrived yesterday," he continued. "You will be watched and graded for the skills needed to play this game. In the end, you will be chosen or you will not. If you are selected, your life will change, if you aren't, you will go home to your mother."

He paused to let his words sink in before explaining their schedule: at three o'clock in the afternoon, they would choose up sides from the twenty men selected and play seven innings—"You will play like it will be the last game of baseball you will ever play. For some of you it will be. Now go do two laps of the field and join the others in left field. Good luck."

Watching the men jog toward right field, he mused that they always went in that direction because of years of running to first base. It was natural to go to the right.

"You think they have the abilities and the skills," a woman's voice said, from near the dugout. "They look raw and stupid. They also look scared to death."

"That's why I do my job and you do yours, Marta. Mine is

to find the diamond inside; yours is to keep the diamonds in the box. I like my job better."

Marta de la Vega watched the young men as they came back around past the dugout. Good-looking fellows, but they also knew who she was; they glanced at her, then put their heads down and continued the loop.

"Yes, raw and stupid. Farm boys who think they can swing a bat. The army would eat them alive," she said to Cortez.

"Luckily, they aren't in the army, where they would be wasted. Here they can help Cuba in the eyes of the world. They are sometimes all that the world sees."

"You sound a little disappointed about Cuba. You aren't becoming a reactionary?"

"Marta, I'm just an old man trying to field the best team he can. These boys live for baseball even though their friends want to play soccer. Hell, I've lost some great athletes to that silly game, ones that could be stars. My biggest problem now is keeping them here. Each year the Americans poach or steal some of our best. Some were bribed right under your nose, so you have your job and I have mine. The revolution has nothing to do with it."

"Señor Cortez, the revolution has everything to do with it. It is the belief that binds these men together."

Cortez withdrew a seven-inch Churchill Espléndido from inside his linen jacket and then extracted a silver cutter. Nipping off the tip, he rolled the Cohiba softly between his fingers as he watched de la Vega. He liked what he saw: trim, athletic, her dark hair sat on her shoulders. She wore a severe blouse over her slacks. Her overall look, while civilian, had a military air about it. It fit her full figure well. He wasn't bothered by her rank of colonel in Cuba's National Guard; he'd dealt with her predecessors and hopefully would be around to deal with her successors. He clicked open the silver lighter he'd found in a fine Zürich shop and toasted the cigar.

"They are very handsome," Vega said.

If the cigar was bothering her, she didn't show it. Nor did

she hide her agenda to look over the prospects. Cortez couldn't stop her but, as in the past, it would be a distraction at some point. Although sometimes her attentions to a young man made them think twice about defecting and leaving Cuba. So if Marta de la Vega wanted a plaything, he could hardly care. But if she fucked with the player's head when he needed him, then he'd make her stop. He had his rules.

"Just watch yourself. Someday you might have to arrest one or two of them; if you are too close you might get caught yourself."

De la Vega looked at Cortez.

"That's my problem. Will they be ready?"

"Yes, the team needs two infielders and two outfielders, and a catcher to back up Ruiz, and God knows we always need pitchers. The tall kid with the black curly hair throws lightning, but like lighting he never throws it to the same place twice. He could be great."

"What about the big man on the right, number twenty-three?"

"You stay away from that one; he's married and he can hit and field as well as Toribio Rodriquez. So you stay away from him."

"I told you to never mention Rodriquez to me."

"It's been years, Marta. Get over it."

"He's the reason I have to chaperone you and your men around the world. I would have been at an embassy or somewhere if it weren't for that fucking Puerto Rican friend of yours."

"Mendez was a great ballplayer, but he's got his job to do. I have mine."

"Yes, but if I were ever to catch him on Cuban soil, I would make sure he never left. There are others who thought they could bribe our citizens with money and fame; most are sitting in *Combinado del Este*. I have a cell with Eduardo Mendez's name on it. They are all parasites that prey on the sons of our working people."

Cortez blew a great cloud of smoke into the still air.

"I know you, and you don't believe that parasite shit," he said to Vega.

"You are very wrong, Señor Cortez, very wrong. I will see that man locked up someday. He will make a mistake."

"I doubt that. Toro is one of the best players in the game and, when I can, I watch him knowing I had a little to do with making him a great ballplayer."

"And if I ever find out that you helped him defect, you will be in the cell next to Mendez."

"Sometimes you get more out of people by making them proud and strong, not fearful. I know what you did to Rodriquez's family. I hear things, so I will play along, but just stay out of my way."

He tapped the ash off his cigar and walked away from de la Vega without bothering to say good-bye.

That evening over dinner with Heinz Altheimer, Jordy Cortez discussed, in the most general and non-specific of terms, the opportunities that awaited them in Amsterdam later that summer. Through Herr Altheimer's contacts in London, it was known that a very large collection of diamonds and other colored stones was to be moved from South Africa through Schiphol airport near Amsterdam and then on to Gatwick via private plane. The quantities or values were not discussed; it would have been impolite to be so crass.

3c

When Fidel Castro's revolution began, it had to start somewhere. In 1956, Castro purchased a sixty-foot yacht called *Granma* from an American in Tuxpan, Mexico. He and more than eighty of his comrades headed across the Caribbean Sea to Cuba, where the incumbent dictator of the island country, Fulgencio Batista, waited impatiently for the brazen band of revolutionaries. Only twenty of Castro's men survived and he was initially believed among the dead, although soon proving that reports of his death were greatly exaggerated.

Castro's party had come ashore at Playa las Coloradas in the municipality of Niquero, the most southern point of Cuba. In the strange way of the world, the province was subsequently renamed Granma, after Castro's yacht. East of Granma, north of the city of Santiago de Cuba, a small village had been redeveloped as a work camp for imprisoned counter-revolutionists and their families soon after the war. Ostensibly a place of reeducation, the camp later evolved into a prison, where families of some of the *beisbol* defectors from Cuba's enlightenment were held. It was, in effect, a camp of hostages. Marta de la Vega, for the last fifteen years, had made it her personal labor camp, where the residents, most believed to be relatives of defected Cuban baseball players playing in America, were "employed" caring for her personal 250 acres of robusta coffee beans that, after being harvested in early winter, were secretly shipped through Santiago de Cuba to Mexico, where they were processed. Coffee growing had been a significant enterprise prior to the revolution, with Cuba commanding a premium price for its product. Now in Castro's Cuba, coffee uses less than fifteen percent of the land that was once cultivated for coffee plants. Vega sold much of her crop to a coffee broker in London and deposited the earnings in a British bank. Even a revolutionary needs to have a rainy-day fund.

A few weeks after her conversation with Cortez near the dugout, de la Vega made one sweeping pass of her quarter square mile of dark green coffee plants in the ancient Piper Cub she had rescued from a scrap pile of derelict airplanes the revolution had deemed "counter-revolutionary." Actually since 2007 it was legal in the eyes of Raul Castro, Fidel's younger brother and now current dictator, to own an airplane if you were one of the exceptional cases necessary to Cuba's economic development. De la Vega's connections, after many years within the government, were more than "exceptional." Vega had the plane painted a grey-green; when on the ground it was virtually indistinguishable from overhead from the green of the verdant Cuban plateau where the camp was located.

Vega landed the plane on the small grass landing strip near the camp and taxied to a fifty-by-fifty-foot hanger roofed with corrugated metal. It looked like a thousand other rusting buildings found throughout this part of Cuba.

A small man in green fatigues walked up to the plane as Vega shut down the engine; when her feet touched the ground he saluted.

"Good morning, Comandante. It is good to see you," he offered, in the same manner a dog would greet its master.

"Manny, make sure she is refueled and ready to go in two hours. I must return to Havana."

Vega began to walk quickly toward a low-slung sprawling building, wrapped by an open porch.

"Did the hurricane cause much damage?" she asked.

"No, Comandante. The winds were not bad this time. No damage was found."

Cubans qualified most everything, especially the weather, simply because hurricanes playing island-hopping tourist, usually made Cuba their first visit to the Caribbean. They were a lot like a cruise ship full of drunken college kids visiting a small beach town. Usually nothing was left standing or unbroken.

"Good, then the crop is fine."

"*Si*, it is excellent this year. Do you have time to visit?"

"Not this trip, I flew over the fields and they do look good from two hundred meters, so I'll have to take your word."

"*Gracias.*"

If he had a tail, he would have wagged.

"Our guests?" asked Vega.

"All are well, two of the children had a brief illness. The doctor thought it was from their diet, but he understood."

"Good, I don't pay him to make judgments; I want healthy employees. That is all."

Even Manuel smiled at the term employee.

"*Si*, he knows. We have also planted the new fields with tobacco with the young plants from the hothouse. They began last week. I have the children keeping back the weeds."

"Good, they learn discipline in the fields. The school?"

"They study in the early morning and late afternoon, as ordered. They work during the day."

"Good, the adults?"

"Nothing more than the usual," Manuel reported, telling Vega more of what she already knew, that the old men stayed close to the barracks and raked the beans as they dried; the women as usual kept the plants.

There were no young men or husbands among the guests at the farm. Young men were trouble, and if their fathers had chosen American baseball, their sons, when they reached age seventeen, were chosen for the military. It was a camp of old and young women, children, and bent-back men. The only phone was in the comandante's office; the next closest phone was at a gas station three miles away near Los Reynaldos.

Marta walked through the small residential compound that enclosed ten small one- and two-room buildings; shotgun shacks would be a more apt term. None had plumbing other than one galvanized water line that snaked through the cluster of houses and up the wall to a single sink in each building's kitchen. Most had a small outhouse standing about thirty feet away from the back door. A well-worn path from the door of each house to the door of its outhouse connected the two structures. Surprisingly, the main street, such as it was for its length of two hundred feet, was lined with large trees all in full bloom. The pink flowers of the orchid trees littered the dirt lane, creating a bizarre parade-like effect. The fleshy flowers stuck to Vega's boots, and she mentioned having them cut down.

Manuel, who actually liked the trees and their spectacular flowers, offered, "They only bloom for a short time, then they are done. The children like the flowers," he added, gesturing for Vega to look down a narrow space between two buildings, where two small girls were decorating straw hats with the orchid flowers.

She watched for a moment, then said, "I guess for now we'll

leave them."

"*Si*, excellent," Manuel answered, the dog again wagging his tail.

At the last cabin, Vega stopped. A young woman sat with an older woman on the small covered porch that extended out from the building; they were shelling beans into a battered pot. A small, terrier-like dog sat atop the single step leading to the low the porch. As Vega came near the house, the white and dark brown mottled animal rose to its feet, growled, and bared its teeth.

"Señora Rodriquez, I suggest you have that mongrel sit, or Manuel will take it away," Vega said.

The woman took a small handful of bean pods and cradled them in her lap.

"Bibi, down," she said.

The dog slowly laid down on the rough planking, although its eyes never left de la Vega.

"How are you, Señora Rodriquez? Is everything satisfactory?"

"Prison is never satisfactory, Comandante, never. But it could be worse; at least here my mother-in-law has clean air to breath. She says it's a lot like the air before Castro."

"That's an incorrect belief. Life is better since the revolution."

"Señora Rodriquez would disagree with you, but then again, she knows her place after fifty years."

The younger woman looked at her mother-in-law, who responded with a nod.

"Why doesn't she speak?" Vega asked.

"I believe she told me once that when her son returns she will talk. Until then, she has nothing to say."

"She's crazy; you all are, and so is Toribio. There was much that he could have had here in Cuba. He would have had the whole of the country behind him; he would have represented Cuba across the world. Shown the world how things are here."

"I guess that's why he left, to show the world how things

are in Cuba."

Toribio's wife resumed shelling the beans.

"We miss him," she said tenderly.

"Where's your boy?"

"Where you will usually find him at this hour, hoeing your tobacco."

"The work is good."

"Slavery is always good for someone, but it does keep him out of mischief. The boys here would look for trouble if they didn't have something to do, and the good Lord knows what kind of trouble they would get into. So I guess I should thank you, comrade Comandante, for attending to their needs."

Vega wasn't sure how to respond.

"I bid you good day," she said finally, with another glance at the two women and their dog.

"She is never any trouble," Manuel offered, as he and Vega walked back toward the office. "She does her work and takes care of the boy. Sometimes he's a handful, but all the boys are."

"Yes, I understand. I had two brothers. He'll be ready for the army in five years."

"*Si*, five years."

Manuel knew that Marta de la Vega's older brother was buried somewhere in an Angolan field full of other Cuban soldiers who'd been sent to Africa to champion the revolution across the world. Her younger brother had been lost somewhere in the mountains of Venezuela during a firefight with Columbian soldiers. Their deaths had done little to move Castro's or any cause forward; Angola and Venezuela are as fucked up today as they were twenty years ago. Revolutions eat up the young men of any nation that challenges its rulers. But at least Venezuela lets it great ballplayers play in professional baseball.

After a brief lunch of carnitas and beans, Vega headed back to her plane. It had been rolled out from its cover and aligned along the short grass runway.

Manuel handed her a small bundle.

"These are from last year's tobacco. Offer them as gifts from the employees here to the officers in Havana."

Taking the bundle, she could feel the narrow shafts of the cigars.

"Did our employees roll these?"

"*Si*, they are learning. An instructor comes once a month to show them."

"*Bueno*, I will see that they find a proper home."

"*Gracias*." One last wag.

As de la Vega's plane bounced down the dirt runway, Manuel waved at his employer just as her wheels lifted off the ground. "Bitch," was his parting comment as he watched her bank west away from the farm.

Thirty minutes later, at five thousand feet over the fields of Cuba, en route to Havana—she would make one stop at Sancti Spiritus to refuel—de la Vega slid open the small window to her left and threw out the bundle of cigars. They were not good enough for her officer friends in Havana. She didn't care what the Americans who bought her cigars in London thought, they were Cuban—that's all that American tourists believed and wanted as they hid them in their luggage for their trip home.

Chapter 4

The evening before Kevin was to leave for London, Gina Cavelli threw a going away party at her Lafayette bar, Geno's. Anyone who knew Kevin was invited, or so it seemed to Sharon as she squeezed through the crowd congregating around the entrance. Men and women lounged about the sidewalk, smoking, holding beers. Normally frowned upon—both the smoking and alcohol in open containers on public sidewalks—everyone seemed to have a pass. It may have also been due to the fact that half the partiers were Lafayette and Walnut Creek cops celebrating Kevin's good luck at landing an exotic job in a foreign country.

"Let the redhead in, you louts," Gina said, as Sharon finally reached the ancient bar. "I'm pouring," she told Sharon, "all on the house."

O'Mara accepted the tumbler from her friend and took a sweet sip of scotch.

"Better?"

"Much."

Geno's was an institution that had graced Lafayette's main street for more years than anyone alive could remember. Gina's grandfather, Geno Alberto Cavelli, had opened the bar soon after the '06 earthquake, suffered through Prohibition, Depression and war, and then, when he passed on to one of those great bar stools in heaven, her father took over and from behind the worn bar's surface had been the titular head of Lafayette's political scene. And now, for the past ten years, the place had been hers.

Young fools with Silicon Valley stock options had offered her ten times its worth, and she politely refused each generous proposal. The mahogany bar itself had been salvaged from a crushed but unburnt bar left by the earthquake, floated across the bay on a hay scow, and then carted by wagon over the hills to the small village of Lafayette. Geno's was as much a county political center as it was libation central: bankers, politicians, and cops came and went (some to jail); the century-year-old bar always remained. It was the first place to which the county's prodigal citizens returned when they eventually came home.

"Where's Kev?" Sharon yelled, over the chorus of voices and music from an antique jukebox, whose tunes seemed to stop somewhere around March 1971.

Gina jerked her thumb toward the far end of the room.

"You need to rescue him—seems his old boss is trying to get him drunk."

"Great, just what we need."

Holding her glass high, Sharon pushed her way to a corner table, where Kevin Bryan stood, a head taller than anyone at the table. His glass (no doubt filled with Jameson whiskey) was being used as a pointer as he talked with the cluster of cops gathered about him. The only one sitting was Captain Horacio Brown, Kevin's old boss. Brown was one of the few who had survived the city council's purge of the ranks.

"If it isn't Sharon O'Mara," Brown said, tipping his tumbler toward her.

She ignored the slurred greeting—it came out "Shorn O'Mora"—and pushed up against Kevin, who gave her a quick kiss on the cheek.

"You should watch what you drink, Captain. There might be evildoers about," she said.

O'Mara and the captain had been at odds over the welfare of Kevin Bryan for a number of years; to Brown it seemed that whenever his friend was involved with the girl, people were injured or worse. More than once, Bryan had come to her rescue and saved a lot of other people at the same time. Brown would miss Kevin, but he was also glad the man would be out of O'Mara's clutches, even if for a few months.

"I'm off duty," he told her. "I'm also glad that you won't be an evil influence on our boy here for a while."

"You two stop it," Kevin demanded. "I might be gone, but I want the two of you to shake hands and call a truce." He looked at his two friends. "I mean it!"

The others surrounding the table, all knowing the situation, took in a collective breath. A détente was requested. Who would be the first to stick out their hand? It was Sharon.

"Here, let's put it all behind us."

Captain Brown pushed his way out of the booth and put his hand in hers.

"To friends," he assented.

"Good. Gina, another round," Kevin called out.

The evening continued, with the crowd gradually thinning, until by closing only Kevin, Sharon, and Gina stood along the bar. The rest of the well-wishers had gone home or wherever they went when a bar closes.

"It's late, and I'm going home," Sharon said. "Basil's been locked up for hours, and I need to let him out. How did you get here?"

"Took a ride with the captain. Can you drop me?"

"Not a problem. Good night, my Italian *principessa*!"

"You promised to never call me that," Gina answered, in a fake huff. Her wild salt-and-pepper hair, piled high on her head, shook as she crossed her arms over her ample bosom. "We promised to keep our secrets."

"What secrets?" Kevin asked.

"None that can be told," Sharon said. "Let's go, time for bed."

After dropping a slightly inebriated Kevin off at his small cottage in the hills of Lafayette, she headed home to Walnut Creek. There would be enough time to say good-bye at the airport later that afternoon. She let Basil out into the small backyard and poured herself a two-finger nightcap of Lagavulin scotch and waited while he completed his business. The stars twinkled and sparkled in the cool of the early morning night. They dazzled like diamonds, like the one night in Baghdad ten years earlier. The night before all hell broke loose.

4b

Green Zone, Baghdad, Iraq, fall 2004

"Lieutenant, the major wants to see you, and he wants you to bring Sergeant Gillis. He's in ops," the private said.

"Roger that, thanks, Private. Find Sergeant Gillis and tell him to meet me in ten," Lieutenant Sharon O'Mara answered.

She crushed a cigarette against the sharp sand with her boot, then pulled her jacket more tightly around herself. A sharp wind blew in from the north; she tasted a cold desert.

It's either too fucking hot or too fucking cold; pleasant has no Arabic word in Baghdad.

She stood just below the top of the levee looking toward the oldest part of Baghdad across the Tigris River. The night hid the grim river flowing past the American Green Zone. The Tigris had seen the Babylonians, the Macedonians, the Persians and more recently the English and the Americans, all there to either enrich themselves or pacify a people hell bent on self destruction. The lights of the city shimmered on the opposite bank. Vehicle headlights probed the darker areas where the power had either failed or been diverted.

"Lieutenant?" a husky voice called out.

Sergeant Bobby Gillis stood at the base of the levee looking up at her. Her first impression had been that Gillis was a big hick, a California valley boy with sandy hair and blue eyes. But six months and a dozen firefights had proved her wrong. Sergeant Gillis was one of those rare humans who was a born warrior, a man of high principle and moral depth, and a natural leader.

"I asked the private to tell you to meet me at ops."

"Yes, sir, he did. But since I was closer to you here than there, I chose here."

"Well, Sergeant, since you are here, we should hightail our asses there. Major Simpson does not like to be kept waiting."

"Yes, sir. Know why?"

"After the past week, who the hell knows anything? There's a whole bunch of new shit happening out there, and I'm not sure we're ready," she said, as she and Gillis fell in step together.

From what she'd seen of that Humvee after an IED ripped it apart, they needed stronger vehicles. It seems that now the local assholes were tying artillery shells together, burying them under roads and playgrounds, and setting them off remotely when an American vehicle passed over them. As a countermeasure, her men had been welding steel sheets to the doors and half-inch plate steel on the floor—Band-Aids at best.

"We have to harden these trucks somehow, or all hell's going to break out," she said, as much to herself as to Gillis.

Sharon's mind was still on the Humvees five minutes later, when the sergeant knocked on the panel door of Major Jebadiah Simpson's office.

"Enter," a voice boomed from inside; there was no aide on duty at the outside desk.

Gillis pushed the door open, and O'Mara followed him inside the ten by ten office cube built into the modern military version of the American doublewide trailer.

Major Simpson was a big man, a Chicago Bears fullback–size black man with close-cropped hair that had already begun to turn salty. He stood, smiling, as the two entered and saluted him.

"The private said ten minutes, and you're here in five, good. Lieutenant, I'm pleased to see you, and nice job on that problem with that shop owner I'm sure he won't be bothered again."

"Thank you, Major. If there's trouble we know where to find them now," O'Mara said. "What's up?"

"Since the two of you are so good at finding things, I've been handed a missing persons assignment."

"Half the people in this country are missing, intentionally or otherwise," O'Mara offered.

She didn't need to explain to the Major that anytime they went looking for someone, the answer was 'never heard of them,' even if the missing person was the questionee's own brother. Often some were found along or in the river, where they became the permanently missing. People were either scared of the U.S. Army, the Iraqi police, or someone in the militia—either Sunni or Shia—or were trying to kill someone in those respective armies. And now there were reports that al-Qaeda was moving in. What a fucking war.

"Yeah, I know," the major said. "We're fighting them, and they are killing each other. But that said, I need you to cut through it and find this guy. He's a nasty son of a bitch."

Simpson picked up a playing card on his desk and expertly sailed it to Gillis, who deftly snatched it out of the air.

Gillis looked at the card with its camouflage back, then turned it over and studied the rugged mustached face of an Iraqi man who looked to be in his forties. His hair was closely cut, his eyebrows thick and black. The face was outlined with a black border with *Sabawi Ibrahim al-Tikriti* written below; *six of diamonds* was printed in the upper and lower corners.

He passed the card to O'Mara.

"Half brother of Saddam, ran their secret police back when they were gassing their own citizens, and recently or at least until he hightailed his ass out of here, was an advisor to Hussein," Simpson said, in response to O'Mara's questioning look.

"How many brothers does that man have?" Gillis asked.

"No one knows," answered Simpson. "Except every time a rock is overturned in the desert, one of them pops up."

With Saddam in prison and his sons, Uday and Qusay, dead, these other rats kept scurrying about, Sharon thought.

"I want you to find him," the major told them. "Captain Harris has the intel. There's a one million bounty on his head, alive or dead. We'd prefer him alive."

"Wow, a million dollars. I could use that," Gillis said under his breath.

"I heard that, son, and you know damn well you aren't entitled to a dime if you catch him. Then again, neither am I. So do your sworn duty and find this son of a bitch. I prefer him alive, but I sure as hell don't want to lose one man over this sack of shit."

"Roger that, Major," O'Mara answered. "Any word on the hardened vehicles? My men are sitting ducks. It's been more than nine months, and something has to be done."

"I know, goddamn, I know. They're my men too. My commanders are out there screaming the same thing; I hope something will get done. There's some refit kits but not enough."

"How many more will die?" Sharon asked.

"It's your job not to let it happen, so do what you—"

Simpson was interrupted by a knock on the door; an aide stuck his head in.

"Pentagon, sir. Line three."

"Tell them I'll be right there, and get O'Mara the package on Sabawi Ibrahim. Lieutenant, Sergeant, good hunting."

The major picked up the phone, and O'Mara and Gillis saluted, then ducked quickly out of his office. The aide handed O'Mara a large manila envelope, a red SECRET stamped on the front and back, their quarry's name neatly typed on a white sticker secured to the top right corner.

"Tikrit, what a pesthole that town is," O'Mara said to Gillis, as they left the ops building and walked between the metal buildings, where the cold wind continued to blow.

Saddam had been discovered in a hole a few miles outside of the town, presumably turned in by his own people. Now there was a full-scale intertribal war going on and the Anglos didn't have a clue as to who was who. O'Mara had seen Saddam's palace before his own people stripped it of anything valuable—it hadn't been to her taste. Then again, there wasn't much here that was.

4c

Walnut Creek, California

Sharon slept in. A personal luxury she had grown to appreciate more and more as she grew older. Anglo-Saxon guilt lingered as she pulled the sheet up and rolled over. As the guilt continued to linger she told it to go make coffee, she would be there in an hour. Unfortunately, Basil didn't share her cultural imperatives and needed a few minutes outside. After his short backyard tour, she crawled back into bed. The clock radio said six-thirty. She took an hour more of R&R.

After thirty minutes of stretching and her personal version of Tai Chi, she took a long shower, then slipped on a thin, overly large tee shirt and wrapped her hair with towel that capped her lithe Irish pink body like a dollop of whipped cream on a strawberry sundae. The tee shirt said GO ARMY. A light breakfast of peanut butter–slathered raisin toast and coffee was set next to her computer. Kevin's plane was at six o'clock; she would pick him up at three-thirty for the drive to the airport—until then there was some serious planning to start. She e-mailed her standard contract to Eduardo Mendez, outlining each party's responsibilities, her hourly and daily rates, and the request for a good faith retainer. In the section outlining the scope and extent of the work, she typed "To Be Determined." He e-mailed back within an hour and attached the signed contract. She wondered if in the future the document might be something for a Cooperstown display; Toribio's signature was directly and boldly below Mendez's. She glanced at the Giant's schedule on the pinboard above her desk; *Yes, they were in town.*

She had considered living off Alain Dumont's inheritance, but knew in her heart that was not the reason Dumont had left her the money. In fact he would have been very disappointed in her if she had. During the short time she'd known the man she had loved him like he was her own grandfather—and a grandfather would never have allowed her to sit on her ass and milk an inheritance. She needed to take the money and make something of it like Alain Dumont had with the millions in gold he'd 'found' during the war.

The contract specified direct deposits and she would know in a few days if the retainer had cleared. One way or another, it really didn't make any difference. She'd accepted the job and now had to figure out how to make it happen. She opened Google Earth and spun the planet to Cuba, a place she never wanted to return to.

Sandwiched between her two tours in Iraq had been a six-month stint learning prisoner management at Guantanamo Bay detention camp, moving from the heat of the desert to the relatively cooler breezes of the tropical Caribbean, although all she remembered were hot, sweaty days spent moving Islamic terrorists dressed in stylish orange jumpsuits from one humid room to another like furniture. Her experiences there had steeled her heart for the second tour in the Green Zone.

Those 180 days in Cuba had dragged as no other deployment in the army. The weather unchanging, the food unchanging, the prisoners unchanging—there'd been days she'd hoped for a hurricane just to bust up the pattern. She took morning jogs alongside the miles of opuntia cacti that paralleled some portions of the camp, somebody's idea of keeping Cubans on Castro's side of Guantanamo before they later put up a high fence as an even better deterrent. The Cactus Curtain, it'd been called. Whenever she stopped at the local Safeway and saw cactus pears fruit in the vegetable section, she remembered the red cactus pear-shaped fruit that decorated the miles and miles of cacti in Cuba. She hoped she wouldn't have to deal with these annoying plants when she made the run to retrieve Rodriquez's family.

She called Bobby Gillis first. Through a strange series of events, mostly dealing with the job of returning the Impressionist paintings for Mr. Alain Dumont, she had employed the retired sergeant as her backup. Now, after he and the Gillis family had been well taken care of by Mr. Dumont's will, Bobby was the only person other than Kevin she could trust in a firefight. He was quick and resourceful and after leaving the army returned to running the family almond and walnut business near Bakersfield. And for this job, his Spanish was flawless.

"Lieutenant, it's great to hear from you," Bobby said, when he answered her call.

"Family?"

"As always, in good health and spirits. Two cousins at Cal, and all the others are doing well in school."

"Have you found the right girl?"

"Always concerned about my love life, and the simple answer is no. Too much to do on the ranch, no time for such frivolities. I leave that to my brothers and sisters. Since gramps died, everyday seems like the next: work, work, work."

"I liked him. He was a good man."

"For some, that's all that's needed to be said. So I assume this isn't just a social call."

"Couldn't get that by you, Sergeant. I need some help."

"Mine to give. What's up?"

"A chance at a Caribbean vacation."

"No such thing when partnering with you. What and when?"

Sharon laid out the story and the job.

"So a simple snatch and grab," Bobby said, with a laugh. "But then again, nothing is simple when it comes to you."

"True, but what do you think?"

"Let's see. We sneak into Cuba, find a family that no one knows where they are, convince them that we can get them out of Cuba, and then nonchalantly walk them out to freedom and a life in sunny California."

"You're quick; I knew you would get the idea."

"The farm's in good hands right now, will be at least until the end of summer before the nuts need to be harvested, so why not? Never been to the Caribbean; a vacation would be nice. When do we start?"

"I'll need two weeks to get things in order and see if I can get one more man on board."

"Kevin?"

"No, he'll be in London on a security job."

When Sharon had filled him in on the details, Bobby said, "Nice gig. Maybe he needs help. Never been to London, but I hear it's nice."

"It's okay, but the beaches aren't as nice."

"Too bad. I'll be up there in a week, just need to finish a few things here first."

He asked what to bring, and Sharon answered that gear would be limited: "We go in as tourists."

"Great, go into one of the most secure places in the world run by paranoid communists and try and find a family no one's heard from in years with no guns. Nothing is easy with you, is it?"

"No, but I'll see if I can narrow down the choices."

"It's like when we went after that relative of Saddam's. All we had was a playing card."

"That's more than we have now. See you next week."

Her next call would be even stranger; to try and convince a Mexican police official, Detective Inspector Xavier Immanuel Lopez, to violate any number of international laws and agreements to join her merry band.

"Sharon, my dearest *amor*, I have missed you," were the first words from Lopez, when she finally tracked him down to a phone number in Mexico City.

"Xavier, I have missed you too," she said, trying not to laugh.

"I heard that snicker; you know that you will always have my heart. I still remember that sunny day on the beach in Cabo San Lucas when we first met."

She remembered it too as well as the four stinking dead Chinese hanging in a shipping container.

"What a way to meet, and all over some fake handbags," she said.

"But we were a good team, were we not? And we did a lot of damage to some very bad people. You helped me clean up some difficult problems here in Mexico with the cartels—all in all we were good together. *Si?*"

"So you're in Mexico City?" she asked him.

"*Si*, a promotion. One well deserved, I might add. Seems they need me here at what you call the home office; I'm in charge of investigating international criminals and their local affiliations here in Mexico. It was your help that put me here. Gracias."

"If I played a small part, all the better. What do you know about Cuba?"

"Cuba, nasty place. Why?"

She told him.

"*Madre de Dios*, nothing is easy with you, is it? Yes, I have had some dealings with the Policía Nacional Revolucionaria. They are a very suspicious people. But, as you say, I scratch your back and you scratch mine, so some favors are in order. A few baseball defectors have come through Mexico before heading north. Why they didn't stay here, I don't know. We have some very good ball teams, but the dollars your American teams offer is ten times what we can offer here. I will make a few inquiries; I have heard that many of the families were relocated for their protection, such as it is. Probably no more than work camps or low-grade prisons."

Lopez said he had a friend who knew a member of the management council of the Los Diablos Rojos, Mexico City's professional baseball team, which had two or three Cubans playing for them.

"I'll ask around and see what I can find. Would that help?"

"More than you can imagine, Xavier. Right now I have nothing."

"*Bueno*, I'll call you tomorrow. When can we have dinner?"

"You never give up, do you?"

"Sharon, my love, Xavier Immanuel Lopez never gives up when a woman as delightful and beautiful as you is still available."

"Who said I was available?"

"You didn't say you weren't. Until tomorrow, *adios, mi amor.*"

Basil nosed Sharon's hip and looked up his mistress. She patted his head.

"That man is a Casanova, Baze. He has the ego of Don Juan and the sensibilities of a stag in season. Maybe I should ask him to go along on this little adventure? No, he'd get in too much trouble—but then again, he is a charmer."

Chapter 5

5a

Between the lane-controlled Caldecott Tunnel boring through the Berkeley Hills, the predictably bottlenecked San Francisco–Oakland Bay Bridge, not to mention overwrought streets and highways en route, the prudent Bay Area commuter understands that at any point they could be bushwhacked. So budgeting enough time to drive the thirty-five miles from Walnut Creek in the East Bay to the sprawling airport on the San Francisco peninsula is imperative. But this afternoon, the gods were either sleeping in or off screwing up someone else's life; Sharon and Kevin made it to within three miles of the airport in forty minutes. Then the gods awoke and decided to take a look at the Bayshore Freeway near Candlestick Park.

"Shit," Sharon said as a black Honda Civic swerved directly in front of her missing her front end by five feet. Then another, this one red, flew by Kevin's door doing at least one hundred miles an hour. The two wove in and out of traffic like it was the first lap of the Indy 500. "Assholes," she added.

Two Highway Patrol cars, lights and sirens wailing, quickly followed. Their skills were good but the two rice rockets were more nimble and faster. They were faster until the lead black car clipped the rear bumper of a grey Toyota Corolla driven by an elderly man. The Civic rose off its two left tires, and then the front right caught the sharp edge of the shoulder and within a blink became airborne. The red Civic slowed and watched his partner summersault, then roll over and over toward the ditch that paralleled the freeway. Tidal water flew up in a huge spray as the black car slammed into the channel.

Sharon slammed on her brakes, just like the dozens of other cars that surrounded the accident. Three cars sandwiched a limousine, others pulled quickly to the side of the road missing the hard breaking cars directly in front of them. Those that could weaved through the chaos and escaped. None looked in their rear view mirrors. The Highway Patrol cars pulled to the side of the road and ran to the half-submerged car. Sharon and Kevin slowly drove past the accident, Kevin giving Sharon the story as they passed.

"Car's a wreck, the kid is halfway out the window, not moving, good God what a shame."

"It's the damage they could have had on all of the drivers I'm pissed about," Sharon said.

They passed the old man in his Corrola; he had parked on the shoulder of the freeway a hundred yards past the Civic in the ditch. Two cars had pulled over to see if he needed assistance.

"The man seems okay, walking around," Kevin said. "Lucky, that car could have flipped over at the speeds everyone was traveling."

"My guess they won't find the other racer," Sharon said.

Sharon was wrong. Just before they left the freeway to enter the off-ramp that led to the airport terminal, they watched two Highway Patrol officers handcuffing a young oriental male as they pressed him against the red Civic.

"Sometimes a little justice is found," Kevin said.

"As I said, assholes," Sharon said as they climbed the overpass of the freeway and dove into the vehicular machine that wrapped itself through one of the world's busiest airports.

Kevin gave Sharon a hug and a quick kiss and said, "That was fun, let's *not* do that again. If we were ten minutes later the freeway would be congested to the bridge. Would probably have missed my flight."

"Always the pessimist, we are here and you didn't," Sharon answered. "Have a good flight, try not to complain too much, play nice with the kids in England."

"Anything else mother?"

"Yes, stay out of trouble. I do not want any late night calls from Scotland Yard or Interpol, okay?"

Sharon heard Kevin mumble something, but did not call him on it. She wasn't too keen herself anymore about long flights.

Kevin watched her pull away from the drop-off lane in the dark green Jaguar XJR sedan. She had once told him about her fondness for the old Jaguar styles but for the life of him he couldn't remember why. He did recall that more than one of her past Jaguars had been destroyed during their adventures. But he was very glad she knew how to drive the car and that the disk brakes had performed as specified. He carried a leather brief-case and towed his one large suitcase to the First Class–Business counter of British Airlines. The woman at the counter checked his passport and printed out his boarding pass. She was all of five feet tall, her hair cut in a modern flip with a pink strand of hair hanging over her left eye. She arched her neck to look up at the man in front of her; her heart skipped a beat.

"You okay?" Kevin said, seeing her hesitation.

Recovering, she said, "Yes, sir, all is in order. The plane is on time. Is there anything I can do to make your trip easier?"

"Make sure the seat is big enough," he answered, with a laugh.

"They are the best; you will find them more than accommo-dating even for an experienced gentleman like yourself. Do you travel to London often?"

"No, first time. I've been through London from Paris but never directly into Heathrow. But I'll be in London for a few months on business."

"If I may, here is my card. I'll be back seeing my family in a few weeks; they live in Kent. If you need a tour guide, ring me up. I'm very good."

"At what?" he innocently asked.

Her heart skipped another beat.

"Being a tour guide, luv."

She slipped him his boarding pass and strapped a tag onto his bag.

"No promises," Kevin answered. "I'll be very busy."

He read the name—Grace Middleton—on her card.

"Ms. Middleton, no promises."

"I understand, Mr. Bryan. But if you have the time. Your gate is A-7. Have a pleasant flight. And, it's Grace.

"Well, Grace, you never know."

"Yes, Mr. Bryan, you never know."

Lucky to arrive and check-in early, Kevin stopped in one of the bars and ordered a Jameson on the rocks. The whiskey helped to settle his nerves, he'd first believed he was over the problem on the freeway, but as he thought about it, his hand started to shake. It was something new, and he did not like it. He forced himself to slowly sip the drink. He looked at the crowds that surged through the terminal, more and more, San Francisco had become a portal of the world for America, especially from Pacific Rim countries. Starting in Hong Kong and heading north to Beijing, every large city in Asia had flights that start or stop in San Francisco, so many that some airlines, especially the Japanese, were adding flights to San Jose's airport. For a few minutes, as hundreds of Chinese hurried through the terminal, Kevin felt like he could have been in Beijing's international airport. He'd worked for years in Oakland's Chinatown and had great friends who were of Chinese and Japanese ancestry, but he did feel a touch out of place when he looked about and noticed that he was the only Anglo to be seen.

As he waited in the airport lounge, he watched a tight group of men, all Chinese by their looks, gather toward the rear of the departure area. All wore a distinctive blue jacket with a red C and T logo; underneath were the words *Chinese Taipei*. Each carried a matching blue gym bag, and every one had their phones out and were taking pictures. Curious Kevin gathered up his bag and wandered over to the Chinese gentleman who seemed to be managing the group; he had to be twenty years older than the players.

"Baseball players?" Kevin asked.

The man smiled.

"Some of the best from Taiwan, heading to London then Holland for the World Port Tournament."

His English was flawless; in fact there was a hint of the American south in his accent.

"My boys are great," he told Kevin. "Some have even played in the Little League World Series in South Williamsport. But these are the professionals. They have their sights set on winning this year—all they have to do is beat Cuba."

"You sound American. My name's Kevin Bryan."

"Danny Yang, Mr. Bryan. Born and raised in Atlanta. Played ball at Georgia and would have gone to the show if I hadn't blown out my Achilles. Now I've coached all around the world and this gig with Taipei is the best."

Yang rolled his eyes and smiled again.

"Baseball, as it's been said, has been very, very good for me."

"Do what you love—what could be better. You said these fellows are pros?"

"We have a small professional league of four teams, all named after animals, kind of like the Cubs and Cardinals. The real source of the game is the Little Leagues throughout the island; it's huge there. Bigger than America. Every town has fields and sponsors. Maybe like it was in the States back thirty years ago. These guys are very good; we should put on a good effort. Some were on the team when we won a few years back. None of the fellows wants to lose to Cuba. But me, I'm concerned about the Dutch; they could take it."

"Changing planes?"

Yang answered that his team had been in the Bay Area for a week and had played some exhibition games with Stanford and University of California teams.

"We tried to do something with the Giants, but they were busy," he said, as the two men took seats in the rear of the lounge. "They won last night. We caught the game with some comped tickets—the fellows loved it. We're just stopping in London to change planes, then into Schiphol airport, bus to Rotterdam. Long night and long day, but three days to rest before the tournament starts. Me, while I love the game, I'm getting very tired of airplanes. When I was in Double A, I hated the buses. Now it's the planes. Such is the life of a baseball gypsy."

As if to reiterate Yang's last comment, an announcement blared from the overhead speakers: "Ladies and Gentlemen, British Airways regrets that there will be a short delay before boarding our flight to London. We expected to begin boarding at seven p.m."

Kevin watched the screen over the desk as the listed departure time switched.

"Damn," he said, softly.

"Isn't it always the case," Yang said. "We rush to get here and discover we didn't have to rush at all."

"Me, I just want to get aboard. Nonetheless, baseball in Holland; never would have thought of it. Giants fan myself."

Yang shrugged.

"Always hated the Giants. I'm from the days when they were in the same division; never did understand that one, and it made for very late-night baseball when my Braves played on the West Coast."

"I remember some great pitchers then," Kevin said. "Glavine, Maddux, Smoltz—good Lord, they could pitch. And the Giants seemed to always be a game or two back. Tough games, was a lot of fun. Five or six Cy Youngs among them."

"Six, if I remember. Maddux won three, but one was with the Cubs. That one doesn't count. Great years; I spent a lot of time in the bleachers when I wasn't playing."

"You look like a catcher," Kevin said.

"And with your height, probably a pitcher. To us guys, the ball from one of you tall fellows looked like it was thrown from the top of a building."

"I did pitch a little, but it was tough to play in San Francisco. Not like the old days of when there were neighborhood fields."

Kevin explained that he had become a cop like his uncle, but was retired now.

"No actually a new job, some consulting," he answered, when Yang asked if he was on vacation. "In London for a few months, then home. Where are you going after Amsterdam?"

"Actually, we play near Rotterdam—not a bad ballpark. Four teams this year: Cuba, Netherlands, Japan and us. Quite a mix. But most of them are good; a bunch could play pro ball if their countries would let them, mostly the fellas from Cuba. Count on some excitement every year when one of their players tries to defect. In fact, I was there when that kid Toribio Rodriquez took off. That was something to see. Now he'll be MVP again with you guys. There's no justice."

"You're breaking my heart, Danny."

5b

He was surprised when the flight steward said his seat was upstairs, until he remembered the setup of a 747. For those in the know and with money, the most spectacular arrangements for flying anywhere are the twenty seats in the upper business class area of the Boeing 747. British Airways called this bubble on top of the aircraft Club World; Kevin called it heaven. He stretched his legs out and was offered a whiskey before the plane even began to taxi. Having nothing more than his phone as a diversion, he was grateful for the extensive list of movies on his personal screen. He realized that if he were in steerage, as Sharon referred to economy, he would have thought he had been put in solitary. After his third Jameson, he fell asleep watching Bruce Willis do strange things with a blunderbuss in some kind of flashback sci-fi movie. He awoke one hour out of Heathrow to a fairly edible breakfast omelet and fruit. What he really appreciated was the warm damp towel and coffee. Sunlight streamed through the windows, and when he looked out nothing but green forests and fields extended to the horizon, quite a contrast to the yellow-brown landscape of a California winter with less than the usual rain he had left ten hours earlier. Then as the plane made a slow pass over London, one tourist spot after another passed five thousand feet below him, the Houses of Parliament, the giant London Ferris Wheel, the Thames, then miles of housing. The flight attendant said it was one o'clock as they rolled to a stop and apologized for the delay.

Customs was a nightmare due to the crowds but not as complicated as he expected, in fact easier than what he had gone through coming back into the United States from Paris with Sharon not more than a year ago. He was surprised as he looked around that as a white guy he was in the minority again; every nationality in the world seemed to be in line, and all in front of him. Finally, after an hour, he rolled his bag through the double doors of the international terminal. The crowd waiting outside the arrival gate shocked him. Hundreds stood three and four deep, patiently waiting for kin and friends. Lining a barricade were drivers waiting for clients, holding up names plastered on paper signs, cheap erasable boards, and iPads. A distinguished man sporting a brushy British mustache and grey suit stood properly off to one side; his iPad said *Mr. Bryan*. Kevin pointed and was swept along with the tide of travelers as they pushed their way out of arrival. The man met him at the opening and immediately took his suitcase.

"Good afternoon, Mr. Bryan. Welcome to London. My name's Barrington. Our car is just across the road in the car park. Traffic midday should be fine; it's mornings and evenings that are difficult. We should be at your apartment in less than an hour."

"Good afternoon, Mr. Barrington. I suppose you know where we are going? I haven't a clue."

"Yes, I drive exclusively for the company, third trip today in fact. Your apartment is in Sloane Square—comfortable neighborhood, pricey but very nice. It's just a short walk to Buckingham and the Tube."

"Buckingham?"

"Buckingham Castle, the Queen's residence."

Barrington said it with a matter-of-fact tone, as he picked up the pace and began to move quickly through the concourse and lobby. Kevin's long legs just matched the man's shorter but still athletic gait.

"I need a coffee, Mr. Barrington. I see a Starbucks ahead."

"You sure, sir? Traffic will start to build."

Kevin looked at the man.

"What's your hurry? I want a coffee."

"I'm sorry, sir, just been a hectic day. Sorry. Please, do you have English pounds?"

It had never occurred to Kevin to do anything about money. He had maybe five hundred American dollars in his pocket; he literally couldn't buy a coffee.

"May I borrow a few pounds, Mr. Barrington? I'll see that you get them back."

"No problem, sir, I'll just put it on the account. But we should hurry."

Still put off by Barrington's desire to move along, Kevin ordered a grande coffee and a strange-looking sandwich. He handed the change back to the driver.

"I put twenty quid on the bill. Keep the change. There is a currency exchange around the corner from the apartment, near the Tube station. You can exchange your cash there. All the other arrangements for the room have been completed. There's even a nice mess, I mean larder, of food put away in the kitchen."

In the parking area, they approached a large Mercedes sedan; the trunk slowly opened.

"I'll put the bag in the boot," Barrington said. "Do you wish to have your carry-on placed there as well?"

"No, Mr. Barrington, I'll keep it with me."

Barrington stowed the bag and opened the rear passenger's side door.

Barrington started the car and maneuvered through the car park and out the pay gate before he answered.

"Yes, sir, quite a tour. Falklands, Belfast, Iraq, home, then

Iraq again. Saw more than I wanted, sir."

"I understand. Even my friend doesn't talk a lot about Iraq, but I know she still can't shake it."

Kevin sipped his coffee and looked out the window. British motorways, such as they are, are heavily used, seem narrower, and are for American sensibilities backward. From the backseat he could see the speedometer, which for a few minutes where the traffic was thin, topped 140 kph.

"No hurry, Barrington."

"Sorry, sir, habit. In and out all day. Sorry."

Kevin could see the eyes of the driver in the rearview mirror; he was squinting as he looked forward, as if concerned about something. The speedometer settled in at about 100 kph.

Kevin sipped his coffee; the sandwich was inedible.

"Military?" Kevin asked.

Barrington acted like he hadn't heard Kevin's question.

"I was wondering if you had been in the military. You carry yourself like an officer with experience," Kevin said.

Barrington took a quick glance at the mirror. "Yes, sir, almost thirty years. Retired—this job keeps me busy and away from the house. Problem, sir?"

"No, Mr. Barrington, absolutely not. A good friend is a retired military officer. She's been through some tough times, but things have worked out for her. Thirty years, that's quite a career."

"Yes, sir. It was." Barrington turned his attention back to the road.

"Will there be someone to meet me at the apartment? I wasn't sure what the procedure would be. The information was only the address and that someone would be picking me up at the airport."

"I will call when we reach the city. A Miss Montgomery will meet you there. She is the head of security and, if I may, quite a looker. Very good at what she does. She is also ex-military. She has everything you will need."

They turned onto a narrow street flanked by a colonnade of

huge trees whose branches arched completely over the narrow road. Cars parked in what seemed like illogical locations and directions on both sides.

"Don't ask about parking, sir, no one has a clue. Park where you can and pray, that's the current London way. Five blocks."

Barrington punched a number into a cell phone and waited for maybe thirty seconds before saying, "No answer, strange. She said she would be there."

He double-parked in front of a stairway that climbed ten steps to a white townhome. Two pillars capped by a half-round overhang framed the front door. To each side and extending to the far street corners were identical townhomes, the only variation being the hedge planting and window boxes of some of the houses.

"Built during the Edwardian period by some speculators, probably made a fortune. But they aren't too bad. The company has owned this one for years." He passed Bryan a key. "You go ahead. I'll bring your bag."

Kevin climbed the steps and looked up and down the street; it was remarkably quiet considering the traffic they had just been through. As he pushed the key into the keyhole the door noiselessly swung open.

Behind him with the suitcase, Barrington said, "That's odd, she's never left it open before."

Kevin put the key in his pocket, each of his cop antennae suddenly alive. He put up his hand to have Barrington hold. Glancing in the man's direction, all he saw was the Glock carefully held in Barrington's right hand; it was pointed at him.

"What the hell?" Kevin demanded.

Barrington didn't say a word but, with the barrel of the gun, waved Kevin to one side of the door, then slid past him and slowly walked down the long hallway.

Kevin knew it was foolish to follow the man, so he did.

Barrington took a quick look around the corner, and put up his hand signaling Kevin to stop. Then Barrington disappeared around the corner.

Ten seconds passed.

"I think you need to come in here, Mr. Bryan," Barrington called from further in the apartment. "We have a problem."

Kevin turned the corner leading to the main downstairs room. Bright sunlight streamed in through leaded glass windows. The butter-yellow walls with cream trim accented the many paintings; the furniture was polished leather. A glass coffee table the center of the furniture arrangement. And sprawled in a most provocative and immodest posture lay a drop-dead gorgeous brunette, a bloody crack running across her forehead that had left spots of blood on the oriental silk carpet.

"You said you were a cop?" Barrington asked.

"Yes."

"Here."

He pulled a snub-nosed revolver from his ankle holster and handed it to Kevin.

"We need to clear the house before I call for assistance. I'll take upstairs; you take this floor and the cellar. Back here in five minutes or less."

Kevin had seen dead people before, more times than he wanted to count. People can do a lot of damage to another human if pissed enough. But in his years as an Oakland and Lafayette cop, he had never seen a more beautiful woman in his life. He slowly walked past the body and through the downstairs rooms; in the kitchen he found a stairway into a basement maze of a wine cellar, billiards room, small gym, and sauna. But no killer.

When he returned to the parlor, he found Barrington standing over the body, talking into his mobile. Seeing Kevin, he clicked off.

"She didn't deserve this. Some son of a bitch will pay dearly. You didn't touch anything, did you?"

"Only the door handle to the basement. I used my handkerchief." He extracted it from his pocket with his freehand. "Was that the police you were talking to?"

"To a degree, this is not a police matter now."

A long blast from a car horn echoed down the hallway.

"Shit, I need to move the car. Too many eyes. This will be taken care of, but we need to get you out of here, now!"

Barrington slipped the pistol back into his shoulder holster and pointed toward the hallway.

"My backup, if you don't mind, Mr. Bryan."

Kevin thought for a brief moment.

"Not right now, maybe later. I hear the streets in London can be dangerous."

"Suit yourself. I need to get you somewhere safe until we figure out what this is all about. This is a major cockup of the first degree. What do you think of the Savoy?"

"Don't you think we should wait for the police?"

"Mr. Bryan, there will be no police. There will be no questions, or at least any for you. You are the most innocent man involved. Sally's been dead maybe an hour, about the time we were supposed to arrive if it weren't for the delays. I don't have the time right now to discuss this with the local constabulary; we need to leave before my associates arrive. I don't know them, and I sure as hell don't want them to know me. Out."

Kevin headed to the hallway and turned to see Barrington kiss his fingertips and place them on the cheek of the woman. He assumed that she had been Ms. Sally Montgomery, but they had never been formally introduced.

5c

Barrington asked for the key from Kevin and locked the front door behind them. Kevin threw his suitcase into the boot. This time he slid into the front seat, checked that the revolver was snug in the pocket of his jacket, and waited for the driver. After they had gone three blocks, he asked, "What's your name?"

"Barrington."

"We Americans are less formal; we call each other by our given names."

"All's the loss, but if you need to know, it's Clive."

"Well, Clive, what the fuck just went on back there?"

"I don't know."

"Yeah, sure, like I haven't heard that before. What are you—MI5, MI6, military police, the fucking Beefeaters? I know, bloody Scotland Yard."

Barrington said nothing, weaving in and out of traffic. They passed a sign that said Sloane Square, then a flurry of street signs: Holbein, Pimlico, and Chelsea Bridge Road. Kevin watched Barrington stuff a black communicator in his left ear. They flew out of the tree-shrouded streets and turned hard left onto Grosvenor Road, the Thames to their right. He barely slowed the car as they raced parallel to the river. More parks flew by, and then housing piled up along the embankment, temporarily hiding the river. A sign said Vauxhall Bridge; they didn't turn. Another bridge, Lambeth, passed on the right. Barrington pressed on.

"Damn it, Clive, what the hell just happened?"

"I'm trying to find out."

Barrington punched another number into his mobile.

As if out of a gothic novel, the Parliament Building, in all its ornate wedding cake flourishes, finishes, and brownness, passed them on the right. Tourists fill every crosswalk and plaza, and they were forced to stop.

"So I guess we're not going to see the prime minister. Wow, there's Big Ben."

"It's the bloody bell, not the building, and the prime minister is somewhere in Africa today."

"That's nice. Do you think he knows what the fuck went on back there?"

"Not likely."

Barrington's mobile buzzed.

"Right . . . right! Be very careful when you remove the body, get what you can. Prints, DN-fucking-A, everything. I want to know who killed her and why. . . . Yes, I'm taking the Yank to the Savoy. . . . No, I'm staying there. Easier to control."

After ordering the person on the other end of the phone to

call him back at five o'clock, Clive clicked off the earpiece.

"I've heard the Savoy is nice," Kevin offered.

"Would you shut up?"

"Shut up? You're telling me to shut up. For Christ's sake, I spend less than two hours in this country and I'm rudely insulted on top of finding a great-looking woman dead in my apartment. With all the closed circuit TVs around, they probably have my smiling face leaving the place."

Barrington turned right and then left at the river. The signage read Victoria Embankment.

"This is pleasant. Nice trees, tourist boats, nice. Say, why don't we stop and chat?"

"No time."

"There's always time," Kevin said.

He extracted the revolver, and from his lap pointed at Clive Barrington.

"There's a nice park. Let's stop there."

"No time."

"Like I suggested, let's stop there, NOW!" Kevin jammed the revolver into Barrington's left side.

Barrington slid the Mercedes to a stop in a bus zone. Kevin swung the door open, slipped the revolver into his pocket and exited the car. He faced a narrow gateway into the park, surrounded by an iron fence. He heard Barrington's door slam behind him as he walked into the park.

"Mr. Bryan, hold right there, please."

Kevin didn't stop, raised his right arm, and gave Barrington the finger.

"I'm out of here. I'm going home."

He heard Barrington's leather footsteps behind him, and when he suddenly turned and stopped, the man nearly ran into him.

"Get my bag," Kevin snapped. "I'll find the Savoy on my own."

"A blind man could find it, the entry is right there."

Clive pointed toward the huge stone building that rose high

over them.

"We need to talk."

"You think? By the way, there's a meter maid or whatever you call them giving you a ticket."

Barrington walked quickly to the car. He pulled a bill-fold-sized case out of his jacket, opened it and held it directly in front of the young girl's face. She studied it for a few seconds, then raised her hands like she was warding off the devil and turned and walked away. People walking through the park watched and then hurried on.

"Big deal, I can make meter maids disappear too, or at least I was once able to," Kevin said, when he caught up with Barrington. "Now, Clive, tell me what's happening, and none of that fucking need to know crap."

Barrington extracted a gold case from his coat pocket, removed a cigarette, and lit it with a gold lighter.

"I assume that Clive Barrington is not your real name. So what is it—James Bond, Daniel Craig, Ward Bond?"

Barrington smiled.

"It is actually Clive Barrington, and you were close with all your guesses. I'm with the London Police in the Specialist and Economic Crime Command. We are working closely with the company that hired you and, I must add, who brought you here against our recommendations. We are more than able to take care of what is required."

"Gee, thanks. So let's get back in your fine car and take me back to Heathrow. Maybe I can be back to California in less than a day. And, take care of it? Is this how London takes care of murder? Sweep it all under the carpet?"

"You can't leave now; you're up to your ass in this. For some reason, your being here got one of my people killed. She was there to fill you in. Now, I've got to deal with you. Tomorrow you will meet with the select group of the insurance people. Outside of a few high officers, they don't know who I am. There's a chance it's an inside operation. Having you onboard gives them some room, since they will be fairly certain you're not one of my people. Sally was working closely with them; she was under-cover."

"My first thought is that someone found out," Kevin said. "She was more than just an employee, wasn't she?"

"You're too much a cop, I can see that. Yes, she was very close; her father was one of my best friends. He was with me in Iraq. So shall we head to the hotel? I'm what we call a float-er, and I work on certain crimes. My specialty is diamonds and jewel heists."

"In San Francisco, we call someone found in the bay a float-er. Probably similar."

"Thanks, that's just what I need, a bloody comedian. Let's get you checked in. It's getting late, and I'm starved."

"You buy."

Chapter 6

"You have got to be kidding. You're gone for less than a day and already in trouble," Sharon said into the phone. "What have you gotten yourself into?"

She put the phone down on her desk and clicked on the speaker.

"I haven't a clue. I'll learn more tomorrow."

When Basil heard Kevin's voice echoing about Sharon's office, he stood up and looked around.

"This Clive fellow has us meeting with the insurance people in the morning. But right now, he's all over the place—haven't figured him out, yet. We went to dinner at a small French restaurant around the corner from the hotel. Great food and even better French fries. Reminds me of that place in Paris we went to."

"I'm more concerned about you than your stomach."

"So am I, but a guy's got to eat. Barrington told me that the word on the street is about a big shipment coming up from South Africa, all legitimate stones, not blood diamonds. He said one of his outside informants told him about it. The company's trying to find out how he knew. All hush-hush, to use Barrington's phrase."

"Ah, the British. I met some good guys in Iraq and some real assholes."

"I think he's one of the good guys. I asked if he knew you. He said no."

"Name doesn't ring a bell, either. Coming home?"

"No, not right now. He thinks there's a connection to all this and little old me. Why, I haven't a clue. I'll know more tomorrow. It's late and I'm beat. I slept a little on the plane, but my body says sleep. I found a Jameson in the mini-bar. Probably cost twenty pounds, but I don't care. After that—sleep. I'm meeting Barrington in the lobby for breakfast at eight. At least that's a civil way to start the day."

"Go to bed; call me tomorrow if you can."

"When are you seeing Bobby?"

"Next Monday; he's driving up. Still waiting to hear from Lopez, maybe later today. It's only two o'clock here. Go to bed."

"Yes, mother."

Kevin clicked off, and Sharon looked at Basil, who had settled back onto his bed.

"What do you think, Baze? Can he handle himself without our help?"

Her phone started ringing; the screen said *X.I. Lopez.*

"This will be fun. O'Mara," she said, again clicking on the speaker.

"*Buenas tardes*, Sharon. How are you this delightful afternoon?"

"Xavier, I'm just fine. Have you learned anything?"

"*Si*. A lot. Seems that it's a nest of snakes and villains down there in Cuba. My manager friend says the family may be held at a farm-camp in the southern region, near Santiago. A woman who is a part of state security has a small plantation near there, where she cares for the families of defecting ballplayers. One of his players' family disappeared when he initially defected, but when he ended up in Mexico, they suddenly reemerged, my guess after paying some ransom money. The woman who runs the place is Marta de la Vega."

According to Xavier's source, this de la Vega was a true believer, but with a fat bank account in Switzerland, or at least that was the guess. De la Vega was also involved with Cuban baseball, as one of the government managers of the players when they were on the road.

"He also said she ships the coffee grown on her farm to Mexico, where it's processed and then sent to France and Switzerland."

"My guess, she's more of a guard than a manager," Sharon said thoughtfully. She asked Lopez if the player's family knew where they'd been held.

"No, they were taken out of the farm in a truck with no windows, then to an airport, where a plane took them to Mexico City."

"Did they remember how long the truck ride took?"

"A couple of hours. They flew out of Santiago on Cubana Airlines."

"So the story about somewhere in the south end of Cuba may be true."

"I'll be up there next week for meetings with your DEA. Can we have dinner? I miss you," Lopez said.

Sharon made a face at Basil.

"Dinner? What day?"

Lopez said he was flying up Tuesday and back Friday morning. Would Wednesday night work?

"I'm staying at the Marriot on Market Street," he said. "Maybe the Tadich Grill? We can talk about old times."

Sharon paused.

"I won't be alone."

The pause was longer on Lopez's end.

"Not that tall fellow, Kevin?"

"He's in London. It's a friend who is helping me with this Cuban thing. You need to meet him, since you two may be working together."

"No time for just the two of us?"

"Not this trip. There's too much to do. We'll meet you at the restaurant at six-thirty."

"You are breaking this hombre's heart."

"Xavier, you'll get over it."

She clicked off the phone and went to scratch the back of Basil's big head.

"He's a piece of work, but priceless all the same."

The big dog cocked his head at her words. This was one of

the times she wished he could talk.

"Is this the right thing to do, Baze? Our needs are fairly small. We now have money in the bank, the car works, and you'll never run out of bones. Most of our troubles seem to be gone, so why am I in such a foul mood?"

She scratched his head again, his ears perking when she said, "Walk?" He immediately got up and trotted down the hallway to where his leash hung.

Sharon lit a cigarette as she left the front porch and started walking up the sidewalk. Their route took them around the block, where Basil could stop and visit some of his favorite spots. The pressure on the neighborhood to change had been growing the past year. Two blocks away a new hotel had opened, and a new apartment building now loomed over the collection of pre-World War II cottages that had held off the town's growth. But being sandwiched between a booming downtown and the BART train tracks had a strange impact on the residents. Some wanted to organize and resist the push from town, others, mostly renters, didn't care. They liked how close the train and town were, but also knew they couldn't fight if the property owner decided to sell. Sharon's house was worth more as a puzzle part for some developer's grand scheme than a resale. Ever since her dealings with a developer over some land near San Jose a few years earlier, her sympathy for growth had wavered. She felt that sometimes a line should be drawn; the argument was always where.

6b
Green Zone, Baghdad, Iraq, fall 2004

Crazy was only the half of it. The word from two Shia Iraqis after the million dollars on Sabawi Ibrahim's head was that the man was holed up outside his ancestral home of Tikrit, 160 kilometers north of Baghdad on the Tigris River. It was likewise the ancestral home of Saddam Hussein, near the site of the hole in the ground where, like a rat, Hussein had been discovered hiding less than nine months earlier. How accurate the intel was from the Shiite's could only be verified by going to Tikrit, a trip that O'Mara was not thrilled to make. There were too many opportunities for IEDs and ambushes; she wasn't going to lose any of her men over some asshole brother of Saddam's. She requested and was approved by Major Simpson for helicopters for the jump to Forward Operating Base Danger, located on the grounds of the ex-leader's presidential palace. From there she and her team would follow up the lead.

"Ten minutes," squawked the pilot over the headset. The roar of the Black Hawk helicopter preempted any casual conversation.

"Roger that," O'Mara shouted.

She looked in turn at the faces of the six men and their equipment jammed in the helicopter, each was deep in their own thoughts. Helicopters were safer than Humvees, but only by a degree or two. The pilot stayed over the river the whole trip.

She caught Sergeant Bobby Gillis looking at her with a big smile, and mouthed, "What?"

He answered with a soundless, "Later."

The landing zone lay parallel to the main road leading to the palace. After disembarking, the Black Hawk left as quickly as they arrived. "Places to go, things to do, Lieutenant," was all that the pilot offered as he saluted and climbed back into the helicopter. The American complex that spread out around the royal palace was immense. After winning the war against Saddam Hussein, the Americans took over the massive complex of buildings that had been one of the presidential palaces Saddam was fond of building. It was now Forward Operating Base Danger. Massive amounts of equipment and supplies had been stacked throughout the collection of buildings. Other smaller palaces and residences, all excessive in their bad architectural design, sat along the bluff overlooking the river and the manmade lake, like gargoyles waiting for carrion. None were to O'Mara's taste and if overdramatic sycophantic architecture were to be given an award, the numerous surrounding mini-palaces abutting Saddam's overwrought monstrosity would have been winners hands down.

From the LZ, O'Mara and her team were escorted to a temporary building and shown where they could bed down. For all intents the billet wasn't that bad; they could have easily been shown a sandy spot full of fleas and scorpions and told to set up their own tents. At least the crapper worked and was a lot better than a hole in the ground.

"Not bad, Lieutenant," Gillis said, looking over the digs. "We have the river to our back and a wall to the south and west. Hell, it reminds me of a gated community they built near Fresno—all the comforts of home."

"Yes, Sergeant," O'Mara said. "But in Fresno the neighbors don't try to shoot you or blow your sorry ass to kingdom come."

"Yes, sir, but some of those Fresno neighborhoods can be tough."

"Yes, I'm sure they are. But these accommodations will make you soft. You might check on room service."

"Yeah, candied dates on our pillows. Can't wait."

"And make sure the men have mosquito dope on tonight—I want no Leishmaniasis from sand fleas."

"Yes, sir."

O'Mara had a hard time understanding how the Iraqi people coped with the diseases spread by the endemic sand fleas and mosquitoes and all sorts of other creepy crawlies that made you sick or even dead if untreated. Aleppo boil was one of the worst: a fleabite–induced bug that could disfigure you for life, and even kill you slowly if not treated. She wanted to go home whole or not at all. And there was malaria, dengue fever, typhus, and so many other things living in the river she forbade her men from swimming in the soup called the Tigris. She only drank bottled water and, when available, scotch—no ice.

The next morning Gillis brought a young man to her office. The man acted scared but defiant.

"I want my money first," he said, in broken English.

When O'Mara looked at the man, he averted his eyes.

"What money?" she asked.

"The reward."

"What reward? Why?"

"I have information. The word is out you are looking for people, Saddam's people. I have information. No money, no information."

"Sergeant, show him out."

Gillis grabbed the man by the arms and began to turn him toward the door.

"Wait, I do have information. I want the reward, and then a way to America."

"What information could someone like you have? Throw him out."

"No, no. I heard you are looking for Sabawi, Saddam's half-brother. True?"

"Who says?"

The kid looked at the sergeant then back at O'Mara.

"There is talk, that is all I know. I was standing in the market and two soldiers, American soldiers, were passing out leaflets that said that one million dollars was offered for the man. I know him."

"How?"

She lit a Marlboro and left the nearly full pack on her desk.

"I was his driver for six months when he was here in Tikrit," the informant answered. He eyed the pack of cigarettes.

"When?"

"Two years ago, he was building a house here, a big palace. So big all my aunts and uncles and my whole family could live in the kitchen."

"That's common knowledge. What else?"

"When he came, I drove. Reward?"

"Maybe, but the reward is for Sabawi, not talk. Talk is cheap here. Where is he?"

"Reward?"

"Sergeant, can we find a hundred bucks for this man if his

intel is good?"

"I'll check with the purser or whoever they have here with money."

"A hundred dollars? I leave my neck exposed to a knife coming here and all I'm offered is a hundred dollars?"

"And you might not even get that," O'Mara told him. To Gillis she said, "Put him in a holding cell for a few days, then we'll find out."

The sergeant took hold of the young man; he collapsed like Jell-O left in the sun.

"Okay, okay. But if you do find him, will I get more?"

"Who the hell knows in this country? What do you know?"

"When you Americans came, he dressed up like my aunt, in a black burqa, and climbed into the back of his fancy Mercedes. He had me drive him to Syria; when we crossed the border he disappeared. I drove it back here."

"That's it?"

"Yes, that is all."

"Gillis, this son of a bitch wants a reward for being a chauffeur. I don't believe it. What's your name?"

"Hussein Mohammed al-Tikriti."

"You will get your hundred dollars, and then I want you to pass the word there's more if your friends have better information than you."

"I could just hear what they have to say, then tell you," the kid said.

"Then you are a cheat, and I will make sure they know it. Where did you learn to speak English?"

"A school here in Tikrit. We all have to learn some English so we can work for the oil companies."

"Get Hussein out of here, Sergeant, and try and verify what he said."

"Yes, sir."

When the door closed behind them, she crushed the cigarette out in the ashtray and thought about what the kid had said.

Syria, great. From one fucked up country to another. Just great.

Sergeant Gillis did find more information; when asked by O'Mara about its source, all he said was that there were many ways to find information in Iraq. He didn't elaborate. She didn't ask.

"Can you get me Major Simpson, Green Zone?" she said to the communications operator the next morning.

Ten seconds went by before Major Simpson said, "Good morning, Lieutenant. What did you find out?"

She told him the long version. She also said that with the collaboration from other sources, Sabawi could be a dead end.

"I concur," Simpson said. "Get your men out and back here. There are rumors that we have a growing al-Qaeda movement here taking advantage of the collapse of the government and the lack of local police. Papers and intel says they want to drive us out, and they are not shy about killing hostages."

Simpson guessed it was the same faction that had bombed the UN headquarters in Baghdad and the Jordanian embassy.

"They're also the ones who just beheaded those American civilians. Bad bunch, very bad," he said.

"Copters?" O'Mara asked.

"Can't, sandstorm coming up from the south. You and your men grab what transports you can and get your asses back here. Just pretend that it's like that pretty coastal highway you have there in California."

"Yes, sir, but Route 1 doesn't have IEDs and snipers behind every palm tree. See you tonight."

"Roger that. Be fucking careful, Lieutenant."

O'Mara walked out into the yard in front of the communications complex. The temperature was actually warm, not blistering hot; her experienced guess was ninety-five degrees. *Almost balmy.* She saw one of her new replacement recruits, a private, Theodore Beckett, whom Gillis had dubbed TeddyB.

"Private, find Sergeant Gillis. I want him here five minutes ago."

"Yes, sir. He said he was going to the mess."

"That man eats more than any horse I know. Find him."

TeddyB took off toward a complex of buildings grouped together on the river side of the base and disappeared among them.

Two minutes later, with the private in tow, Gillis jogged toward her, a chicken leg in one hand and a Coke in the other. By the time he reached her both were gone. He dropped the remains in an empty fuel drum that had CRAP lettered on the outside.

"Sir?" Gillis said, as he pulled up short, dust settling around his boots.

"The major wants us back in Baghdad ASAP," she said. "This thing's been a no-go from the start. Maybe the son of a bitch will die in Syria and save us all a bunch of shit. We need transport, so see what you can rustle up. I want to be on the road in less than an hour. It's one hundred miles of fucked-up highway between here and the Zone. I want to be there by six tonight. Can we do it?"

"Old Bobby Gillis will make it work."

He turned to the private.

"TeddyB, find the others. I want them right here in ten, got it?"

"Yes, Sarg. Got it."

They watched the kid sprint back toward the mess.

"Most of the men are in the mess cramming food. They never know when their next meal will be," Gillis said to O'Mara. "I guess Baghdad, tonight."

"*Insha'Allah*, Sergeant. God willing."

6c

London, Present Day

Kevin walked into the Thames Foyer of the Savoy and spotted Barrington pouring himself a cup of tea. The Thames River filled the great window beyond the small tables filled with guests having breakfast. The room like the hotel itself was lush and extremely British after the multi-million pound renovation. He sat in the gold brocade chair next to Barrington.

"Good morning Mr. Bryan, sleep well?" Barrington said.

"Like a lamb, thanks for dinner."

"My pleasure. We have a busy day ahead of us, tea?"

"Coffee."

Barrington signaled to the server. Another tray with coffee and scones arrived within minutes.

"Any more information about yesterday?" Kevin asked. "You said Ms. Montgomery was a friend's daughter?"

"Yes, Sir Thomas Montgomery. We fought all around the world together. He was a good mate. I knew her since her birth; stood in for her Christening, Thomas was somewhere in South Africa then, nasty business. Then again, that's what we're in for, all the nasty stuff. She was smart and well educated. Why she came into the police service is beyond me. She once said, 'If it's good enough for Da, it's bloody good enough for me.' I'm glad he and her mother aren't alive to see this."

"They're both dead?"

"Yes, they were driving west out of Jerusalem toward Tel Aviv, when some Hamas thugs stopped the car in the middle of the road. Thomas tried to protect his wife; he killed two before they were both shot dead. That was ten years ago. She's been my charge since. Sally said she could take care of herself."

"I'm very sorry. My first suggestion is she might have known who killed her. The doors were not damaged or forced, no signs of a struggle. Whoever it was left through the front door—CCTV?"

"My people are checking, but it's a long shot," Barrington answered. "They haven't found her automobile, mobile, or her purse, either."

"They are called handbags, not purses," Kevin said, with a straight face.

"How the hell do you know that?"

"Long story, that I'll bore you with someday. Maybe the killer took the car and her bag, and anything else he thought he could get away with."

"The house produced little of value," Barrington replied. "It was clean and comfortable, and was used before as an apartment for other guests of the insurance company. My people have now cleared it and found nothing."

"Cause of death?" Bryan asked.

"Blow to the head and strangled. Cold-blooded assholes. I swear I will kill them when I find them."

"I might stand by and watch. If you need help, just ask. She didn't deserve this."

"No she didn't, but then again, no one deserves to die like that.

Bryan's first meeting with the insurance company took place at their offices in the glass spiral tower at 30 St. Mary Axe, affectionately called *The Gherkin* in reference to its pickle-like shape. The ovoid structure towered over surrounding buildings in the heart of London's financial district, an impressive if stark reminder of its predecessor, the Baltic Exchange building, which had been destroyed a decade earlier by a Provisional IRA bomb attack. Somewhere in a warehouse, the remains of the Baltic Exchange were stored for reconstruction at some future location, at some future date.

"Interesting," Bryan said, when they had arrived and he was gazing up the sloping face of the building.

"Yes, it is, and everyone has an opinion," Barrington replied, as he paid the taxi driver. "I'm not an architectural critic, so I stay away from the fights, but I have to admit the views are spectacular from the upper floors."

They took the elevator to the thirtieth floor; it opened to a modern and very shiny marble and steel lobby, where a cute girl sat at the front desk. A shock of turquoise hair draped over her right eye.

"New color, Lydia?" Barrington said.

"Yes, Mr. Barrington. Do you like it?"

"I think it's brilliant, almost matches your eyes."

"Oh, Mr. Barrington."

She adjusted her gaze upward to look at Kevin.

"He is with me," Barrington said. "Has the meeting started?"

"Yes, sir, they are in the usual place. Coffee?"

She looked again at Bryan.

"Starbucks," she added.

"Yes, thank you, Lydia. This way, Kevin."

Bryan walked quickly to keep up with the military strides of Clive Barrington, who stopped at the glass doors to a conference room where five people sat around a long table. All of London stretched out beyond them in the window; the five all had their backs to the glass.

"This is the committee formed to oversee security," Barrington said, before they entered. "None have experience with security, except for the man on the left. Dorsey is his name. He's a retired MI6 field agent."

"Double dipping?" Bryan asked.

"Absolutely, his pension and a nice consultant's fee. To be honest, he was the loudest voice against hiring you."

"Beyond yours? Great, can I go home now?"

"Maybe before the day is over, Mr. Bryan. Who knows? And by the way, they do not know about Sally."

Barrington tapped on the glass and pushed the doors open.

After introductions, Kevin was more confused than ever. Seated to the right of Dorsey, the others were called Smith, Jones, Brown, and Davis. They all looked like they had walked out of the same private school, gone to the same overpriced tailor, and underpriced barber. He told himself to try and not remember their names.

Brown said, "Mr. Bryan, you come well recommended by our American partners, but I'll tell you right up front that we do not think this is necessary. Mr. Dorsey here can certainly take care of any issues that come up. It is only because our American friends are paying the bill that we have even entertained your company."

Jones added, "We have had no thefts in the last ten years."

Davis pushed his narrow wire glasses down his nose and looked at Kevin, started to say something and was interrupted by Smith, who said, "Well, he's here. Maybe Dorsey can find something for him to do."

"He can go home," Dorsey said.

Kevin was getting pissed. It was one thing to be marginalized; it was wholly different to be insulted in this demeaning and passive-aggressive attitude that bounced around the shiny mahogany table.

"Gentlemen, I'm a cop and a damn good one. I do not have to justify myself to you or your man, Dorsey. I was asked by a friend to help, because he and his partners thought that you hadn't a clue as to how to deal with all this. And I am beginning to believe he was right. I have had a very eventful entry into your country, and considering what I am hearing from you gentlemen, I would just as soon walk out the building, go to St. Pancras, catch the train to Paris and kiss this all good-bye. But I have a contract, *with your American owners*. So let's put all this petty English stiff upper lip shit behind us and get on with finding the problems and holes in your system."

He pulled his cell phone out and set it on the table.

"If not, I have my friend on speed dial, and even though it is two in the morning in San Francisco, he would surely like to hear the news now rather than later."

He lit up the phone's screen and slid it across the table toward Brown.

"Well, I never," Brown said.

"Most probably, but that's not my problem. So if I'm staying, let's get started. If not, then Mr. Barrington can drive me back to my apartment," Kevin looked at Barrington who nodded, "so I can pick up my bags and get the hell out of here."

Two hours later he was still there, albeit even more shocked by the overall lack of continuity, cross checks, and collaboration amongst the men around the table. Each thought the other was doing something, where in reality they were doing nothing. Even Dorsey began to warm to Bryan's suggestions, and Kevin could see that he was also surprised by the lack of an overall interconnected security.

"There are too many gaps in the process," Bryan told his new coworkers as he pointed to the map of Schiphol Airport sitting on the conference table. "Based on the diagrams and Dorsey's report, we have people walking between arrival and departure locations; we have cars driving between this airport and that hotel. At any spot, they can be engaged and taken down." Kevin looked again at Barrington, who wore a smile.

"Here and here, they are exposed and vulnerable. This may have been okay ten years ago, but these people are more sophisticated. They aren't like Cary Grant playing John Robie, sneaking in through windows and escaping across rooftops. These people are experienced teams, some ex-military, smart, well armed, and very well paid. They are international, and the diamonds they steal are in Thailand or Israel the next day being recut, polished, and all their I.D.s burnished off. A week later, they show up in New York, Dubai, and Tokyo for some expensive bauble or trinket."

"We appreciate your mentioning one of our greatest actors, and I think we understand now what you are saying and we now know it all too well," Brown offered. "What do you propose?"

"First of all, never repeat the transfer twice. Each one must be different, unpredictable yet extremely well planned. Predictability and repetition are the easiest to compromise for obvious reasons. Over time, expectations are made, even by your own people. They get lazy. But it is those around the process—agents, pilots, aircraft personnel, drivers, guards—any one of them can be compromised, even people in your own offices. If they don't know what they are involved in, all's the better. One man—one process—one show. Here's how I would do it."

He pointed to the need to compartmentalize the information, the fewer people that knew the whole process the better, and began to layout the process at arrival. They ordered in lunch, then Kevin broke down the various parts on the white board. By late afternoon, everyone had bought in.

"I'm impressed. You really know your stuff," Barrington said, the others shook their heads in agreement.

"Years of being a cop and thinking like a criminal. In my Oakland years, I was on a team whose sole directive was to anticipate criminal behavior, where it might start and where it might come from. From there it was easier to anticipate and understand criminals' motivation and opportunity. We went by the old urban legend—so the story goes, an American bank robber named Willie Sutton once answered, when asked why he robbed banks, 'Because that's where the money is.' We looked for places where the money was and acted accordingly. We were right more often than not. Same goes for here."

He and Barrington rode down in the elevator together.

"I've got to cut you loose tonight," Barrington said, as they left the building a few minutes later. "My mother misses me, I'm heading home after I drop you off."

"Where's that?"

"South of here in Kent, near Royal Tunbridge Wells. Nice part of the world there. We have a family home, and I'm the eighth descendent to manage the place. I say manage lovingly though. The family's owned it since before Henry VIII; it was given as a result of some nefarious deeds by an ancestor. The Barrington line has cared for it since."

"Is there a Mrs. Barrington?"

"Other than my mother, no. My wife Martha passed away more than twenty years ago, but I have a pair of very fine children. All grown and successful on their own."

"Like to see your home someday."

"I'll see what can be arranged."

Kevin told Clive that he'd walk back to the hotel. The weather was comfortable and his suit coat was more than adequate for the evening. He headed down Threadneedle Street to Queen Victoria Street; it was close to the end of the business day and the sidewalks were full of people heading home. He had never seen a more crowded and hectic mass of people. He remembered it was Friday; his whole sense of timing was off due to some latent jet lag. He had two days to himself, London was his, yet for some reason he felt lonelier than he had in years. A touch of melancholia, he thought, nothing more. He reached the Thames and Victoria Embankment and paralleled the river until he saw a patch of green, where a sign said Inner Temple Gardens. He sat on a bench overlooking the river. Some children were playing nearby, their very pleasant looking nanny watching them with a phone to her ear. Kevin pulled out his phone, punched in Sharon. Four rings later, she picked up.

"Anything more on the girl?"

"No, and the strange thing was that all day it was never brought up. Barrington didn't say anything, and after I met the security committee—now that's a strange lot—he never mentioned it again. Nothing, except that he told me no one else at the meeting knew anything about the girl's death, all too strange."

"You were a good boy?"

"After I told them I was heading home if they didn't quit being assholes, they settled down. I was amazed at their attitude; aloof would be too simple a term. All so passive-aggressive and so proper. It was as if they couldn't be bothered—what's a few million one way or another? And I have a couple of days to myself, Clive is going to his country home—I have until Monday.

"Country home, my, my. Lots to do, great museums, enjoy."

Someone sat down on the other end of the bench and Kevin turned away slightly, glancing toward where the setting sun lit up the buildings beyond the park.

"I'll check out the magazines in the room," he told O'Mara. "This security-consulting gig might actually be something good, but I'll wait and see. Hey, do you mind?"

"Do you mind what?" Sharon said.

"Not you—somebody's here smoking a cigarette right behind me."

As Bryan turned toward the bench's other occupant, he felt

something hard shoved against his ribs.

"Hang up now, Mr. Bryan. I need a word," the man said.

Bryan focused on the man: thin face, pasty complexion, brown eyes, dirty grey cap in an old school shape, worn maroon tie cinched around an even older shirt collar. The cigarette dangling from the right corner of his mouth balanced the sharp scar under his left eye. It wasn't the scar or the hat or the cigarette that made him hang up, it was the hard tip of the suppressor on the pistol he saw and felt jammed in his ribs, hard. It would leave a bruise the size of a twenty pence piece on his white Irish skin, just above his kidney.

As the connection went dead, "Hang up now, Mr. Bryan," echoed in Sharon's mind. The speaker had emphasized the word *now*—an order not a request. She quickly punched in Kevin's number and got his voicemail. *What the hell?*

Chapter 7

Sharon tried calling Kevin's number four times over the next ten minutes—nothing. It was then she realized that she knew nothing about Kevin's itinerary, who he was meeting with, his friend in Lafayette who got him the job, nothing. The only thing she knew was the Savoy, and some guy named Barrington. Otherwise, nada.

She rang the hotel and asked for Kevin Bryan's room.

There was a lengthy pause, and when the woman reengaged all she could offer was, "We have no one staying here by that name, ma'am. Sorry."

"Mr. Barrington's room then, please."

Another pause.

"Again, ma'am, I do not have a Mr. Barrington staying with us either. Maybe they haven't checked in yet. I can leave a message if you would like to leave your number."

Sharon ended the call and looked down at Basil, who for some dog reason she couldn't fathom, had gotten up from his bed as soon as she called London and plopped down next to her, his damp jowl on her jeans. It was as if he knew or sensed something.

"You could find him if we were in London, I know you could," she said, scratching the furrow high between his eyes. "What the hell is going on?"

Her phone screen lit up and then buzzed. The incoming number was blocked.

"O'Mara."

"Miss O'Mara, my name is Clive Barrington. Has Mr. Bryan tried to reach you?"

"Where the hell is he? If that man is hurt or injured, I'll come there personally and punish you. Where is he?"

"That's what we would like to know, and I understand your concern."

"Barrington, you haven't even the remotest understanding of my concern. Why aren't you listed at the Savoy? Why isn't Kevin listed either? What happened?"

"We have an arrangement with the hotel and its security. How we are listed isn't an issue, but Mr. Bryan's whereabouts is my concern at the moment."

Barrington told her he'd been on his way home for the weekend.

"We had a surprisingly productive day, better than I thought we would, in fact. Mr. Bryan is very good, and extremely helpful," he said.

"Is this about the dead woman?"

There was a long pause before he asked, "How do you know about that?"

"Kevin told me, and he told me about all the cloak and dagger shit that went on afterward. Is it about her?"

"You Americans. My, you people get excited," Barrington said. "Mr. Bryan acted the same way."

"Mr. Barrington, do not patronize me, ever. My friend is missing, and it was on your watch. You seem to know that he's missing, and it's been less than an hour. Hell, I don't even know if he is missing or if his phone is dead or if he's drinking in some pub at Piccadilly Circus. But your call tells me something is wrong, so what is it, Mr. Barrington?"

"After the death of Sally Montgomery, I had my people watching Mr. Bryan after he left the meeting. As I told him, he is the only person involved in all of this who could not have killed her, but his arrival was more than a coincidence of timing."

"Was she murdered?"

"Yes, she had been hit with something heavy and rounded.

My forensic expert thinks it could have been the butt end of the handle to a pistol. It caught her just right—massive bleeding under the skull. She died from the attack. Maybe it was not intentional, but the room had been disarranged, as if from a fight or something similar."

He was silent for a moment and Sharon waited, knowing they were both mulling over the details.

"If she was to be killed, why go through all the messiness of a struggle?" he said, finally. "The killer had a gun, so why not shoot her?"

"Maybe too noisy, or as you said, not intentional. You said you were following Kevin. What happened?"

"He had walked from the meeting to a park near his hotel. He sat down on a park bench and made a call."

"I think he called me."

"That's what I thought; it looked as though he made only one call. Then a scruffy-looking man came down from the street above the park. There were three other open benches nearby, but he chose to sit next to Mr. Bryan."

"He was smoking," Sharon said. "I heard Kevin telling him to stop. That's when Kevin hung up."

"Then they both stood and walked through the park toward the river. The man was close, too close. Our guess is that he had a pistol or other weapon held against Mr. Bryan's ribs. Bryan towered over the man by a foot. It was something to see, I'm sure."

"Not funny," Sharon snapped. "Why didn't you do something?"

"My man was a hundred yards away. By the time he was able to quick-time it close enough, a black BMW sedan pulled up to the curb. The man pointed to the open door, Bryan climbed in and the man followed. The car then sped away, back toward the center of London. We didn't get a plate number."

"What the hell is going on?" Sharon said, curious and worried at the same time. Stolen diamonds, a dead woman—now she herself was talking to an undercover policeman. And Kevin had been abducted in brazen fashion.

"Mr. Barrington, what the fuck is going on?"

Kevin Bryan sat in the backseat of the car into which he'd been forced, jammed between Mr. Bad Hat and another mug, who could have used a bath two weeks ago. The driver was a woman, though Kevin wasn't entirely sure of the flavor. The hair was cut short, straight, and dyed extreme purple on the iridescent side of the color spectrum. From her left earlobe dangled a bangle-like earring in silver and beads; the color of the glass beads matched her hair. When she turned her head, he noticed that the large bead stuck on the side of her nose also matched the earrings. Between the split in the seats, he could see her very tight black leather pants. From the turn of her thigh he assumed she was female, but today he wasn't sure about anything. He was beginning to believe, now quite strongly, that he should have taken his own threat seriously and left for Paris seven hours ago. He would be at a nice bistro, maybe with a wonderful glass of Sancerre and Claudette Leclair. His two BMW bookends reminded him of winos he'd arrested in Oakland, only scarier.

"Where we going?"

"Shut up," Bad Hat said, still holding the suppressor against Bryan's ribs. The barrel of the gun rested against Bryan's arm.

"No really, where are we going? I have a date later tonight, then the theater."

Purple Head snickered, but then said, "You heard him. Shut the fuck up!"

She wore an extremely tight pink tee shirt. Kevin couldn't read what it said across her ample bosom, but if it read *Sid Vicious*, he would not have been surprised.

"Testy bitch, aren't you? Nice hair color though—you get that from a bottle, or the same jerk who did your tats?" he said to her, eyeing the two snakes inked into her left forearm and wrapping their way up to the hand grasping the steering wheel.

"Oh, I get it. You use a takeaway hairdresser and tattoos shop. Very chic."

"I said shut up. Billy, get his wallet." Stinky reached across Bryan's chest and toward his jacket pocket as the girl slowed the car into the queue waiting at the stoplight. When they were effectively boxed in, Kevin jerked his left arm up, dislodging the pistol from his ribs. The gun fired with a concussive snap. The bullet clipped the right shoulder of the woman before shattering the driver's side window; she screamed and let her foot off the brake. The BMW jerked forward and slammed into the rear of the Range Rover directly ahead. Purple Hair was thrown across the steering wheel, blood spraying across the front windscreen as the airbag simultaneously exploded.

Kevin drove his left elbow into Bad Hat's chest, easily breaking three or four ribs; he jabbed his right elbow into Stinky's jaw, with every intention of breaking the man's face. The forward momentum of the collision only added to the effect. The pistol went off again, this time punching a clean hole through the front windshield. Purple screamed. Bryan wrenched the suppressed pistol from the man, who was more concerned about trying to find his next breath than the gun, and with one long arm reached across to the door and pulled the handle, at the same instant pushing Bad Hat with all his might. When the door flew open, the man fell to the ground with a muffled bellow. Kevin tumbled out after him and stomped hard on Bad Hat's right hand. Quickly securing the pistol against the small of his back, under his coat, he jogged away. Horns blared from behind him in the jammed queue as he rounded the next corner and spotted a cab.

"The Savoy," Kevin said to the driver, simultaneously punching in Sharon's number in his speed dial.

"Cern'ly, gov'nor, cern'ly," the cabbie said, with a Cockney twist to his words.

7b

"Hold a second, Barrington, hold," Sharon said, when th second call came in and Kevin's name flashed on her screen. Not waiting for Barrington to answer, she switched.

"What the hell happened?"

"And I miss you too. Seems they have incredibly incompetent third-rate kidnappers in jolly old England. Some young thugs just tried to kidnap yours truly. I left them stuck in a traffic jam. I think one has a gunshot wound in her shoulder, another with busted ribs and hand, and maybe the third with a broken jaw. Not sure about the last one though—could've just broken his nose."

"Good Lord, Kevin. I've got your new best friend on hold. He says the last time they saw you was when you were being shoved into the backseat of a car."

"That son of a bitch was following me? Not surprised, although a lot of good it did me."

Sharon was already doing so, when he said, "Can you put me on with that British asshole?"

"I heard that, Mr. Bryan, and I have been called worse," Barrington said.

"Take it to heart, it was meant in only the most sincere way," Kevin told him. "Do you know who those people were?"

"Where are you?"

"Answer me first."

"No idea," Barrington said. "I'll check with the police and see if anything turns up. My guess, the car was stolen and you looked like an easy mark."

"He's six-foot-six, if you hadn't been paying attention," Sharon said. "Now who would fuck with someone that big? Has to be something else, not just some inept British version of a random street mugging. Maybe they weren't the first string, but they were sent by someone."

"I agree," Kevin said. "They were well equipped and even though they screwed up, it was all too neat and tidy, rehearsed. If it weren't for the traffic, I'd probably still be sitting in the backseat on my sorry ass, wondering what the hell is going on."

He didn't mention the Glock 17 he'd confiscated, its six-inch suppressor barrel digging uncomfortably into his butt and spine as he sat in the back of the taxi.

"Probably not locals. The Embankment road is always jammed," Barrington added. "It was crazy to think they could make a quick escape on a Friday afternoon. Idiots."

"I'm arriving at the hotel now," Kevin told them. "I'm going to the American Bar for a drink. Sharon, I'll call you later, and Barrington, I'll wait for your call or see your sorry ass in the bar."

"It'll be a call. I'm halfway home."

"I guess the traffic's not that bad for a senior police official."

There was a pause.

"Sometimes, Mr. Bryan, you can be an ass."

"No arguments here, but he's my kind of ass. Later, Kev," Sharon said, and clicked off.

The American Bar in the Savoy is a strange place. Down a few steps from the marble and dark-wood lobby, the bar is always full of tourists and guests, and the ice in short supply. It is known for its fancy liquor and total lack of a heart when it comes to price. Bryan's triple Connemara Cask Strength Irish whiskey, neat, would cost his client a night's rent in an Oxford hotel. The specialty bar menu ran to twelve pages. He saw no one eating anything other than peanuts, so after finishing his drink, he headed for the Savoy Grill on the lobby level—best way to get even with Barrington was through his pocketbook. The restaurant was a Gordon Ramsay establishment; he was sure the executive chef must be out since he didn't hear any screaming coming from the kitchen. He tried to order a hamburger but ended up with flank steak in a peppercorn sauce. It was good, but what he really wanted was a burger.

He was finishing the steak when Barrington stomped into the restaurant.

"Don't you answer your mobile?" Barrington demanded, so English, with enough emphasis on the 'i' that it sounded like 'bile.'

"Mo-*bile* what?" Kevin replied, not amused. "Dinner? Sit down, you look hungry."

"Mobile phone, your bloody cell phone."

"I turned it off. I wanted to eat in peace, but a lot of good that did me. Your lordship still found me."

He held up his empty fork.

"The steak is great, the sauce divine."

Barrington took a quick glance around the room. Their exchange had caught the attention of a few well-dressed diners on their way to the theater, another table held a foursome of Japanese businessmen. He frowned, slid into the booth.

"Did you find them?" Bryan asked.

"There was a patrol car further back in the queue. When the car didn't move, and they saw someone jump out, the officers investigated. They found one badly banged-up occupant in the rear seat, one lying on the street nursing crushed ribs and fingers, and a bloody woman in the front, her shoulder pretty well shot up. You do that?"

"No, it was actually her partner. Not a good shot" — Bryan held up a thumb and forefinger, splayed to about five inches — "missed her head by this much. She was lucky; he could have really spoiled her day. Any I.D.?"

"None, but we are checking their prints."

"Shocking," Bryan said, taking a last bite of steak.

"Did you know them?"

"I've been in your country just over a day, and you've been bird-dogging me the last twenty-four hours since I landed. How could I have met anyone who wanted to kidnap me? And why were you tailing me — not that it did me a lot of fucking good?"

A waiter came up to their table as Barrington was filling his glass from the bottle of a reasonable Burgundy that Kevin had ordered.

"Let me do that, sir," the waiter offered.

Bryan had to smile at the death stare Barrington turned on the waiter.

"I'll have what the gentleman had," Barrington said, in

clipped tones.

"Rare?"

"Like the gentleman's, thank you."

"I hope you like well done, Clive," Kevin said, as the waiter departed.

"I'm English. I like everything well done."

The two men stared at each other. Each bounced thoughts around in his own head, like it was the finals at Wimbledon. Kevin was the first to break serve.

"You might check the butt of this against the DNA of Miss Montgomery. You never know."

He passed a green folded copy of the *Financial Times* to Barrington; it was far heavier than all the weight of the business news contained in its pages.

Barrington accepted the parcel, not missing the addition of the suppressor barrel, and placed it in his lap.

"Where did you get this?" he asked.

"I liberated it from a guy with a bad hat and terrible aim. He's the one who sat next to me on the bench. Could be the same blunt instrument that hurt Sally, just saying."

"Miss O'Mara seems like a nice girl. Your girlfriend?" Barrington asked.

"No, and leave it at that. We go back a long time, worked on a few projects together."

"Like land developers, Chinese gangs, Nazis and the like?"

"You do excellent homework. Then you know she's not involved. She is a good friend and someone who always, as we say, has my back."

"And you have hers, or at least that's what the rumor is."

"I do my part."

Barrington finished his meal and pronounced it excellent.

"The meat was too well done," Bryan responded, when Barrington asked his opinion. "For the best, I like a small place near Saint Germaine in the Sixth, in Paris. There, it's all you can eat."

"So American."

"Always with the shit. Listen, Clive, I like you, but since my feet landed on this island, it's all been murder, meetings, and kidnappings. I feel like I never left home, so the sooner we can conclude all this crap, the happier I will be."

Barrington's answer was to reach into his pocket and extract his mobile. He looked at the screen, then took the call. After thirty seconds all he said was, "Hold them until I get there. . . . I'm at his hotel. Right, yes, sir. . . . Yes, tomorrow at nine. I was hoping to go home for a few days. . . . Yes sir, when it's over. Good night."

"Mother?"

"Close enough. The diamond company is getting impatient. He says they need to move the products from South Africa and soon. They want to do it next week."

Bryan sipped his wine.

"Too soon. Not enough time," he told Barrington.

"I know, but they are paying the bills. Me, I'm just a cop doing my job for minimum pay."

"Ahh yes, minimum wage—and you with a fifteenth-century estate in the country. Ahh, the privations."

"Your friend Sharon was right. You are an ass."

7c

Jorge Cortez stood on the chalk of the right field foul line, watching his team jog around the ball field at the Neptunus Familiestadion. The city skyline of glass facades, such as it was, rose starkly upright beyond the elevated rail lines that wrapped the stadium to the south. The occasional hum and clatter of the trains was all that intruded into this small bit of the Americas planted in the suburbs of Rotterdam.

They'd been late to arrive, their charter jet held up on the tarmac at the Havana airport for three hours while something was apparently being fixed. Although Jorge's guess was that the issue hadn't been mechanical but instead extra time taken to check passports, faces, and verifications—all the usual stuff when Cuban citizens tried to leave the motherland. Some of his players sweated like babies from fear, which Jorge found amusing. With all they put up with in Cuba, they were still afraid of flying. They'd arrived at Schiphol international airport in the early evening, five hours behind schedule. Then the tour bus operator, obviously no friend to the People's Republic of Cuba, had demanded to be paid up front in Euros before the two buses and their drivers would move the team forty miles south to Rotterdam. He'd watched Marta de la Vega argue with the man, who obviously did not know Spanish; they found a rough common ground with English. She ended up giving the man her American Express card to cover the overtime pay he was demanding. Again, Cortez found it all amusing. Communism and American Express. Did she use the rewards points?

The Rotterdam hotel was the same downtown hotel they always stayed in, acceptable and clean. He guessed that the security detail operated by de la Vega wasn't interested in trying anything new. The bus ride took over an hour in the late-evening commute traffic. For some of the men, it was their first time out of Cuba and on an airplane; the traffic both astounded them and lifted them out of their exhaustion. His players stared out the windows in wonder at the Christmas-like display of material wealth rolling past them: Mercedes, Audis, BMWs, automobiles they had never seen in real life.

Cortez lit a cigar. He had heard that smoking might be now outlawed in the stadium; he didn't care. He was an important guest and would act like it, and besides, igniting one of his country's finer products would have to be seen as a touch of nationalistic pride, like lighting up a joint in Dam Square in Amsterdam. To each country their own brand of tourism and national pride.

Marta de la Vega walked up and asked if the other teams had arrived.

"Yes," he answered. "The Taiwanese team arrived three days ago. They look tough. But then again, they always are."

"This is all a waste of resources."

"And your point is?"

"There are serious issues in the world and we spend our

time playing a children's game," she said. "Our money could be better spent."

"This is for the glory of Cuba and the revolution."

"Bullshit, it's a way for you to get out of Cuba, and maybe help some of these young men to America."

"Marta, I'm insulted. You know more than anyone that if that were the case, I'd be in one of your reeducation facilities right now instead of smoking a fine Cuban cigar and watching our young men play a game they all love."

He blew a great cloud of blue smoke into the fine Dutch air. He was sure he was violating some international treaty by smoking, *but too damn fucking bad.*

"I have work to do, so why don't you bother someone else," he said to de la Vega.

"I have no time for this," she hissed, before turning and walking back toward the gate in the left field fence. A dark BMW was parked just outside the ball field. A thin, almost gaunt man stood next to the car. He too was smoking a cigar.

"Back to the hotel," was all Vega said, as the man crushed the cigar on the pavement.

Marta de la Vega saw nothing to be happy with in her job as head of security; it was a position that guaranteed failure. During the past fifteen years, she had been involved with at least seven of these Port Tournaments, and during each of them Cuba had lost players. They defected or simply walked away and escaped. Many ended up in America. Often they continued to play baseball for some minor league team in a city no one had ever heard of. But a few, like Toribio Rodriquez, made it big, and in fact so big that they couldn't be ignored and because of that every ballplayer on the Cuban team wanted to follow in Toro's cleat marks. They all dreamed of Chavez Ravine, the Miami Marlins, Yankee Stadium, and the most recent World Series champions, the San Francisco Giants. They dreamed of hitting homeruns into San Francisco Bay.

The preliminary games were scheduled to begin the next day. Someone called them friendlies. Cortez wasn't happy about the mixing of soccer terms with baseball, but there was little he could do, and the press knew what they knew. He was there to play baseball, not change a culture.

Cortez crossed the infield to the dugout his team was using. Bags of gear and boxes labeled 'gloves' lay in piles. Bats were still stacked in their cardboard boxes. Cartons labeled 'Mizuno,' 'Wilson,' and 'Louisville Slugger' sat next to the uniform shirts of the Cuban players, who were out on the field stretching. Cortez was pleased; the local equipment supplier, one of the few in Europe, had done well.

Cortez had already checked that morning with his account in Zürich; the deposit from the supplier had cleared. It would just about cover his personal expenses during the next few weeks.

"Señor Cortez?" an American voice said.

Jorge turned toward the sound and faced a man of obvious Chinese extraction, stocky, muscular, clean-shaven, and wearing the nation of Taiwan's baseball uniform.

The man, who introduced himself as Danny Yang, stuck out his hand.

"You're the new manager of the Taiwan team. Welcome to Holland," Cortez said, with an answering handshake. "I heard they had an American as their manager. The face doesn't go with the accent."

"Atlanta," Yang replied easily. "My grandparents came from China after the Second World War, settled in Georgia. I went to Georgia Tech on a baseball scholarship. Been in the game all my life, now here."

Cortez looked at the man, who was easily thirty years younger than himself. These Americans always told you more than you asked for or needed. Even this fellow, with his Oriental face and Southern drawl, passed on more information than Jorge would ever care about.

"It's a good game," he said to Yang. "I have been doing this for more than fifty years. Even my skin is beginning to look and feel like an old catcher's mitt."

"Sadly, no. Don't smoke, but thanks," Yang said, when Jorge

offered a cigar.

Cortez opened his cigar case anyway and tucked a Cuban in Yang's breast pocket.

"For later."

"Thanks, real Cuban, I'm sure. Maybe I can sneak a puff later."

"You do that. Your team, how old?"

"Most are in their twenties, but there are a few old men in their thirties. They could never give it up. We beat both Cal and Stanford teams last weekend while we were in California. Good for the men and yours truly."

"Cal?"

"University of California in Berkeley. Good ballplayers, but our experience won out. A couple of the fellows may turn pro after the tournament."

"That's nice," Cortez said, ready for Yang to move along.

"Gotta go, my boys are warming up. Maybe get a drink later?"

"We'll see," was all Jorge offered in reply, as Danny Yang walked away.

A gangly fellow separated himself from the team and jogged over to Cortez.

"Coach, I want to thank you for allowing me to come with the team. I know I have a lot to learn, but this is so much like heaven. I want to thank you."

"Paco, my boy, you deserve to be here. With your speed and skills at the plate, I think you could become another Toro. All you need is experience. And this has always been a good way to get it, playing against others who aren't Cuban. There are lots of nuances to this game and each team brings something different to the field."

He pointed to the Taiwanese players, who had gathered in the far left corner of the field.

"Those boys are very good. Some could be playing for the major leagues in Korea and even Japan in the next few years. A few even have played for Australian teams. My son, baseball is played all around the world and, even though it's our national sport, for others it's just a game. Very few make a living at it. At least in Cuba, you can live well."

"I know that, sir, and I appreciate it. But I'm afraid."

"Of what, Paco? What do you have to be afraid of?"

The young player mentioned hearing his teammates talking about poachers.

"They tease you with money and hopes to play in America, to hang your cleats next to those of Rodriquez and Céspedes. There are rumors they are paid millions," Paco said, not meeting the older man's eye.

Cortez nodded.

"The rumors are true. They are paid a lot of money. I have known dozens of men who fled our homeland to play ball, but I also know that some have been left on the side of the road in America. They played a few years, and like children spent all their money and have nothing. Baseball can be very good to a young man with skills, but blow out your knee and you are left with nothing. In Cuba, you will be taken care of. Remember that."

Paco looked at the Taiwanese players, then at his own teammates; it was a study in contrasts. The Taiwanese were joking and laughing—he couldn't understand what was being said, but he knew they were having a great time. Whereas, his own teammates seemed sullen. Sure, there was joking, but a pensive air hung about his friends, like waiting for a storm. He had heard rumors that at least three of the men were thinking of defecting. That meant maybe even more were planning something. A couple Latino men had been seen talking with a few of the players at a coffee shop near the hotel when de la Vega or her people weren't around. This was dangerous, even criminal, according to the lectures and instructions they were given on the plane. He thought he was a very good player with excellent baseball skills, but since no one had approached him, he was now doubting his abilities. Maybe he wasn't that good after all, maybe the Americans did not want him. He slowly walked back to his Cuban teammates.

Chapter 8

Camp Danger, Tikrit, Iraq, fall 2004

"This is fucked," Sergeant Gillis said. "We can fucking borrow two of their Humvees, we just have to sign for them and promise that we'll return them."

"Promise them anything," Lieutenant O'Mara answered. "But keep your fingers crossed. We need to be out of here before daylight. I want to be forty klicks south of this fucking pile of crap when the sun hits the horizon. It's one hundred fucking miles of shit, and I want lunch in the Zone."

The lack of helicopters to return to Baghdad wasn't a shock. O'Mara was used to the program: fly in, hump out. In this situation, it was drive out: south from Tikrit on Iraq's infamous Highway 1, one hundred and five miles of some of the nastiest asphalt in the whole world to reach Baghdad. Four lanes—sometimes, two lanes—often, traffic jams near mud and concrete-block villages, sand storms, and the occasional IED that made the hairs on the back of your head tingle. The only way was fast and with authority. When necessary, go around not through, stop for nothing or no one. And, if necessary, shoot first, ask questions later.

As the sun broke the flat horizon to the east, they were six klicks west of Samarra and eighty miles north of Baghdad, with only light traffic on the opposing two lanes. There was no eye contact between the Iraqis and the soldiers; it was as if the Americans didn't exist. They were strange beings from another planet just fucking around in their country. In time, like every other invading army, from the Mongols, to the Turks, to the English, they too would be gone, and the citizenry could resume their normal day-to-day life of hating each other.

By nine o'clock, the heat pushed its way into the cabs of the Humvees, along with the dust. Their gear filled every square foot of the interior; weapons sat tight to their knees. To be heard required yelling, so no one said much.

O'Mara watched the Iraqi countryside fly past at fifty miles an hour, a flatness unlike any American landscape she remembered. A mustard-yellow landscape of plowed and fallow fields paralleled the road, occasionally varied by gray-green touches from dense groves of palm trees. The architecture, such as it is, was one-story blockhouses with colorful signs in Arabic. Occasionally, a sign in English would appear, suggesting food or cold drinks. Outside of the word "gas," nothing seemed to be spelled correctly. She smiled at some of the versions of the word 'restaurant.'

Highway 1 near Al-Dujail was four lanes with a flat median of sand and broken palm trees. Eighteen months earlier, the U.S.-led invasion of coalition forces had rolled up this highway toward Tikrit with every intention of grabbing Saddam; it had taken nine months to find him. The shoulders of the highway still carried reminders of the invasion, with burned tanks and vehicles littering the landscape.

Gillis, in the lead vehicle, spoke over the headset.

"Lieutenant, road block ahead."

"Roger that. Can we bypass?"

"Can't say yet, but buildings are tight on each side. Makes it a box."

"Roger, is it one of ours?"

"The sergeant in Tikrit said that there were no schedule stops between Tikrit and Al-Dujail. If this one's official, it's got to be Iraqi Army. Official or unofficial, it sucks," he added.

"Probably a shakedown," O'Mara guessed.

They were forty miles from Camp Taji. She asked the corporal in her vehicle if he could reach the camp on his radio.

"Yes, sir," he answered.

"When they see us, they'll either flee or puff up. I suggest we not give them the chance," Gillis said, over the headset from the lead vehicle.

"Is the other side open?"

"Yes, sir."

"Cross over."

"Roger that, on my mark, we go left."

Gillis counted down from five, then cut hard left and bounced through the median. O'Mara's driver followed. Two seconds after her Humvee crossed the asphalt, the road behind them exploded into chunks of roadway and gravel. Debris rained down on both vehicles as they sped toward the onrushing, northbound traffic."

"Fuck, that was close!" Gillis yelled.

"Too damn close, Sergeant. I wish you could count faster."

"Us California farm boys can only count on one hand," he came back.

"I don't even want to know what you do with the other."

For the next two miles, they wove in and out of the oncoming traffic. Trucks and old Japanese-made cars spun to the road's shoulders and into the ditches on each side. Gillis never gave a thought to stopping; to stop was to maybe die. It had been a trap from the beginning, all set up to stop any American vehicle and blow them to their infidel heaven. He was not going to have that happen to his squad. By the time they pulled back into the southbound lanes, three miles later, adrenalin had kicked in and Gillis's pedal foot was almost to the floor of the Humvee. The engine screamed.

"You can let up, Sergeant," O'Mara said, over her mic. "We survived that IED. I don't want you doing what they couldn't."

"Yes, sir."

An hour later, they slowed outside the American Base Camp Taji. One of Saddam's Republican Army's bases before the war, the camp was now home to elements of the 1st Calvary Division.

"You hungry, Gillis?" O'Mara asked, earning a collective

smile as she glanced around at the crew in her vehicle.

"Yes, sir," was the emphatic answer.

They wove through the opposing concrete barricades that would slow any suicide vehicle to a crawl and met with the American squad guarding the entry. After a couple of calls, O'Mara's team was waved in. Heading into the main portion of the camp, they passed slowly through the "boneyard," literally the last stop for myriad derelict tanks and weapons that had been collected from across the area.

"Must be thousands," O'Mara said, looking out at the mess of Russian tanks, guns, and rocket launchers—the debris of a lost war. They were lined up on either side of the road as far as the eye could see.

"All shit now," Gillis answered. "And there's others across the country. Saddam loved his military. Now it's all crap, not even good for scrap. It'll be here a hundred years from now, when the next dictator takes his turn at butchering his own people."

"Thanks, Gillis. I needed that bit of cynical optimism."

Their sobering tour ended at a building whose sign said Mess. An hour later, they continued into Baghdad and the Green Zone, a small island of reasonable sanity in a sea of blood and broken bone.

"I'm playing at the DFAC tonight. You want to join me?" Gillis asked, as he and O'Mara stowed their gear and weapons. "They finally tuned that piano, or so I'm told. Will be nice to wrap these fingers around something that doesn't smell of gun oil."

"I have to meet with the colonel, but it sounds like a better diversion than what I was thinking," she answered.

"What's that?"

"Washing my hair."

"Stuff it under a cap. Besides, it looks great as is. Red with dusty flecks of Iraqi sand suits you."

"Can you play one-handed? I know people, remember that. And another crack about my hair will get your nose busted."

"Jeez, sensitive aren't we?"

"I'm always sensitive when someone tries to fucking blow up my squad. Just pisses me off, the cowards."

"Agreed, but they didn't and we weren't. That's the half of it in this shithole."

"Time?" O'Mara wanted to know.

"In an hour. I'll buy beers, and a few of the men will be there. You going to try that song?" he asked her, meaning the Hoagy Carmichael number from the old wartime Bogart film *To Have and Have Not*.

"Lays good for you and that smoky voice," he told her.

"Now you're busting my voice—have you no limits, Sergeant?"

"Just saying, you and Bacall would make a great pair."

"And you're more like Walter Brennan than Bogart . . . just saying."

O'Mara, after setting a personal best by showering and washing two sand dunes out of her hair in under forty-five minutes, strolled into the DFAC; the sound of Gillis's fingers strolling the ancient piano rescued from one of Saddam's palaces filled the low-ceilinged dining room. A screen was already set up in one corner. O'Mara was handed a beer. She lit a Marlboro, sat down next to Gillis.

"So, this is what heaven's like?" she said, only half joking.

"In some distorted and twisted universe, yes, and for now it's ours. You ready?"

"You sure about this? Public singing scares me more than a road full of IEDs."

"You will do great. Besides, most of these idiots don't even know who Bogart and Bacall were. It's my job to expand their education."

The black-and-white film flickered on the screen, cued to the start of the scene where Carmichael beckons Bacall to the piano. Sharon stood and slowly began the song, as the men tapped their shoes and the piano top. The rhythm, with a touch of tribal and a bizarre waltz backbeat, echoed around the room. When O'Mara sang the final line, "how little we know," the men applauded.

"Not bad, not bad at all. You sure you've not had any training?" Gillis said.

"If you mean singing to cattle and horses, yeah, I had some when I was a kid. But no. No training, just me and the wide, open spaces. Only scared the dog then."

"Lucky dog."

For the next two hours, Gillis played hits from the American Songbook. A few of the men sang along on a few of the tunes, and occasionally wiped away tears. "Make It One for My Baby" was the big hit of the night. Everyone, including the nineteen year olds, had a soft spot for the Sinatra standard.

As O'Mara walked back to her bunk, the sky above, for the first time in weeks, was clear and sharp. A three-quarter moon hung like a notched, cold steel disk over the city that had been old before the crusades and thousands of years before Christ was born. Wars and invasions had washed over this country since before the Bible was written, its people and culture now an amalgam of every warrior and trader that stormed the mud walls and gates. She wondered what she would leave, what small contribution to the unending farce that was politics and religion in a world that only believed in yesterday and not tomorrow. At the top of the ancient levee that wrapped along the Tigris River, she lit another cigarette and then quickly took three steps to the right. The sniper's bullet snapped through the air in the space where she'd been standing, *so predictable*.

8b

London

Most nights, Kevin Bryan found it hard to fall asleep, always something buzzing in his head, some thought bouncing around until either he got up and turned on the TV or just waited it out and eventually fell asleep. No pattern or reason, and sleep aids only helped the pharmaceutical company's pockets, not him. But his second night in London was different; after a final whiskey in the bar and a parting handshake from Barrington, he was asleep in his suite less than ten minutes later. Only when the wake-up call buzzed, did he awaken the next morning. He hadn't felt this good in years, and a peek out the window revealed a crystal blue, cloudless sky extending across the London skyline from the giant Ferris wheel called the Eye to the Tower Bridge. This day proved wrong the oft-heard rumors that it was seldom sunny in London.

Barrington was waiting for him in the dining room. Bryan ordered a simple breakfast of bacon and eggs; the Englishman drank tea and chewed the crust off a slice of toast. He watched as Kevin downed a third cup of coffee.

"You Americans drink coffee like it was cheap wine."

Kevin set the empty mug back on the table and looked at Barrington.

"If you start one more sentence with 'You Americans,' I'll pop you in the nose. What is it with your attitude, Clive, even at this time of the morning and on such a gorgeous day? And a Saturday, no less. What gives?"

Barrington studied Kevin for a moment, then simply said, "The funeral. With everything else pressing, I have to make sure that the family and Sally receive the best we have to offer. They knew she was a cop but not what she did. The funeral is Wednesday, and you and I are supposed to be in Amsterdam that day."

"Amsterdam? Why? From what you've said it's at least a week away."

Before answering, Barrington looked out the window toward a large barge that was working its way up the Thames. The broad expanse of glass in the dining room matched the view Bryan had five floors up.

Barrington took a deep breath.

"That's the purpose of this meeting at the insurance company, to review the procedures and schedule for moving the diamonds from South Africa to Amsterdam, where the packages will be broken down and then distributed across Europe."

"Why not here?"

"The experts and people who know the business are there, not here. Simpler, I guess, and cheaper than moving fifty people around. Bring the diamonds to one place, one security detail, one process, one route."

"And all gone with one successful operation," Kevin mused. "There's an old fable about putting all your eggs in one basket — drop it, and you have one big omelet. You think that's why Ms. Montgomery was killed and the three Stooges tried to nab me, to screw up the transfer? That tells me someone else has to know what was going on."

"My assumption too," Barrington said, nodding. "The problem is, we don't know how many people know what's going on. Could be dozens inside the insurance company and the diamond company."

"Wonderful. A giant sieve with little bright sparkly things falling through the holes."

"Cute, but you're right. You met them; they are diamond sellers and control the whole process from mining to marketing. Their attitude is simple. They will dig more if these are stolen. Unfortunately, they insured the stones, and the insurance company would rather not have to pay out for the theft. That's what we're here for, to make sure it doesn't happen."

"What exactly was Ms. Montgomery doing?" Bryan asked.

"Her undercover activities led to an interesting bit of intelligence, a connection between Zürich, Amsterdam, and Cuba. There is an old Swiss family that has been in the robbery business for more than a hundred years — the Altheimers."

"Sounds more like a disease than a family name."

"In many ways they are. They made their fortune selling guns to those who needed them during World War Two. In fact, they sold guns to both the Greeks and the Albanians, who used them on each other. Later, as Europe quieted down and the Russians and Americans got into the weapons business, the family moved on to high-end goods, such as cars and gems. Sally found that they would offer stones to some of the biggest retailers around the world at very good prices."

"Low prices, because they were stolen."

"You're catching on, yes, stolen. Seems these big American and European chains weren't all that particular about where the stones came from, as long as they could be assured they weren't conflict diamonds or blood diamonds. Seems even they have some scruples."

"Sally found out how?"

"She worked in a jewelry store in Geneva as a buyer. She met the senior male member of the gang, Heinz Altheimer, when he came one day to offer her a million dollars' worth of very good stones, all colors. The prices were high, but not as high as they should have been, and he left the door open for more if they were interested. She said she was. The insurance consortium put up the money, and the stones were purchased. It took a while, but many were matched to some thefts that occurred about five years ago."

"Seems this gang is not in a hurry to turn over their inventory," Kevin said.

"So it seems, and that got us to wondering who may have been behind other thefts."

"You said the senior male member, this Heinz Altheimer. So there's a senior female member?"

"Yes, his mother, Tanja. She has run the family since the fall of Berlin and the collapse of the Soviet Union. They made a lot of money from the rise of the Russian oligarchs; they even restarted their arms business, albeit on small scale so as not to run afoul of the major players, the governments themselves. Often they traded old Soviet guns, AK-47s and the like, to African gangs for diamonds."

"Where'd they get the guns?"

"Cuba."

"Well, I'll be damned. How did you find that out?"

"Seems that some of our friends in France found a number of crates full of weapons stuffed in a shipping container with bags of coffee. The rifles still had their tags on. Soviet-era AKs circa 1960s, still greased and wrapped up all nice in paper and excelsior. The container arrived in Marseilles from Veracruz, Mexico. We are sure the containers started in Santiago de Cuba, where they were loaded with bags of coffee. The gun crates were buried under tons of dried coffee beans—Cuban coffee beans."

"Cuba grows coffee?"

"Actually, very good coffee. It was one the first things lost at the start of the Cuban revolution, the plantations. But they are coming back, I'm told. The containers were then shipped south to Beira, in Mozambique, on the eastern coast of Africa."

"You followed them?"

"Not exactly. We put a satellite transponder on the box and followed it minute by minute until it was off-loaded at the Beira terminal. Our people there watched them unload the containers, and they were met by some very unsavory people driving very nice Range Rovers."

"You English will sell to anyone."

After a moment, Barrington smiled.

"True, but only for cash," he said.

Kevin flagged down a waitress and held up his cup for a refill from the pot she carried.

"I assume that the Altheimers come back into this about now?" he asked Barrington, when the waitress had departed.

"The containers on the dock were also met by Heinz Altheimer. We know he flew in on his jet from Zürich, with one stop in Addis Ababa to refuel. He left one hour later; the guns and coffee remained."

He inclined his head toward the cup Kevin held.

"Our man says later the coffee was just dumped, minus the crates of guns, of course."

Kevin smiled.

"Of course. The assumption is that Mr. Altheimer picked up his payment for the guns when the containers arrived."

"Yes, only we were told later that the buyers were disappointed. It seems that the guns were defective, missing their firing pins. Needless to say, the Altheimers are trying to correct the problem."

"A problem that you may have had a small part in?"

"A small part. But the bigger issue is the Cuban connection and the multilayered systems that have been set up by the Altheimers. Too many options and resources moving around the globe."

Both of them were silent for a moment. The squawking of police cars and the roar of motorcycles interrupted their reverie; four massive black Jaguar sedans followed the police on the Embankment Road visible out the window.

"The prime minister," Clive said, nonchalantly.

"You mentioned Santiago de Cuba," Kevin said, after the motorcade passed.

"Yes, a number of containers left Santiago for Veracruz. Most stayed there for coffee packaging and processing. Only the one that went on to Marseilles we followed."

"So it's a simple guns to coffee to diamonds thing?"

"You Americans."

"How does that connect to Amsterdam?" Kevin said, getting more intrigued by this contract every minute.

"The rumor, and it's a very good one, is that a senior official with the Cuban government, Marta de la Vega, is the grower of the coffee. She has a plantation about a hundred miles from Santiago; she also has access to many of the military facilities in the Granma province. We put one and one together."

"And maybe get diamonds. So again, why Amsterdam?"

"Vega's with the Cuban national baseball team, as one of their managers, and she is with the team now. They are playing in Amsterdam. We think that where she goes, Altheimer and the diamonds will follow."

"A stretch, don't you think? Might not be that simple. Is there someone else?"

"Mr. Bryan, most things are simple, once you sort them out. Right now there are too many parts, too many options. If she is in Amsterdam and is involved, we want to know why and what's her connection to Altheimer. And we don't know if there is someone else. Right now we are concentrating on Vega."

"This isn't just about stolen diamonds, is it?"

"No, there are thousands dying in Africa, killed by weapons coming out of Cuba and a few of the other collapsed states in the Soviet sphere. We need to stop them. I want to know if they are involved with the death of Sally Montgomery."

"Let me change my little song," Kevin added. "It should go, guns to coffee to diamonds to baseball."

8c

AT&T Park, San Francisco, A few days earlier

"The count's two and one to Toro, two out, Whyte's on third," the play-by-play guy said. "This is a spot for one in the dirt, see if he'll go fishing."

"Agree, partner. This pitcher's got his number today. He's oh for two. Toro's been in a bit of a slump since he came off the disabled list. What is he—four for his last fifteen at bats? Hasn't had that kind of a run since last spring," the color man offered.

"Ball three, in the dirt."

"Could see that coming a mile away, so could Toro. There's a story out there that the Cuban government has started putting pressure on these fellows who defected. They want them back to play for the Cuban team in next spring's World Baseball Classic. They haven't done well in the Classic and want to turn it around."

"Hard to do when most of your team wants to flee the country. Strike two, fouled off to the right field Club Level."

"Just missed that one, trying to go to the opposite field. Yeah, Cuba's been embarrassed by their showing in the Classic since they took second back in oh-six against the Japanese. Cuba's done all right in the World Port Tournament in Rotterdam the last few contests. Can you believe they play baseball in Holland? Hard to imagine."

"It's a world sport and growing, partner, I tell you. Here's the pitch—strike three. Low outside, and he had Rodriquez completely off balance, confused."

"Totally. If he's that way in two weeks at the All-Star break here at AT&T, the home-crowd fans are not going to be happy."

"I have faith he'll pull out of it. It's end of the fifth, and Giants seven, the Padres six."

On cue, Toribio Rodriquez jogged out to his position in right field and began to warm up his arm with throws to the center fielder. The San Francisco crowd filled the air with a buzz that was unique in the sports world. Every professional baseball stadium's vibe is different; in San Francisco, years of consecutive sellouts had turned the crowd into a brash multitude of loud experts. They had seen the best and demanded better from their teams. More than once this season, they had risen as one voice to cheer in a winning run or the final strike. If a united crowd's willpower could carry a ball into the surrounding bay, it would only be in San Francisco.

Toro tossed the ball back to the centerfielder and turned and looked out into the bay through the metal fencing that filled the archways directly behind right field. He took a deep breath. He was still reeling from Sharon O'Mara's call to his private cell phone early that morning before he left for the ballpark.

"I think we can get them out," Ms. O'Mara had said. "The less you know, the better. We are going into Cuba in a couple of days, and we have a good idea where they are."

He'd told her that he'd been thinking it over, not sure that she should take the risk.

"Maybe I can work something out with the government," he said. "I know these people. If you are caught you will be arrested or . . . worse."

"Then I won't get caught. It seems that the person behind this is Marta de la Vega. Does that name sound familiar?"

"She's the one who has my family?" Toro said, feeling as if he'd been punched in the gut. An image of the long-ago coach lying in the street flashed in his mind. "Vega was the government agent working to make sure that the ballplayers don't defect. She chased me when I escaped," he told O'Mara.

"Everything points to her," O'Mara answered. "And from what my friends are saying, there are others she has also imprisoned. There are many in Cuba who would like her gone. It seems that she has placed herself outside the party of true believers and revolutionaries and into the group of 'get all you can while you can.' We are receiving some help from inside. If everything works out, we will be back before the All-Star game."

"I'm worried for you and your friends. If anything were to happen—"

She cut him off: "Nothing will happen other than getting your family out. Got to go, but I will call you when they are safe."

Toro threw the warm-up baseball back to the Giant dugout; it had become his trademark, winging a throw more than two hundred feet on the fly. More than a dozen times he'd thrown out, from deep right field, a runner at home plate who challenged his arm. Players and third base coaches were a lot wiser now and the challenges were fewer. Toro also knew that his arm was, like the rest of him, getting older. There would come a day when runners wouldn't stop at third. They would challenge, and some might win.

For ten seasons, Toribio Rodriquez had prowled the right field of San Francisco's AT&T Park, its third or fourth ballpark label since its opening in 2000. While the park may have suffered an identity crisis every few years, due to mergers and acquisitions of corporate sponsors, the fans never did. Some still called it PacBell Park, it's birth name, and others just loved it for the location, the food, and the vibe. And it didn't hurt that the team had made the playoffs and won a couple of World Series during the past decade and a half. Everyone loves a winner. Toro felt this love and respect from the catwalk seats and promenade twenty-four feet over his head. Here, at the top of the right field wall, were three rows of seats; these seats, this loyal band of fans, called themselves the Toroistas. Someone had even recorded a CD of Cuban salsa songs that extolled Toro's triumphs and successes as a player. For any other player, all this might have gone to their head. The Cuban ballplayer was honored and took every opportunity to work in the community and do what the team wanted. But today his mind wandered. He was putting someone directly in danger, a danger caused by his ego and blind desire to play baseball.

He was lucky that a smashed baseball flies considerably slower than a bullet; with a bullet, you never hear the sound of the gun that kills you. But a baseball is hard, and the bat is hard, and the snap of the two colliding is distinctively particular. After years of playing, Toro could almost tell how far the ball would go by that singular, unique *thwack*. The struck baseball, with its flat-line drive trajectory, rocketed toward the distinctive brick façade and its eight arches that ruled the fair side of the ballpark's right field wall; the ball cleared his head by fifteen feet. Instinct is a ballplayer's friend, and while Toro's head was still thinking of O'Mara and Cuba, his body was reacting and racing hard toward the second arch. The baseball struck high and off one of the sharp light-colored concrete frames that wrapped the arch, deflecting the ball high and back over the onrushing Toro; it hit the green grass and began bounding back toward first base. Toro pushed himself away from the wall and spun around, looking for the ball; it was rolling toward first and away from any help of the sprinting center fielder. Toro glanced at the runner. The batter was already halfway between second and third, and Toro could see the third base coach's arm pinwheeling, telling the runner to go for home.

Not in my park, mi amigo. Not in my park.

Toro never slowed, never slid, never stopped. He raced to the ball at full speed, everyone in the park sure he would overrun it. The runner was exactly halfway from third to home, forty-five feet left for an inside-the-park homerun against the most feared right fielder the game had know since Roberto Clemente. Toro lowered his right arm until it brushed the grass, snagged the ball with two fingers, and with his momentum going toward home, slung the ball like a Jai-alai player throwing a *pelota* against the wall. To say it was on a string would be wrong. Toro threw the baseball like it was riding a laser beam; his catcher only had to turn a crisp ninety degrees after receiving the strike to meet the sliding runner four feet from home plate. The runner didn't have a chance; "You're out!" yelled the umpire.

Toro's instinctive skill and luck had held the moment. As the crowed whooped overhead, he quietly hoped that Sharon O'Mara's skill and luck would do the same for her and his family.

Chapter 9

From 36,000 feet the Gulf of Mexico looks like any other ocean, maybe a touch bluer. Whether it was called a sea, a gulf or an ocean, it was still salty and wet as far as Sharon was concerned. At least she'd won the draw on the window. In the seat next to her, Bobby Gillis was asleep, his legs stretched out into the aisle. Who wouldn't be after the last three days?

"Can you be here in Mexico City the day after tomorrow? I think we can make this happen. My friends in Cuba can help," Senior Inspector Detective Xavier Immanuel Lopez had said to Sharon over the phone.

"Impossible," she'd replied. "Too much planning to do. Gillis is here now"—her old sergeant had been at that moment seated on her kitchen floor, Basil flopped across his legs—"and we are expecting you tomorrow."

"I can't make it," Xavier told her. "My boss's boss wants me here. But if you can come to Mexico City, there is much to tell."

"Like what?"

The what was actually a who in the regional Cuban police in Santiago de Cuba province, a man who knew exactly what Lopez wanted to know. This Cuban cop was very aware of the coffee plantation in the northern area of the province, but the owner, Marta de la Vega, was powerful and over the years had paid handsomely for the privilege of being left alone. The officer told Lopez that he hadn't been pleased with how de la Vega conducted her business; it was contrary to the ideals of the revolution, and he would be very glad to have the whole plantation closed.

"It's not my job to reform Cuban land policies," Sharon said, after hearing what Lopez had learned.

"Yes, but a little embarrassment wouldn't be too bad."

"Not if it gets us landed in a Cuban jail, or worse."

"Then come to Mexico City. I have a plan."

Sharon had heard that line a thousand times in the army, and often such plans were completely fucked when boots hit the ground. Nonetheless, the following evening, she and Gillis had walked through the crowded corridors of Benito Juárez International Airport in Mexico City. While they waited for their bags, she looked at her phone. Two messages from Kevin Bryan, but it was the middle of the night in London, and he could wait. She felt a tap on her shoulder and turned to face the randy mug of Inspector Detective Xavier Immanuel Lopez.

"You are a delight for these eyes, *mi amor*, a true delight," Lopez said, with his typical Latin flare. "And this gentleman is the war hero I have heard so much about?"

"Hardly that, Inspector," Bobby Gillis said. "I did my part."

"And modest. Sharon, where do you find these men, heroic men such as your friend, Mr. Bryan, and Mr. Gillis?"

Lopez shook the large hand of Bobby, saying, "But I apologize, we must hurry. There is much to do and little time."

The inspector put his hand in the air, and in seconds a massive black Humvee pulled to the curb and a young man in military fatigues exited the front passenger seat. He held a small but very effective looking MP5 secured to a shoulder strap. He saluted the inspector, then opened the rear door for Gillis and O'Mara. They got in, followed by Lopez.

Once settled in, Lopez offered them bottled water; Bobby responded with a crack about the water.

"Our water is excellent here in Mexico City, but I can't say that about many other places," Lopez replied. "So I recommend bottled water wherever we go."

"Thanks for the tip," Bobby answered, watching out the window at the traffic racing past their vehicle.

Only a fool or a drunk would drive Mexico City's highways at night. Sharon was sure that the driver was neither, but she had never seen such intense and well-practiced driving. No, she had to amend that thought; Baghdad sometimes demanded skills just as crazy-scary.

The driver continued weaving through the traffic, carried along by blaring horns and squealing tires from near misses. After an hour, they turned into a gated community and waited as the driver talked with the guard. Fifteen-foot-high gates blocked the entrance; a gaudy amount of gilded filigree and flourishes covered the black superstructure. After a few moments, the guard signaled to someone in the guardhouse behind the gates, which slowly opened.

"We pretend we are an egalitarian society, but that's all a façade," Lopez said, as they watched the guard walk back to the gatehouse. "But these are difficult times in Mexico, and security is critical."

"Is this where your office is?" Gillis asked, looking up at the gates as they passed.

"No, my friend, this is where my home is."

A little later, Sharon stood on the stone plaza that extended out from the rear of Inspector Lopez's hacienda and looked over the broad expanse of Mexico City visible below. The city's lights disappeared on the horizon. In some vague way, it reminded her of Los Angeles but felt older, much older.

"She is quite a city, Sharon, is she not?" Lopez said, approaching. "There have been people living here for more than a thousand years, almost nine million people now, and when you include the whole region it is larger than Los Angeles and San Diego combined. And I think it is prettier too."

He handed her a tumbler.

"I believe Johnnie Walker Red, *si*?"

She took the drink and smelled the distinct aroma mixed with Mexico's highland tropical air.

"I thought it would be hotter," she said.

"It is not like the desert and Cabo San Lucas. Here it is mild and comfortable most of the year."

"You have a wonderful home."

"Gracias. It has been in my family for almost one hundred years. We have always been civil servants and that has not always been easy in this country, but then again, we are also survivors. We are like the chameleon—we change as needed to survive."

"Opportunists?"

"I don't think that is the right word," he answered. "If that were the case, we would have left years ago. No, Mexico is our home and always will be."

"I am surprised that you are not married," Sharon said, sipping her scotch. "You would be quite a catch."

"I was once, many years ago. She died, and that broke my heart. It has taken a long time to heal. I have two children, actually young men now working with the government in trade negotiations. One is in Chile and the other in Argentina. I see them three or four times a year."

"I'm sorry, Xavier. I didn't know."

"How could you? But thank you. Your friend seems strong and knowledgeable."

"Bobby spent three tours in Baghdad; he's tough and smart. He was my sergeant for one tour, and we have been friends a long time. You will see how good he is when the time is right."

"Well, the time is right. Shall we go in?"

Bobby watched as his two partners walked across the terrace, a servant handed him another beer and took away his empty. He walked toward them.

"Hold a second, Xavier. It's Kevin," Sharon said, glancing at the screen as her phone buzzed.

"Where are you?" Kevin wanted to know.

"Bobby and I are in Mexico City, at Xavier's home. We've moved up the program to retrieve the family. There's an opportunity."

"Sounds too damn hinky, if you ask me. Too many questions with no answers," he said, after Sharon went through what had been discussed with Lopez and his source in Cuba. "You mentioned a coffee plantation—did the name Marta de la Vega come up?"

"Yes. Hold a sec. Let me put you on speaker." She signaled to Xavier. "Go."

"Does the name Marta de la Vega mean anything to you, Xavier?" Bryan asked.

"Yes, she is the woman holding the families on her coffee plantation north of Santiago de Cuba. That is where we will be heading the day after tomorrow."

"Well I'll be damned. Full circle."

"What's full circle?" Sharon asked.

Kevin told them about the coffee and the weapons and diamonds.

"*Madre de Dios*," Lopez said. "And there is a connection to the baseball team as well."

"Seems to be, but I'll know more after we get to Amsterdam. You be careful. I know if I told you not to go forward with this, you would just blow me off, so just listen. Sharon, you be damn careful. And Bobby and Xavier, if anything happens to this girl, you two won't be able to find a place dark enough to hide, and I mean it."

Neither man said anything, but they both knew that if anything happened to O'Mara, it would probably happen to them at the same time.

Bobby's snoring startled Sharon out her daydream. She stared out the plane window at a cruise ship on the water below. Its long wake pointed toward Latin America, the bow aiming north toward the United States.

The plan with Lopez was simple: they would go in as musicians with a salsa band from Mexico City that Lopez helped to unofficially manage. The Fiesta del Fuego was underway in Santiago de Cuba. To alleviate any overt suspicion, they would be just one group among the dozens entertaining the revelers. Bobby had injected that Sharon didn't play an instrument and could barely hum a tune. She had thanked him for the support, after punching him in the arm. Xavier's band had traveled to Cuba many times for various festivals, and three of the musicians were cops whom Lopez had known for years, and in fact, they were pretty good. After Bobby played some Chicago blues on the grand piano in Lopez's music room, much of the inspector's concerns about his ability to blend in drifted away.

According to Xavier's man in Cuba, Marta de la Vega's other job was with the national baseball team, which was currently playing in Europe, Rotterdam to be specific.

"Baseball in Holland. That's a new one on me," Bobby said.

"An international tournament. Vega's one of the watchers to prevent defections, but they still lose one or two a year," Lopez explained. "According to my baseball friend here in Mexico, three of his players are from Cuba by way of Rotterdam. They wanted to play in the United States but weren't good enough, and now they can't go back to Cuba."

"It's always tough to be a pro athlete," Bobby offered. "So we have a small window?"

"*Si, pequeño*. We are lucky. The fates, they are with us. The tournament runs for another week, and coincides with the festival. I'll be traveling with you for a series of meetings with officials in Santiago—some problem with cigars and illegal imports—usually not my job but, with a little help from my oldest son, I asked to tag along with the trade group. We'll be in first class—you'll be with the band."

"Thanks, why am I not surprised? Always wanted to be a roadie."

"The officer will meet us at the hotel. He has all the information about the camp and its location."

"Why the hell would some Cuban cop want to help us?" Sharon asked.

"As I said, he's a true believer in the revolution. His father fought with Castro. But Vega, he says, is what's wrong with

Cuba now. There's too many opportunities to bend the rules, and she uses the system to pad her pockets. He can't do anything himself, but if she could be embarrassed and publically humiliated, then she may just disappear. Helping those who are her *guests* to escape would do a lot to shine a bright light on her activities."

Now, a day later, the dark green coastline of Cuba extended across the horizon outside the plane's window; the coast had a rough vertical face of stone and vegetation that reminded Sharon of some of Hawaii's islands, the dryer side. Mountains rose high beyond the coastline. Patches of fields in disorganized plots seemed interconnected with twisting roads. The city of Santiago de Cuba flashed by her line of vision, tucked behind the green palm-covered hills, just as the tarmac rose up to meet the plane. She hadn't liked Cuba when she was at Guantanamo, and she wasn't too keen on it now. As they exited the plane, standing at the top of the stairway leading to the tarmac, Bobby said, "It feels and smells like the swamps of Iraq."

9b

Santiago de Cuba, Cuba

At Antonio Maceo Airport in Santiago, Bobby Gillis and Sharon O'Mara pushed and wound their way through the lines of tourists that had flown in with them from Mexico. Most were pasty-faced Canadians who had come for the sun and rum, not necessarily in that order. The waiting room was packed with arriving and exiting guests. Those leaving looked hungover, faces and bare arms pink to lobster red, sporting palm frond sombreros and carrying all manner of stuffed, cheap plastic bags advertising Cuba. Gillis and O'Mara passed through customs with nothing more than a stamp on the tourist cards Detective Lopez had acquired for them in Mexico City.

"Don't let your passports get stamped," he'd instructed,

handing them each of them a card, "it could lead to difficulties back in your United States. The American customs officials wink at all this American tourism; they just don't want to have to acknowledge it with a stamped passport. But don't lose that tourist card. If you do, you will have to swim back."

Sharon watched Lopez go through the lobby doors and out onto the sidewalk to be greeted with a warm hug from an official in a very crisp blue-grey Cuban police uniform. Lopez then scanned the crowd and, spotting her and Gillis, waved them over.

"Comandante Alberto Acevedo, these are my friends, Sharon O'Mara and Roberto Gillis. They are here for the festival, playing with our band from the Mexico City police. They are the people I mentioned last week when we talked."

Lopez said this loudly enough and in Spanish, so that the two bored army guards standing just ten feet away could hear him

"Señor Inspector Acevedo, *mucho gusto*," Sharon said, extending her hand.

Bobby followed suit.

"May I suggest we go elsewhere to discuss the arrangements we talked about, Xavier," Acevedo said, in English. "Your band will travel in the van we have provided; there is room for their instruments in the back. The driver knows their hotel, and he will take them there. You and your friends will travel with me. I have arranged a quiet lunch for the four of us. You can catch up with the band later this evening."

"Excellent, Alberto, excellent. Sharon, are you ready?"

"Ready as we will ever be, Xavier," she answered, not sure if 'ready' was the right word for what they faced.

And she and Bobby weren't ready for the searing heat and suffocating humidity. Acevedo's car, a bastardized version of some type of Russian vehicle that was old twenty years earlier, was not air-conditioned, in fact, had never been air-conditioned except when the windows were open. And all that did was to push hot air through the cabin; increasing the car's speed made it feel like someone had turned up a fan from one of hell's ovens. Within seconds, Sharon was sweltering, and the thick air made breathing difficult. Her time in Guantanamo again flashed across her watering eyes.

The restaurant wasn't air-conditioned either; the four sat at a table on a wooden deck that extended out over the Bahia de Santiago de Cuba. Sharon guessed the temperature dropped by one degree due to the water sloshing about under the cracked and rotted boards. Umbrellas made from palm fronds shaded their table from the oppressive early afternoon sun. They sat for almost ten minutes before a less-than-attentive waiter took their drink order. Everyone, including Acevedo, ordered a beer.

"Nice," Sharon commented to Acevedo, as she looked across the harbor at the derelict buildings, fish-processing plant with its broken windows, and the two or three dozen boats that lay sunk up to their gunwales along the shore. One boat with a less-than-energetic rower slowly crossed the bay.

"You must be a politician," Acevedo said. "I would not call this nice; it is barely tolerable. The few dollars in imports and tariffs we get barely keeps the staff paid. Everything costs more than it's worth. I should know, my family owns this restaurant."

"That's why the quick service?" Gillis said, as he sipped his beer from the recycled bottle.

"They don't know me," Acevedo explained. "My cousin owns it. He has great difficulty with the demanding employees and the union. Everyone seems to think they are owed something."

"Kind of comes with the territory," Sharon added. She lit a cigarette.

"Maybe. It is a system that almost everyone alive in Cuba has lived with their whole lives—most were born after 1959. It is a system I know in my heart can work, but the difficulties come from the few who use their power and standing for their own purposes, people such as Marta de la Vega. She has been a thorn in my side for more than fifteen years. She has very powerful friends in Havana. I would like nothing more than to clear out that farm she has. But every time I try to do something, my commander says no. So what can I do?"

"Has Inspector Lopez told you why we are here?" Sharon asked him.

"Yes, but not in great detail. All I know is that it has to do with her plantation."

"We have come to take Toribio Rodriquez's family to the United States. Our sources tell us that de la Vega has them on her farm."

"*El Toro?* She has his family? *Madre de Dios!* When he plays in Miami, we can sometimes get the broadcast on the radio and some of my officers can get the baseball game on their computers. He represents Cuba very well; we are proud of him."

"Then why do you think the government won't let his family leave?" Sharon asked.

"We are a proud people, and some in the government do not understand why he left. They want him to acknowledge Cuba."

"And the government?"

"*Si,* and the government. But we the people understand him; he is one of us, not them. We celebrate every victory of our sons playing in America. We are proud of them, every one of them. But what the government demands makes it very hard for them to return. I would, in my heart, want to see every one of these great players come and play on the Cuban national team. We would be unbeatable."

"You may be right," Bobby said. "There are five or six players who might make the All-Star team from Cuba, more than any other country. But, Señor Acevedo, you do not talk like a Cuban revolutionary."

"I believe in Cuba and the revolution. My father tells me about Cuba before Castro, when it was an island of corruption and sin. We are better now but sadly poorer. We can provide for ourselves, but it is my children I worry about. What will they have, how will their dreams be fulfilled? The corruption is still here, only different. That is why when"— Acevedo nodded at Lopez—"my friend asked, I offered to help."

"My friend, we thank you, and we understand the risks you take," Lopez said. "With your help, we can return many of these people back to their families elsewhere in Cuba and reunite Toribio with his wife and child."

"I did not know they were Toro's family, but I know them. The child is no longer a child," Acevedo said, "but I understand they are all well."

"So, Comandante Acevedo, tell us about this farm that Marta de la Vega has," Sharon asked.

"Gladly, Señorita O'Mara, gladly.

He told them that de la Vega's facility was an old coffee plantation that had been very successful before the revolution. Many people in the region had worked there, for good wages by Cuban standards. The coffee was shipped mostly to Europe, primarily Spain and France. The owners were American, from Miami, Acevedo had heard. After the revolution, they had abandoned the plantation and the storage buildings.

"Time began to destroy what remained," Acevedo said. "After a while, only a few people still lived there, and no one cared. About fifteen years ago, when I was just a young police recruit and fresh out of the Cuban army, I heard that someone had returned to the farm and forcibly removed all those people who had lived there for more than thirty years."

"Let me guess. Marta de la Vega?" Sharon said.

Acevedo nodded.

De la Vega had rehabilitated many of the houses and the storage buildings and prepared a grass runway for her airplane. Within a year, she had replanted the fields with young coffee plants and a modern irrigation system for the dry months. She also had about fifty hectares of tobacco, Acevedo estimated.

"At the time, I wondered where she found her employees. None were hired from the local area, and many on the property wore army uniforms—from a branch of the government I had never heard of."

"I take it you were suspicious," Bobby said.

"Yes, very suspicious. I always want to know what is going on in my district, even if it doesn't concern me. We unfortunately have many camps like this around Cuba, places where those who do not approve of the government can relearn what they forgot growing up. To learn honor, respect, history, and the goals of the revolution."

"The reeducation camps," Sharon said.

"Such a harsh term, but if you will, yes. Sometimes things need to be done to secure peace and freedom."

"Sharon, I suggest that we allow the comandante to finish," Lopez said.

"Gladly."

"Thank you," Acevedo answered. "De la Vega has a small contingent of men, who patrol the grounds in dark green Toyota pickup trucks. One has a machine gun mounted in the bed."

"Sound more like the technicals we had to deal with in Iraq," Bobby said. "Fast-strike suicide machines."

"Yes, they are there to secure peace and freedom," Sharon added.

"Are you listening?" Lopez said, looking a Sharon. "These people are not amateurs, and no one cares what happens to you here."

"Thanks for that, Xavier. I'm getting all warm and cozy about all this as is. How many men, would you guess?" she asked Acevedo.

"Ten to twelve. They work in teams, with someone there at all times. One truck is always roaming the property. But the guards they do not stay on the property. Most live near Los Reynaldos, about three miles east. Vega also has an overseer that takes care of the coffee and the tobacco she grows. I think he lives in the house near the entry."

According to Acevedo, the tobacco was shipped north for curing, was an average cigar filler, and not very valuable.

"All the best tobacco is grown on the far western end of Cuba. There are rumors that they have brought in instructors to show how to properly roll and shape cigars, then they can sell the finished product," he told them.

"The coffee?" O'Mara asked.

"The dried coffee beans go to Mexico in shipping containers out of Santiago de Cuba, and after that I don't know where."

Señor Acevedo would be shocked to learn the coffee was being used as a disguise to smuggle weapons out of Cuba and into Africa, Sharon thought. And he is quite free with information, here in a country where no one gives away anything for nothing. This man is a curious fellow, a little too forward and almost trying to be too helpful. Maybe the less he knows the better.

"We will need a large truck or even a bus," she said aloud. "I'm thinking that we're going to try and bring out more than just the Rodriquez family. We can't leave any of those people for de la Vega. Can you find us something like that?"

"I have some sources that we can use, but why take more than who you came for?" Acevedo asked.

"My experience with people like Vega is that they take their vengeance on those who remain. So we carry as many as we can."

"Fifty to sixty, all ages, some very old," Acevedo replied, when asked how many might be in the camp. "All are there because someone in their family escaped to America to play baseball. *Madre de Dios*, it is only a game."

"*Si*, Señor Acevedo. Only a game, but to many it is the game of their lives," Bobby said, as he finished his beer.

"Comandante Acevedo, my friend," Lopez said, looking at the policeman. "There is time for you to avoid all this. We will tell no one who helped us if we are caught."

"I understand, Xavier, but we will go through with this as discussed. You don't know the roads and back roads. And besides, I am going with you."

"Not a chance, Comandante, not a chance," Sharon said, shocked by Acevedo's demand. Now she was very, very curious.

He shrugged.

"You have no choice. If you don't, I will have you arrested and sent home on the next plane."

"Now, now Comandante, please no need for this," Sharon

said, placing her hand on Acevedo's. "You caught me off guard, of course you can go. I just wasn't prepared for you to help as much as you are. You're under great risk by all this. So, yes you can go." Sharon looked at Bobby, who had a big grin on his face. "And of course Comandante you can help us with weapons? The idea of a machine gun mounted on the back of a pickup truck concerns me greatly."

"*Si, si.* I have access to a few Russian-made rifles, they are in good shape. Will that do?"

Sharon turned to Booby, "And you were wondering where we were going to get weapons?"

9c

The meeting to look at the transportation was arranged for four o'clock that afternoon. Acevedo left a note at the hotel that he had found a truck and the address. It was conveniently near the restaurant where they had lunch. He would meet them there. Lopez was scheduled for a meeting with the local trade people at three. He would join them back at the hotel before the music started. Sharon and Bobby walked through the city in the heat of the afternoon.

"Reminds me of some of the seedier places along the river in Baghdad," Bobby said. "Temperature's about right, it smells of diesel fumes, and the quality of rust on the steel buildings just adds a fine piquant quality to the view. And the smell of fish just makes it swell."

"We've seen a lot worse," Sharon said.

"True." Bobby didn't add anything for a block or two.

"What's got you edgy? I know you, what is it?" Sharon asked.

"What was that with Acevedo, all the shuck and jive about his going with us?"

"I don't trust that son of a bitch. There's too much at stake, he's being a little too helpful."

"Yeah, I got that too. What's the play?"

"We watch and see, but be ready. This thing can go bad, real bad, real fast."

"Now you're talking Lieutenant, now you're talking. It's the old keep your friends close, but your enemies closer."

The truck turned into an ancient International Harvester yellow school bus that had seen better days before the revolution. But, after Bobby had inspected the engine and the tires, he said it might live.

"We shouldn't need more than a hundred miles out of it in two days, three days tops. Thirty-five miles in and about the same coming out. I think I can squeeze that out of it," he said. "I want to make sure we have enough gas and that the tank doesn't leak. Other than that, I guess we're good."

"The road is rough but serviceable," Acevedo said. "In spots, it has been washed away by storms and rough bypasses have been built. One crossing has a bridge that may or may not be there. I have not been up in that part of the province in more than a year."

"Any more good news, Comandante?" Sharon said.

Up until this point, she'd been mentally taking notes. Now she looked at the map Acevedo had provided, the pathway into de la Vega's camp was drawn in pencil.

"I have two AK-47s. Do not lose either one. One is mine, the other was in my commander's closet, he's gone for a few days. He won't miss it. They are the only weapons, other than my pistol."

He handed her the rifle.

Sharon had handled AK-47s while in Iraq—she was shocked by these. They looked almost new; there wasn't the usual scratching at the magazine slot, no dings in the wood stock. She thought about what Kevin had said a few days earlier. Yes. This could be one of those pieces from the arms cache.

"I can't believe this, Bobby," Sharon said, looking at the piece of Soviet military craftsmanship. She took the magazine offered by Acevedo with its recognizable curve to its shape. She peered into its end—it was fully loaded. Even the bullets looked new. "I wish we had a chance to try these before we take off, but they do work—don't they Comandante?"

"*Si*, they are some of the finest," Acevedo said. "They were only issued to us during the last year. I have personally fired these myself, they are very good."

"I hope so." She gave Acevedo a smile that Bobby instantly recognized. "Bobby what do you think?"

"Another wonderful, fun ride down sure-to-die trail." And he turned back to the bus. "We can get maybe forty or fifty on board. Maybe a few more if we squeeze and the younger people stand."

"Great, we won't know what we'll have till we get there. It will take longer in than out."

"Say again? We will have a bunch of people with us," Bobby said.

"Yes, but we will know what to expect on the way out."

"Yeah, and they will send out the army to block every road on the trip back to Santiago."

"Maybe, but with you by my side, Tonto, I just know we will make it."

"That's what I love about you, Sharon O'Mara. Your unbridled optimism."

Sharon and Bobby spent the remainder of the day acquiring fresh fruit, bread and crates of bottled water for the return trip. The water came from one of the hotels that Acevedo suggested; the fellow they dealt with looked remarkably like a relative of the comandante. All Sharon could do was shrug and hand over American dollars. One day in and one day out is what she wanted; what they would end up with would be another matter. If subtlety was what she wanted, they wouldn't find it driving through the Cuban countryside in a fifty-foot-long yellow school bus. She was far from optimistic.

Standing next to the dubious vehicle in the heat of the warehouse, Sharon said, "We go tomorrow afternoon."

After a shower in the relatively modern downtown hotel in

which they were staying, she slipped a white cotton top on over dark shorts and tied her hair back in a ponytail. Sandals finished the feet and a large straw hat finished the head. For the first time in more than a week, she felt refreshed and relaxed. Basil was staying with a friend, so no worries there. But her cell phone worked intermittently and there had been no calls from Kevin in the last two days. She wasn't sure if it was that he hadn't called or couldn't get through. There was no way of knowing.

She met Bobby in the hotel lobby and was shocked by his total Cuban look: white guayabera shirt, khaki slacks, woven espadrilles, and a straw hat. With his deep farmer's tan, he fit right in with the natives, and being fluent in Spanish didn't hurt either.

"You look good, Señor Gillis, damn good, *muy bien*."

"And you look delicious, for an officer and all."

"Cut the officer crap," she shot back. "That's history, and after what we've been through, Lord knows who was the real officer back in those days, but thank you for the compliment. Sometimes a girl just has to dress up."

She asked Gillis where the band was playing.

"Small club about a block from here," he told her. "I'll sit in for a couple of sessions on the piano. Xavier and I checked it out after we came back to the hotel. The damn thing is actually in tune. Should be fun—his friends are good, sort of salsa meets Chick Corea. And I knew about eight of the pieces they played. You want to have some fun with that song we did in Green Zone?"

"I don't think so. Once was enough."

Looking like tourists, the two walked through the city's narrow streets, festooned for the Fiesta del Fuego. Hot as it was, the *fuego* part was redundant. Cuban bongos, whistles, and clanging cowbells echoed through the alleys and streets. Colorful flags and banners hung from balconies and rooftops. The outfits the men and women wore were in total contrast to Sharon's view of the Cuban government. Some costumes worn by the amply endowed women would have shocked even the regulars at San Francisco's Gay Pride Parade. She began to believe that these people knew how to make the best of their situation.

The club was up a relatively quiet alley; the thick stucco walls of the jazz club actually lowered the temperature inside to almost tolerable. It was packed with Cubans and tourists. Sharon asked for scotch and got beer.

"That's all we have, Señorita," was the rough translation.

At least it was cold.

Cuba's location gives it advantages over most of mainland North America, in that hundreds of cultures from Spain to Angola have left their rhythms and beats. In many ways it is like New Orleans, someplace that extracted and distilled the sounds of cultures and races, mixed in the climate, and poured out a delicious cocktail of beer- and rum-soaked melodies in as many styles as there are provinces on the island.

Sharon watched as Bobby and the Mexicans played a mixture of timba, salsa, and American jazz classics. Their beat was infectious, the rhythms base and sensual, and even though most of the musicians were amateurs, their skills were as good as any performer playing in the Caribbean bars of New York and Miami. The crowd ate it up. After the last set, she, Bobby, and Xavier joined the throngs watching the seemingly endless parade of drummers, dancers, costumed posers, and over-the-top floats. As the parade ended, locals and tourists fell en masse behind the last musicians and danced down the main street in the heat and cigar smoke of this ancient Cuban town.

The next morning, over a weak cup of coffee and questionable plate of eggs, Sharon sat with Xavier and Bobby.

"He still wants to go?" she asked.

"Yes, won't have it any other way," Lopez replied. "I asked him if there was something else behind his demand. He said that for fifteen years de la Vega has thumbed her nose at the revolution and his authority. I have known Alberto for maybe ten years and he is a dignified man. He does not like what she does but can do nothing. We are a chance to change that. He wants no one hurt, just embarrassed—that should be enough to get her out. His hope is then to return the people we rescue back to their families. He's been working with some of the church groups in the province. Once we get them back to Santiago, he will take care of them."

"And the Rodriquez family?" Sharon asked.

"He will help you get papers and cards so they can leave with you through Mexico. That's the best he can do."

"That, hopefully, will be enough." Sharon did not say anything to Xavier about what her gut was telling her about Acevedo. And Bobby didn't say anything either.

Bobby spent the rest of the morning going over the bus again and again, looking for anything that might break down. After making a two-page list, he gave up.

"It is all we have, we just have to accept it," he said to Sharon.

"We'll be fine. And besides, this will be easy, *no problemas*. In and out, bing-bang-boom."

"Yeah, it's the bang-boom part that bothers me."

Chapter 10

As Sharon explained it to Bobby, Xavier, and Alberto, surprise was the key. She opened the large package that Acevedo had placed on the table and unwrapped three Cuban police uniforms—dark blue slacks, steel-grey shirts, blue epaulets, grey web belts, and blue baseball-style caps. She handed out the costumes to Bobby and Xavier.

"We will appear at the gate in full gear and demand to see the top hombre," Sharon said. "It's a good guess that he's not there, and according to our intel from Alberto, de la Vega is still in Rotterdam with the ball team. In fact he said that the games are being shown on Cuban TV. We'll put pressure on them, hard. But not let them get to a phone or cell phone. We need to keep them puzzled and confused. Alberto, you will keep them occupied; it's a good bet they will know you, or at least who you are."

Aerial photos provided by Acevedo had revealed ten houses on the street, six on one side, four on the other. Sharon's plan was to quickly find the Rodriquez family and explain the mission.

"I hope to use her to convince the others to come with us," she said. "They will all be afraid and unsure. Hell, they have lived paranoid lives, and now us. Who can you trust? My guess is, they think they are there because of the government, not some opportunist and thug. We will have less than an hour to change their minds. If we get half to come, I'll be surprised. They will trust us less than they do de la Vega."

"I get that." Bobby said. "It hasn't been bad or, at least, any worse for them than being outside the fence. They probably get food, medical aide, a place over their heads, and work. What we offer them, the unknown, will scare the hell out of them."

"We won't push it. Our goal is Toribio's family," Sharon added. "Anyone beyond that, Comandante Acevedo will take care of."

"We pick them up and then come back here, then what?" Xavier asked.

"The comandante has graciously given us some tourist cards. They will go back the way we came. Simple."

"With you, nothing is simple, Lieutenant," Bobby said.

She didn't correct Bobby; any leverage with Comandante Acevedo would be to her favor.

"Lieutenant?" Acevedo asked, a surprised look on his face.

"Yes, United States Army. Two tours Baghdad, retired."

"I was in the army too. You never retire, only change chairs." She smiled at that.

"We go at three p.m. Once we get through the gate, my guess there will be a lot of improvisation and guessing."

"Your guess is my order, Lieutenant," Bobby said.

"We will have sunset at about eight-twenty, light falls fast. I want to roll into the gate at eight-thirty, headlights on the guards. Then we move into the camp, fast and with authority."

The bus ride in the late-afternoon heat drained them. Once they left the main road, it took an hour to go twenty slow, tortuous miles over roads that were deeply eroded and in places washed away. They climbed over one thousand-foot ridgeline, and then another, before they entered a long valley. The hills continued to rise to the east, climbing another fifteen hundred feet higher than the village of Los Reynaldos. It was six-fifteen by Sharon's watch.

"We'll wait here until seven-thirty, then move slowly on up the road to the camp. Bobby, I want to be at the entry at precisely eight-thirty."

"*No problemos.*"

"You'll jinx the whole deal if you say that one more time. I see *problemos* everywhere," she told him.

She climbed down from the bus and lit a cigarette. Acevedo and Xavier joined her, and all three stood in the shade of the bus. Acevedo produced a cigar, which Sharon lit for him. Xavier surprised Sharon by waving off the cigar that Acevedo offered.

"Why are you doing this?" Acevedo said. "You are a smart woman and from what Xavier says, you don't need this. So why?"

He exhaled a cloud of soft smoke. It hung in the still, late-afternoon air and, like Acevedo, waited for Sharon's answer.

"A contract, someone asked me for a favor, and I agreed. And the request was from someone I respect, Toribio Rodriquez."

"A ballplayer, *Madre de Dios*, they are just baseball players. Look at him; he left his family to play baseball. Don't you think that's irresponsible?"

"Maybe, but we all have dreams and hopes for something better."

"The luxury of the rich American, thinking of something other than tomorrow's dinner."

"Comandante, I didn't make this happen to your country. You Cubans brought this on yourselves. Me, I just have a job, and I will try to do it the best I can. I appreciate that you are here, how dangerous it is for you, and thank you. But for now, I need to get the family out of Cuba and reunite them with my client. Simple."

"Yes, simple. Except for the politics and the corruption in my country. This is why I am with you, an opportunity to change that. It may be a small gesture, but it will be something."

"Thank you Comandante, for everything you have done," she said again, when Bobby signaled that it was time to get going.

The plantation was in a broad valley left between two ranges of high hills. As they crested the hills to the west of the camp it was already deep in the shadow of the setting sun. Night would fall quickly. Bobby ground through the gears as the rickety bus wove along the rolling road that led to the gate of the camp. Surprise was not an option after all; the meshing of the old gears in the growing gloom could be heard a mile away. Gillis stopped the bus at a double gate of chain link; more chain link fencing extended left and right and disappeared into the woods. There was no guard.

"What the fuck?" Bobby said, pointing to a hand-painted sign that read *Privida. Prohibido el paso.* "That's it? That's the security? What a way to run a prison. Is the chain locked?"

Sharon went to the gate and saw that the chain loosely held the gates together, no lock. She scanned the road in both directions; light was visible from windows of houses maybe a quarter mile past the gate. She slowly pulled the chain free and left it hanging on the right-side gate, then one at a time pushed the gates inward. Bobby slowly followed in the bus. She climbed back onboard and looked at Lopez and Acevedo, who each shrugged.

She leaned over to Bobby and quietly said, "I do not like this."

"Roger that, Lieutenant."

"Do it, Sergeant."

Bobby slowly accelerated, and they bounced noisily along the rutted earth of the entry road. As the road flattened out, the ruts disappeared. Sharon stood next to Gillis, the AK-47 on the bench seat next to her. She had checked the clip and the rifle; it seemed to function. But she had not had a chance—not that she could have, given where they were—to fire the weapon. All she could be sure of was that it would make a good club.

Outside, everything was growing darker and darker; the only waypoints were the lights ahead in the small village, glowing more brightly as the bus neared the cluster of buildings. Bobby headed for them like a ship heads toward a lighthouse, knowing that danger lurks on all sides. They passed the first two houses flanking the road; the shadows from the twisted branches of the overhanging trees enveloped the bus, flowers fell from the branches and settled on the hood. Two more houses in, Bobby stopped in the middle of the road and shut down the engine.

On both sides of the bus, on narrow porches in front of every house, sat the residents of Marta de la Vegas' prison camp. Somewhere a radio played a ball game that everyone along the dirt roadway could hear: "Next up for the San Francisco Giants, Toribio Rodriquez. Toro's been hitting better this past week, like something has inspired him, partner. What do you think?"

10b

Sharon turned to Xavier.

"Did we just drive into a trap? What the hell is all this? No guards, nothing."

She looked back out at the people on the porches; everyone had stood and was looking at the group in the bus.

"Dónde está la familia Rodriquez, por favor?" Bobby asked, loudly enough through the driver's broken window for all the residents to hear.

There was no reply, just murmuring.

"Rodriquez, por favor. Toribio nos envió!"

Sharon moved forward to the stairwell of the bus door. She leaned toward the door and nodded to Bobby who pulled the rusty mechanism that opened the door.

"Ask again," she said to Bobby. He did—still no reply. No one walked off their porches or even attempted to approach the bus. Sharon scanned the house nearest to the bus. A woman had stood up from a chair, another woman remained seated. A young boy, maybe almost a teen, stood next to the woman. It was on their porch that the radio broadcast the Giants game.

"Did my husband really send you?" the woman said in broken English, as she stepped down from the porch and waited on the stone path that led from the house to the street. A small terrier dog stood on the porch behind her, watching.

Sharon approached the woman, who stood straight and defiant.

"You are Señora Rodriquez, Toribio's wife? And how did you know we spoke English?"

"Si, I am his wife. That hombre has an awful accent—sounds like a Mexican. I assume you are Americans, so—are you? The uniforms say police, but you don't act like them."

"We are friends. My name is Sharon O'Mara. We are going to take you to see your husband."

Sharon indicated the two people still on the porch.

"Señora, is this Toribio's mother and your son?"

"Si."

"We are not going anywhere with them, Mother," the youngster said. "It's a trick."

"Possibly, but what can we do if it is? Miss O'Mara, this is my son, Carlos, and Toribio's mother, Angela. My name is Elena. Have you seen my husband?"

She pointed to the small black box on the low table.

"We only hear about him on the radio."

"Yes, I saw him just a week ago and talked to him the day before yesterday. He sent us to bring you and your family to him. And if these other people are willing, we can bring them too."

By this time many of the residents had crowded around the bus and were listening to Sharon and Elena Rodriquez, although it was obvious that none of them could speak English. O'Mara didn't think they understood any of what she and Elena were saying.

"Most of these people won't go, in fact, many like it here," Elena said. "We are the only ones left of the 'baseball widows.' The others left and joined their husbands, or at least that is what I was told. These people work the farm; they know nothing about the reasons why Angela and I are here."

"Mother, tell them to go away. It will only cause us more trouble," Carlos said.

"I think this woman is telling the truth. Why would she risk everything to come here?"

"We can't trust her," Carlos argued.

He pointed at Acevedo.

"I know that man there, the policeman. I saw him talking with de la Vega in Los Reynaldos."

Sharon turned to Acevedo, who had followed her out of the bus.

"You talked with de la Vega?"

"Of course," he answered. "We have had many conversations over the years."

"We've got company, Sharon," Bobby said, and pointed to the pair of headlights moving toward them from up the darkened street. "Now what?"

In the same moment, Xavier grabbed Acevedo and spun him around.

"I thought you were my friend, you bastard."

He threw a punch, knocking Acevedo to the dirt road. The man reached for this pistol, but Xavier kicked him in the arm, paralyzing it, the pistol still in its holster. He swiftly bent down and withdrew Acevedo's pistol, motioned for him to stand.

The residents scattered at the commotion, most running back to their houses. The pickup truck with the guards drew closer, a hundred yards away and closing fast.

"Put a gag on him and hide him behind the bus. We need to deal with these guards," Sharon said to Lopez. Turning back to Toribio's wife, she said, "Elena, I need to know right now if you want to go with us."

Elena looked at her mother and still defiant son.

When the older woman slowly nodded, Elena said, "Yes, we will go with you. Carlos, we have nothing here. We can go to your father in America. You will have everything you want."

"He left us, why would I care? He is nothing to me. I can't even remember him."

To the astonishment of both her daughter and grandson, Angela Rodriquez spoke.

"Carlos, I raised your father until he was a man, and like you he was tough and proud, sometimes too proud. You are like him, with a fire in your belly, a fire that will consume you. You will find nothing here in this forsaken land. Your future is elsewhere. Tell this woman that you will go with her."

Carlos looked at his grandmother, a tear slowly etching its way down her weathered face, then at his mother. In an instant, his whole life had changed. Was he willing to change with it?

While the young man wrestled with his possible future, Xavier and Bobby walked casually toward the front of the bus, its headlights now illuminating the approaching vehicle. One man stood in the bed of the small pickup, holding onto a cross-bar handle that had been secured to the roof of the cab; the flare of the bus' headlights off his AK-47 couldn't be mistaken. The truck stopped twenty feet in front of the bus, and the driver's and passenger's doors flew open.

Screaming in Spanish, the driver demanded to know what was going on. Then he asked for Comandante Acevedo. Bobby strolled up to the man and held his hand out as if offering to shake hands. Not sure what to do, the man tentatively put his hand out. A second later, Xavier fired one shot over the head of the man in the truck's bed, yelling for him to drop the rifle. In Bobby's other hand appeared a pistol that was now aimed at the face of the driver. The man on the passenger side fumbled, trying to retrieve his pistol, which he dropped to the ground when Xavier pointed a rifle at him. Xavier then ordered the man in back to throw his weapon over the side. He did immediately.

"You get down. You two against the bus," Xavier called out. "Bobby, zip them."

Gillis pulled a handful of PlastiCuffs from his pocket and quickly secured the wrists of each of the guards, then lined them and Acevedo against the bus.

"Comandante, next time it might be a good idea to find better men to do the job. These men would as soon pee in their pants than fire their weapons. Lucky for them," O'Mara said.

The look on Acevedo's face was not what she expected. He acted like nothing had changed, his demeanor nonchalant.

"What do you know that I don't, Acevedo?"

The smile grew on his face.

"Do you think that I would let you escape with these people? Captain de la Vega pays very well to watch her people. She knows how incompetent they are. Take Manuel here, nice fellow but couldn't wipe his own nose."

Not understanding, the overseer hesitantly smiled when he heard his name.

"There is no way for you to get out of Cuba," Acevedo continued. "All the airports and ports are watching for you, I have made sure of that. Those travel passes are also worthless. They have been told it is something to do with drugs, and you know how Castro hates drug dealers. They may even shoot first, then ask questions. I expect the three of you will end up in one of our prisons, one not as nice as this one."

"Acevedo, you are a pig," Sharon said, aiming her flashlight on his face. "I also know that you are probably the man supplying AK-47s to Vega, and she gets them out of the country. What would your boss Fidel do if he found out you were nothing more than a cheap gunrunner? A gunrunner that sells Castro's guns."

At the mention of the guns, Sharon saw a flash of fear in Acevedo's eyes.

"Yes, we know about them," she told him. "Did you know they end up in Africa in the hands of thugs and warlords? How does that fit with your holier-than-thou Cuban communism? You are a pig. Maybe I'll send a note to Fidel and his brother. Bobby, get them inside the house and secure their hands and feet. Señora Rodriquez, are you coming with us or are you staying?"

Elena looked at her son's face.

"Go get your things, Carlos. Help your grandmother; there is a small box with photos and a few other keepsakes I want to take. Put what you can in a pillowcase. We are leaving."

Carlos Rodriquez looked at his mother, then the four men standing next to the bus—four men who represented Cuba's finest.

"Yes, mother."

Acevedo and the guards were left in the small front room

of the house; Carlos found some rope and helped to bind their legs. None of the other residents came to say good-bye, and three of the houses were now dark, but O'Mara knew that they were watching. She also knew that within ten minutes of leaving someone would come to the house and release the prisoners.

She thought about using the guard's truck, but it was too small to carry seven people. It would have to be the bus. She pointed to the truck's tires and Bobby walked into the house and returned with a small knife; in seconds all four tires were flat. Carlos helped his grandmother up the stairs of the bus and then placed three pillowcases of clothing and personal items on the front seat. Elena joined them, holding the small dog.

"What's her name," Sharon asked, not the least surprised at the four-legged addition to their party.

"Bibi. She is Angela's favorite. She never leaves her side."

Elena watched Sharon scratch the head of the pooch. The dog looked up at her and sniffed.

"She likes you, that is good."

"I have a soft spot for dogs," O'Mara said, before turning to Bobby. "Unless you want to spend the rest of your life in a Cuban hole in the ground, I suggest we go, pronto."

"Si, si, Lieutenant, pronto."

He gunned the old engine and worked the gearshift. The bus lurched backward; he executed a passable three-point turn and headed back out the way they'd come in. The lights of the small cluster of homes disappeared from view as they rounded a curve. Trees and palm fronds were reflected in the headlights as the bus bounced back along the pothole-filled road.

"Are you all right, Señora?" Sharon asked Angela.

"Let's say this is not how I thought the evening would end," the old woman said, holding onto the hand of her daughter-in-law.

With her free hand, she lightly touched Sharon's hand.

"But the Lord works in mysterious ways, and he has his angels."

Bobby navigated down the windy hill road and then through

the empty streets of Los Reynaldos. Few lights were on, and the village seemed deserted. Minutes later, they came to Highway 1, the primary east-west road in southeastern Cuba.

"Where to, Lieutenant?" Bobby said. "We are at the proverbial crossroads. It is going to be very difficult for us to get off this island now. My guess is Acevedo is free and making calls."

"Go left."

"Roger that, then where?"

"Home."

"And how are we going to arrange that?" Xavier asked.

"I have friends," Sharon answered, looking at the road sign across the intersection. It said, *Guantanamo, 25 km.*

10c

"Guantanamo?" Bobby said, as he turned the bus left and onto the main highway, which after a hundred yards turned out to be only slightly better than the road through Los Reynaldos. "How the hell are we going to get on that base? It's stuck out in the middle of nowhere."

"Si, I agree with the sergeant," Xavier said. "Why would they let us in?"

"Won't know until we ask," Sharon told them. "Bobby, when we reach the outskirts of Guantanamo city, head around it to the north and then down the east side of the upper reaches of the bay. It's mostly swamps and farmland, not much else."

"They will be waiting for us. There will be roadblocks."

"Maybe, but I think that Acevedo will be looking for us to head back toward Santiago. He'll start there, set up stops and barricades in that direction first. We will have an hour before he begins to look this way, or at least I hope so."

She estimated they were twenty miles from the base. After bypassing Guantanamo city, their target would be a gatehouse at the northeast corner of the base.

"Señorita, Sharon, my love, I do not wish to be a pain in the ass and to question your judgment, but how do you know such things?" Xavier asked.

He held onto the frame of one of the bench seats and stared into the oncoming darkness, barely lit by the headlights.

"I was stationed there for six months, part of the army company that watches over some of al-Qaeda's finest. Lots of free time, so eventually I got to know the base and the surrounding territory. The gate is manned but is seldom used. There is no transit of workers and civilians like with other closely guarded army bases, so it's more to keep an eye out for lost tourists who try to come in to take a look. We go there and take our chances."

"Certainly a lot better than trying to steal a boat or getting back onboard a plane," Bobby added. "Acevedo will make sure they are closed up tight. In fact, I pity those people trying to leave in the next few days. Every Yankee and Canadian will be double checked and then checked again. And redheads may find themselves in jail."

O'Mara looked in the large mirror over the sergeant's head at his smiling face.

"That a crack about redheads, Bobby?"

"No, ma'am, not at all, just saying."

The bus lurched hard right, then left. A pothole deep enough to swallow a tire up to the axle passed by on the left.

"If this keeps up, one of these will be big enough to eat the whole bus," Gillis said, gripping the wheel hard. "Hold tight."

He again swerved left, then right. For a brief second the right side of the road seemed to disappear into nothingness, then the shoulder reappeared.

"I think the road collapsed back there," Bobby told them.

"Road? All I saw was nothing. Good job," Xavier said.

They passed through the northern edge of the Cuban city of Guantanamo. Like every small town, there were infrequent lights in some of the windows but few people about and still no police or roadblocks.

"At the next corner, go right," Sharon instructed. "There's some propaganda posters and signs about the base, or at least there were a few years ago. Then keep following the road south. The gate will be hard on the right through a series of switchbacks and controls.

"Afraid of suicide terrorist bombers?" Bobby asked.

"You know the army, Bobby. Someone thought they might try to break into the prison and release the prisoners. The army will do what it will do. Here, right."

The four-way intersection had two unassuming concrete block one-story buildings on two of the corners, a petrol station on the third, and bar on the other. The other buildings were dark, but light and music spilled from the bar's open windows and doorway. Two old 1950s Dodges and a '57 Chevy Biscayne were parked out front of the bar, fins high. Next to the Chevy was a black Toyota pickup truck; two policemen leaned against its side, smoking and talking to two very fully developed young women. The officers ignored the bus as it slowed at the corner, but then as Sharon watched out the window, one of the men opened the truck's door and extracted a microphone on a spring cord. As Bobby rounded the corner, the man looked up at the bus, then spoke into the mic. He glanced up again and turned to his partner.

"Secret's out. Bobby, let's see how fast this old piece of American steel and muscle will go."

"How far to the base?"

"Maybe two miles."

Bobby couldn't see the speedometer on the darkened console, and it wouldn't have made a difference. One of the first things he'd noticed had been that, like much of the equipment on the bus, it didn't work. Neither did the fuel gauge. He hoped the ten gallons they'd put in that morning would be enough.

In the distance, the bright lights from cargo cranes and buildings on the naval base broke the horizon. Bobby judged that they were doing at least forty miles an hour; everything on the bus rattled and strained from the effort. His fear was that something would just lock up, the engine, the transmission, hell, maybe even the brakes.

"Be careful, señor, there is a deep dip in the road ahead as we cross a stream," Carlos spoke up, from his seat near the front. "Some of my friends and I come down here to look at the base and swim. We always joked about what was on the other side. Watch out, it's coming up."

His warning was nearly too late. The bus took a dive down, banged hard against the road, then lurched back up, its front bumper almost scraping the ragged pavement.

"Goddamn. Everyone back there okay?" Bobby said.

Sharon picked herself off the floor of the bus and aimed her flashlight at the two women, who were wrapped around each other.

"You okay?"

"Si, we are okay. Is the bus still running?"

"Bobby? What the hell?"

"Carlos will tell you, but I think we have other trouble than this damn road. Look out the back."

Sharon shifted her gaze to the back windows and saw the flashing blue-and-white lights of a police truck. It was the one they'd seen at the bar, and it was gaining. Then it too disappeared in the dip of the road. She hoped the driver would fail to outmaneuver the hole in the road, but a second later the truck reappeared and increased its speed.

"Damn," she said, softly.

"Carlos, how far to the gate?" Bobby asked.

The young man was now standing directly behind him, holding onto the steel piping secured to the back of the seat for balance.

"Maybe a kilometer. There are bright lights, lots of fencing and armed—"

The explosion of the glass window at the rear of the bus made everyone turn to look, everyone except Carlos, who tumbled into the stairwell to Bobby's right.

"Sharon, Carlos has been hit," Bobby yelled.

Sharon danced her way up the aisle to the stairwell, Xavier close behind. Carlos was jammed headfirst down the steps.

Xavier grabbed the boy by the feet and with Sharon's help they laid him on an open seat. Another window exploded at the rear of the bus, showering the seats with glass.

"Elena, are you hurt?" Sharon yelled.

"No, we are okay. What about my son?"

"Sit down and stay down," Sharon said, when Elena stood.

To emphasize the order, another window exploded. The headlights of the truck were now only a hundred feet behind them. The interior of the bus was lit up like a Broadway stage, as the floodlights mounted on top of the truck flashed on. Another bullet punched a hole in the front windshield, a foot to the right of Bobby.

"SHARON, we have to do something, and I mean right now," Bobby yelled, as yet another bullet hit the windshield. "They are getting better."

"I'll handle it," Sharon said. "Xavier, how about the boy?"

"Hit in the shoulder, knocked him cold. But not too bad, if we can get him to a doctor."

"Where's one of the rifles?"

"Third seat back, or at least that's where I left it. Might be on the floor."

Another bullet shattered a side window.

"Do something, my dearest, or we will all be dead, either from bullets or in a crash by that sergeant of yours."

Bobby snorted loudly in response. "I heard that."

Sharon worked her way down the aisle on her hands and knees, trying to avoid the glass on the floor. She waved the flashlight under the seats; halfway to the rear, she saw one of the rifles sliding across the floor. She grabbed its leather strap, yanked it toward her and crab-walked to the rear door. The spotlights and the truck were now not more than forty or fifty feet behind the bus. She would only have two seconds of surprise before the men on the truck would see her and shift their target from the whole bus to her. She fingered the safety, prayed that the firing pins were still in the rifle, chambered a round into the AK-47, took a deep breath and stood upright into the full glare of the spotlight. The burst of bullets caught the policemen by more than surprise; she aimed at the grill between the two headlights. Seeing the muzzle flashes, the driver slammed on the brakes just as the radiator exploded in steam and engine parts. The truck's hood flew up, completely blocking the driver's view. The shooter leaning out the passenger-side window lost control of his own rifle; it flew up into the air and disappeared into the night. The fifty feet suddenly became two hundred feet.

"Go, Bobby, go," O'Mara screamed.

She worked her way back to Xavier.

"How is he?"

"We need that doctor."

Bobby made a final turn and was instantly confronted by a gate, floodlights, and flashes of barbed wire to the left and right. Completely blinded, he slammed on the brakes. The bus slid dangerously off the main roadway and onto the gravel before jolting to a stop. Bobby switched off the engine.

"I hope these are Americans and not another police barricade," he called back to Sharon.

"And that they don't shoot first and ask questions later," Xavier threw in for effect.

"This is the territory of the United States. If you have weapons, throw them out," a loudspeaker boomed. "Throw them out now, or you will be fired on."

The announcement was repeated in Spanish, as Sharon pitched the AK-47 out a shattered side window. She found the pistol and the other rifle, and tossed them out.

"We are Americans, and we have a wounded man inside. Can we leave the bus?" she yelled out into the lights. "We need your help."

"Everyone out with your hands up," a voice ordered. "Now!"

Bobby was the first down the stairs, followed by Sharon.

A Marine sergeant appeared in the glare and walked up to them.

"Who the hell are you two?"

"Actually, there's six of us. One, a youngster, has been shot,"

Sharon said.

"We heard you coming a mile away, first the bus, then the gunfire. Corporal, get the injured off and to medical. You," the soldier said, looking at Sharon, "since you seemed to be doing the talking, have a lot of explaining to do. Why the hell are you Americans here?"

"Actually, two Americans, one Mexican police officer, and three Cuban nationals," she answered.

"As I said, what the hell are you doing here? You are not going in until I know. I don't need another provocation with the Cubans today, ma'am, not today."

"Let me make introductions," Sharon said. "Then if you allow me to make one phone call, we can sort all this out."

Two hours later it was cleared up, or as best as the commanding officer would believe or wanted to believe. Carlos was doing well in sick bay; some of the best trauma surgeons in the American navy were stationed there, and the boy responded to their care. Elena and Angela Rodriquez were sitting comfortably in the waiting room of the hospital. The attending nurse allowed them to keep Bibi with them. Xavier was being questioned about his role in this—the word from Mexico was that his superiors were not happy with his adventure. The call Sharon made was to Army Colonel Jebadiah Simpson, her commanding officer in Iraq; he was now at Army Intelligence. He took her call immediately. Simpson was now involved with international surveillance of terrorists and their operations. When she explained what she and Bryan had learned over the last few days about the new triangle trade of guns, coffee, and diamonds, he was more than intrigued. With his help, her party was given sanctuary, such as it was.

There were phone calls and foot stomping by the Cuban authorities. When they were told through channels beyond Sharon and Xavier about Comandante Acevedo, the only response was that he had disappeared. And Marta de la Vega had also disappeared from her hotel in Rotterdam.

11a

Chapter 11

Kevin Bryan was surprised when Barrington said they were taking the train to Amsterdam—"Easier and faster than going through Gatwick," he'd told Bryan. From London's St. Pancras station, they traversed the tunnel below the Channel, took a turn north in France, and made one stop to change trains in Brussels. A little more than five hours later they pulled into Centraal Station, in the heart of the historic and now often infamous city of libertine ethics and libertarian values, Amsterdam.

Bryan waited on the train platform with the luggage as Barrington finished a mobile call.

"The plane is arriving from Johannesburg in the morning," Clive said, as they climbed into the car rental bus. "So we have some time to do a little research."

"What do you mean, research?"

"Cuba is playing Taiwan this evening in Rotterdam. I thought you'd like to teach me what baseball is all about—it's still a mystery to me."

"I don't believe you. We come all this way, and you want to go to a ball game. What's the angle?"

"Seems that Ms. Marta de la Vega, of Cuban prison and gun-running fame, is going to be there. She's their government minder. Get out of line, and she'll send you away. Might be fun to ask her a couple of questions."

Kevin checked his cell phone and saw that there were no calls from Sharon.

"Still nothing?" Barrington asked.

"Nada. That girl drives me nuts—she's damn good but does not communicate well. They should be in Cuba; she said they were going through Santiago de Cuba, then on to the plantation where the Rodriquez family was being kept. If they have cell phones, she should have called."

"From what you've told me, she'll be fine. Our problem right now is Vega and connecting her to the guns and the diamonds. There's a missing link, so we need to talk to her."

At the rental counter, Bryan was dumbfounded when the attendant pointed to a SMART car, with its truncated rear end and questionable power supply. The lack of large and roomy automobiles for Barrington and his police service was one thing, but there was a limit to how far Kevin could compress his six-foot-six frame.

"There is no way the two of us can fit into that thing, Clive."

"It's what the service allows me for my budget. That's it."

"Tell you what, put it on my bill and we'll get a real car."

Kevin glanced around the lot and spied a sleek, sand-colored Mercedes.

"Is that available?" he asked the cute attendant, with her iPad clipboard and rental list.

The attendant, all five-foot-one-inch of her, looked up at Kevin, and smiled.

"Yah, it is available, sir. But it is more money."

"Excellent, put it on this," Kevin said, pulling out his American Express card. "By the bye, do you know the way to Rotterdam and this ballpark?" He handed her a piece of paper with the ballpark's name.

"No, but we have GPS," she answered with a smile.

Ten minutes later, after the blonde Dutch girl finished giving the two men instructions on how to use the car's GPS system, she pointed to the street that passed in front of the rental office, indicating their starting point.

"I feel like bloody Dorothy and this is the Yellow Brick Road," Clive said.

He looked at the GPS screen; a voice said something in a language that neither of them understood. He looked back at the screen.

"Turn left next corner, and serves us right that we get a machine that only speaks Dutch."

"She was cute," Kevin said.

"Yes, there was that."

For the next hour and a half, they alternated between watching the GPS screen and stopping and checking their respective mapping systems on their phones. Eventually, they found the Neptune Stadium in Rotterdam. The billboard and electronic signage flashed that the game between Cuba and Taiwan was scheduled for seven p.m., leaving them an hour to kill. They parked in the small lot near the stadium and walked to the stadium entry.

"At least the drive was comfortable," Kevin said. "And they drive on the civilized side of the road here."

"You did a fine job. We only missed being killed twice by my count. Where did you learn to drive?"

"I was a cop for almost twenty years. There's a lot of skills we learn—evasive high-speed driving is one of them. Besides, after all the thrills you've given me, I thought I would return the favor."

"You are a bastard, no doubt about it."

Kevin felt a wash of déjà vu wash over him as they walked into the stadium. While not nearly as grand as a major league ballpark, this had all the trappings and feel of a high-quality minor league field or even a great college ballpark. There was even an aroma of hot dogs hanging in the humid air as they purchased tickets. Hearing the crack of a bat, he instinctively spun toward the field and watched a baseball sail high to the right field fence and clear it by ten feet.

"Nothing better than a ball game, no matter where," he said.

"Cricket. Now there's an international sport," Clive answered.

"You'd argue over the time of day, wouldn't you?"

They were sitting ten rows up on the right field side; Kevin could see the backs of the Taiwan players' jerseys, and one name stuck in his head until he figured it out.

"I'll be back in minute. I need to talk to someone," he said to Barrington.

"Talk with someone, who do you know here?" the other asked, watching Kevin head down the steps to the backside of the fence behind the Taiwan dugout.

"Danny, Danny Yang," Bryan called out to the man standing next to the dugout watching his team hit batting practice.

Yang turned at the sound of his name.

"Well I'll be damned," he said, and walked casually over to Kevin. "It's Bryant or something."

"Kevin Bryan, Danny. Glad to see that you and your boys made it."

He reached down over the low fence to shake Danny's hand.

"How are you doing?'

"We've won five games and not lost any. Good numbers too. If this rain holds off, we may win another."

"Good for you."

"What the hell are you doing here?" Yang asked. "I thought you were going to London."

There was no reason to tell Danny Yang anything about anything. Kevin responded that he'd had a little time and decided to come to Amsterdam for a day or two.

"Then I'll be back to London," he said. "Saw something in the paper on the train about the tournament and thought, what the hell. Playing Cuba? I hear they're pretty good."

"Good? These Cubans are great. Their pitching is almost major league stuff, their fielding is the best of the four teams, and their hitting has taught my fellows a lot. They're three and two, so right now we're playing for the quarterfinals, probably face these guys again in the finals. They are all in chaos though, everything screwed up."

"Why's that?"

"Seems that their manager, an old baseball wizard named Jorge Cortez, has disappeared as well as a witch of a woman, Marta de la Vega. She was the government chaperone, if you know what I mean. Acted like a fucking Nazi with her players."

"You're kidding. So who's minding the team?" Kevin asked, while wondering what the hell just happened.

"The assistant manager, some kid named Luis or something. Haven't met him yet. The rumor is going around that they may not be able to even field a team. Seems a couple of the Cuban players took off. More will probably follow. It's a shame, because my kids really want to beat these guys."

"Sorry to hear. But good for you, I guess."

"Yeah, always politics when we come here, especially with the Cubans. My assistant manager was with this team when that kid Toribio Rodriquez bolted a while back. It wasn't too much of a shock. I saw him play the Braves a few times when the Giants were in town. That kid's a serious ballplayer. Now, with all these others in the show, these Cuban kids have their eyes on the big bucks. Really quite a shame. I know how hard it is; these two worn-out knees prove it."

Kevin glanced back at a puzzled looking Barrington and put up one finger. Barrington gave a questioning look back.

"You play well, Danny. Sometime when you're in San Francisco, give me a ring."

He handed Yang a business card.

"I'll buy you a dog, a real San Francisco hot dog."

"Damn, a private investigator," Danny said, looking at the card. "That why you're here?"

"No. As I said, just in Amsterdam and saw the advertisement."

"Thanks for stopping, and I will take you up on that. You never know. Now, if this rain will hold off."

Kevin climbed the steps back to where Barrington sat, sipping from a paper cup.

"That's not tea, is it?" Kevin asked.

"Yes."

"Figures. We come to a ball game, and you ask for tea. Earl Grey, right?"

"Yes. So?"

"You British."

"What the hell was all that about?"

Barrington used his paper cup as a pointer to indicate Yang.

"Fellow I met on my way over. Danny Yang, the manager for the Taiwan team. Nice guy."

"Okay?"

"Seems that your little trip here has now become a conundrum and a mystery."

"How so?"

"Our dear little Miss Marta de la Vega has disappeared, bolted the scene, scrammed."

"Bollocks. Why?"

"Yang didn't know, but to put frosting on the hot crossed bun, it seems that the Cuban team manger, Mr. Jorge Cortez, has also disappeared."

"Damn, there is a rumor about him and the Altheimers as well."

Kevin's look didn't mask his annoyance.

"And when were you going to tell me the tasty bits of that one, Clive? This guy Cortez may be involved?"

"Possibly. When we've crossed-checked Cortez with Altheimer, they would often be in the same town at the same time."

"There's no place you can hide anymore, is there?"

"Not if you're a bad guy and governments are looking for you," Barrington said.

"I assume that within an hour or so, you'll have some idea as to where they might be?"

"We can only hope." Barrington looked at the sky. "Rain, let's get started back to Amsterdam before it starts. We English have a nose for it."

Within minutes it started to mist heavily and a sharp wind rose off the North Sea. By the time they reached the car, it was raining heavily. They heard the announcer over the loudspeakers say something, then repeat it in English: "Tonight's game has been cancelled."

"No rain checks?" Kevin mumbled.

"What?"

"Nothing, Clive. Nothing."

11b

As Kevin pushed the rented Mercedes over 140 km along the Dutch autobahn in the rain, Barrington was on his mobile, barking orders and demanding answers. Afterward, he stared out the car's window, tapping his phone on the glass.

"Where to, Clive? Those diamonds are coming in tomorrow. Do we meet them, or keep trying to chase down Vega and Cortez?"

Barrington increased his tapping.

"Our first obligation is to our clients," he said after a moment. "We meet the plane. My people are letting Interpol know; they will upgrade the airport police watching the plane. Go to the hotel and we'll get a little sleep. The plane isn't due until tomorrow at nine a.m."

Kevin's cell phone rang with a familiar Irish lullaby that was Sharon O'Mara's ringtone.

"You're late, where the hell are you?" Kevin demanded. "What? . . . Guantanamo? You alright?"

After asking about Gillis and Lopez, he pushed the speaker button on the phone.

"Clive's with me. We're in Amsterdam."

"I leave you alone for a few weeks, and now you're wandering around the fleshpots of Europe with your new BFF."

"Stop it. What about Toro's family?"

Sharon went through what happened and why they ended up in the American territory at Guantanamo. Then it was Kevin's turn about Vega and Cortez.

"My guess is that Acevedo's first call was to de la Vega, and that's the reason she bolted," Sharon said. "Not that I have anything to add about what's going on in Holland or about the diamonds. I've reported to American Naval Intelligence about what went on at Vega's plantation. Other than being seriously pissed at Lopez and me, I think they will pass on the information about Acevedo to the Cuban officials. The Cuban government will be more concerned about the theft of guns than the people on Vega's farm. I would think that Cubans are not big fans of entrepreneurial capitalism, when it comes to opportunistic Cuban citizens stealing their guns and selling them on the black market."

"Clive's chasing Vega and Cortez through the airlines," Kevin told her. "With the EU now one happy family, they will only get caught if they do something stupid. They have to get out of Europe somehow, and they will be found."

"Clive, you take care of that man, you hear me?"

"Ms. O'Mara, I have a great affinity for the Irish, so I will do my best."

"The only thing about me that's Irish is my hide when I get too much sun. Other than that, I am one hundred percent American girl."

She relayed that the State Department had given the Rodriquez family temporary visas to get to Jamaica—"We'll get the first plane out after we get there, Lopez to Mexico and Bobby and I to San Francisco," she said. "Elena Rodriquez has talked to her husband and is crazy to see him. He's taking a few days from the team and coming to Jamaica to see them. The Giants are playing in New York, and he'll rejoin the team in Atlanta. I'll be there with them when they get together, but not sure when they will get off Jamaica.

"We have the diamond shipment coming in tomorrow. When that's safely delivered, we'll get back to London," Kevin said. "After that, I'll be on my way back to San Francisco. Take care."

"You too. We'll talk tomorrow."

Clive looked at Kevin.

"I need a drink."

"Thought you would never ask."

Kevin woke to the sound of knuckles banging on his hotel room door; he looked at the clock on the bedside table—5:03 a.m.

He wrapped one of the hotel's fluffy white robes around his naked body and walked to the door. When he peered through the security eye, Clive Barrington's face filled the tiny window.

"Shit," Kevin said.

He opened the door, rather, Barrington pushed his way in.

"I thought you said six?"

"That was my hope, but I got a call. The plane is making good time and will land at eight o'clock at Schiphol. I've ramped everyone up an hour so, my American friend, get your bum in gear. We need to be out of here by five-thirty."

Bryan spun around, grabbed the clothes he'd laid out the night before, and headed into the tiny bathroom. He was showered and dressed in less than ten minutes. They picked up coffee and a bag of croissants from a Starbucks across the street, as they waited for the valet to bring up the rental. Clive drove.

"An hour early. Not unusual," Kevin said. "Good tailwind?"

"Planned. We wanted to make sure that only a few people knew about the real schedule."

"You son of a bitch. You don't trust me. You think I might be part of the operation to steal the stones? Goddamn."

"I couldn't trust anyone after Sally's death, no one. And you flying in from the U.S. at just that moment only made me more suspicious. So I withheld some tidbits of information."

"Kind of critical information, Barrington. Like the whole fucking reason I'm here, to make sure nothing gets fucked. And now I'm not sure I trust you, either. I've found that when something is worth doing and planning for and has big bucks written all over it, the bad guys will go to great lengths to make it happen. Sometimes they're even smarter than the cops, and with twenty million in diamonds, they will try to be even smarter."

"It's not twenty million, it's a quarter of a billion in diamonds. A quarter of a billion *euros*."

Kevin let out a soft whistle.

"Goddamn, Clive, that's over three hundred million dollars. We need to communicate. These failures only piss me off more.

If you think the Altheimers are juiced up to get twenty million in diamonds, what the hell will they do to get three hundred million dollars worth?"

"Anything they can. The plane is the weakest link. Once it hits the ground, we will have armored trucks and escorts to move the stones back into Amsterdam. We have been monitoring the plane since it refueled in Dubai."

"Why there? That's just a tad out of the way."

"The plane's owner was on board for the leg from Johannesburg. He's also one of the investors in the diamond firm."

"Just one more little issue of security you neglected to tell me. I'm not feeling the love here, Clive. No, not really."

"Sorry, they are over Switzerland right now, or should be. My people will be waiting when they touch down."

"And I bet their people are waiting as well. Is everything we discussed done? All I asked for was a little help, just one little thing," Kevin said.

"It's been done," Barrington answered.

Kevin pulled the rented Mercedes into the parking lot next to the last industrial looking building on the south end of Amsterdam's sprawling Schiphol airport. The main terminal, three runways away, was more than a mile distant. Signs across the front of the long one story building listed airfreight and logistics companies. Kevin recognized a few from his police days working Oakland's airport back home. The monogramed tailfins on cargo airplanes of various sizes, parked on the opposite side of the building, were visible over the top of the flat roof. Queued up along the front of the building were parked a half a dozen armored cars and an assortment of security personnel in full SWAT gear and body armor. All waited outside the fence and gate that led to the taxiways and runways.

Clive's really pulled out the strings on this one, they're either waiting for our shipment or a riot to break out.

They walked to a small folding table set up near a gate that opened out onto the tarmac of the airport. Kevin watched a Lufthansa 747 jet, easily a half mile away, touch down on one of the main runways. Standing next to the table were two men, both wearing bulletproof vests over their Armani suits. Kevin was not impressed by their demeanor: too casual, too matter-of-fact, and too damn mechanical. It also occurred to him that by now maybe forty or fifty people knew something was going on, none of this was a secret now.

"Clive, this sucks. Too many know, and too many are involved."

"Such is a government operation, even here in Europe. No one wants to be left out."

"Mr. Barrington, they are five minutes out," one of the suits said, as he put a walkie-talkie back on the table. "Shall we move?"

"You know what to do. We'll be right behind you." Barrington picked up one of the half dozen walk-talkies on the table.

"Yes, sir."

Leaving the security and SWAT teams, Kevin followed Barrington through narrow hallways of the freight office and out onto the concrete apron on the airport side of the building. The smell of aviation fuel was strong in the damp air, and the lush grass between the runways still glistened with the sheen from the overnight rain. He watched a massive Airbus A380 double-decker slowly approach from south; it followed the Lufthansa 747. He had never seen an airplane that huge. Its wide body seemed to hang in the air as it dropped lower and lower toward the runway.

"I assume that is not the plane we are waiting for?" he said to Barrington, in a wiseass tone.

"No, though I have been told the sheik does have one of those as his personal plane. But ours is further to the west, a more realistic Gulfstream IV."

"What, couldn't afford a V?"

Barrington ignored the remark. "Our jet will land on the far runway, then taxi to us. The primary runways beyond are for the commercial traffic. After landing they will take at least ten minutes to get here, assuming normal commercial ground traffic."

"They couldn't land closer—too much can happen," Kevin said.

"Don't worry. It will be fine, the airport is secure." Barrington turned and looked the one hundred feet to the security fence and gate at the end of the building. The Dutch SWAT team was still queued behind the fence.

Kevin scanned the sky to the east and through the clouds spotted a small flash of morning sunlight reflecting off the airframe of a plane. The difference in size between the Airbus and the Gulfstream was like an eagle and a fly. He watched the G-IV carve a sharp turn and drop quickly to the commercial runway that crossed the far side of the commercial runway. It landed smartly with practiced ease and rolled out toward the end of the runway, then turned and slowly headed back on the taxiway toward the waiting contingent of guards and security personnel. It paused and waited three-quarters of a mile away for a commercial airliner to taxi in front of it.

"Now the tricky part," Kevin began, but was cutoff as the air was shattered by the whomp-whomp-whomp of rotor blades skimming not more than thirty feet above their heads. Kevin instinctively ducked, as the black helicopter flew straight toward the approaching jet. The copter pulled up like a horse being reined in and floated five feet above the ground directly in front of the jet. The G-IV pilot slammed on the brakes as he started to cross the primary runway.

"It's all fucked. So fucked. So *goddamned* fucked," Kevin said, watching the activity more than thousand yards away.

As the helicopter touched the pavement, three men quickly dismounted. One of them walked to a point directly in front of the cockpit and fired one round from his rifle into the window above the pilot. When there was no response, he fired an automatic burst, shattering the cockpit glass. At that, the engines immediately shutdown.

"We need a car now," Kevin yelled, to no one in particular. When he looked around all he saw were stunned policemen watching the action. "Damn it Barrington, get a car, get something."

A second man pointed his rifle at the plane's door, which slowly dropped open, pulling its stair with it. The man was gesturing and into the open doorway. From where Kevin and Barrington stood they obviously couldn't hear what he was saying or see the person or people inside the plane.

"Go, go, go," screamed Barrington into his radio. "Get to them now, damn it, now."

Barrington's security team ran for their trucks, all of which were parked outside on the unsecured side of the fence with the SWAT team. One man fumbled with the keys to the heavy padlock securing the gate. Three of Barrington's Interpol men, in full assault gear, began jogging toward the plane.

"This is so fucked, I can't believe it," Kevin said to Barrington, as they watched two of the armed men from the helicopter run up the G-IV's stairway and into the plane. Seconds later, they bounded back down the steps, each carrying a large black case in one hand, assault rifle in the other. Under the cover of the man who had shot up the cockpit, they climbed back into the helicopter. In one smooth motion, the copter lifted off the tarmac and headed low and fast south away from the airport. It flew directly under the belly of an approaching Boeing 777.

Kevin watched the three Interpol men running toward the plane pull up short, their hands on their knees; they hadn't made it halfway. From flyover to escape, he estimated that no more than four minutes had passed.

11c

"They were good, damn good," Barrington said to Kevin as they stood together on the ground at the nose of the plane and watched the confusion build.

The crowd around the G-IV now included airport police, Barrington's men, the team from Interpol, and city emergency personnel. One man, the pilot, was being attended to by paramedics. There was gauze wrapped around his head, a spot of blood on the white bandage. Another man, also in the white shirt and epaulets of the sheik's private air service, stood next to the gurney on which the pilot sat. The copilot was talking with a policeman. A blonde woman and a tall, Arabic-looking man stood off to one side, also talking with police.

"I'd start with the blonde," Kevin said. "She's with the company, right?"

"Yes, Helga Dortmund. Been with us for six years," Barrington said.

"Us?"

"She's mine. The diamonds were to never leave her sight."

"Gone now, wouldn't you say?"

"Shut up."

They walked up to Dortmund. Kevin had to admit he hadn't seen such a striking woman in a long time. She wasn't beautiful in the classic Sophia Loren sense, with soft curves and an inviting smile; hers was the angular beauty found in a serrated Ka-Bar combat knife. Her eyes followed the two men as they approached, reminding Kevin of a tiger he'd once seen in the San Diego Zoo. The cat had never moved, but its eyes watched every visitor as if it were still in the jungles of India, scoping out its next kill.

"Are you okay, Helga?" Barrington asked, eyeing the bruise forming on the side of her face.

"Yes, this is nothing. They were on and off in seconds," she said.

"We saw. Did they say anything?"

"The one that came up the stairs first demanded, 'The key to the cases, now.' It was like they knew everything."

"I told you we needed a safe," Kevin injected.

"And I told you it would be too heavy," Barrington snapped. "Then what?" he said to Helga.

"I handed them the keys. One man watched the cockpit. When one of the pilots started to open the door, he yelled at them to close it and stay where they were. The co-pilot pulled it closed."

"What language?" Kevin asked.

"What?" she faltered, as if taken aback by the tone of his voice.

"Language, a simple question. I assume you speak a few languages."

"Four," she replied, and then thought for a moment. "Spanish, the man yelled in Spanish. The woman asking for the key told him to shut up."

Kevin and Barrington looked at each other.

"Woman?" Kevin asked.

"Yes, she was the first one inside, but we never saw their faces. They wore ski caps. Only her eyes—they were grey. And they also wore gloves. After they had the cases, they left."

"And what was the sheik's guy doing this whole time?" Barrington asked, pointing to the man in the uniform.

"*Pinkeln in seiner Hose,*" she offered, with a snort.

"What did she say?" Kevin asked Barrington, as they left Helga.

"Peeing in his pants."

For the next ten minutes, Bryan and Barrington talked with the pilots and went through the jet's interior. Outside of the shattered cockpit windows and AK-47 bullets stuck in the sensitive overhead electronics above the pilot's seats, little else was damaged. Airport personnel were securing a pushback tractor to the airplane's front landing gear, preparing to tow it back to the freight gate.

"The sheik won't be happy," Kevin said, as they walked back to the gate.

"He will bill us later, I'm sure."

Barrington's mobile buzzed.

"That Mother?" Kevin asked.

Clive checked the screen and nodded.

Kevin waited while Clive talked to the command center in London. He kept saying 'good,' 'good,' then 'jolly good.'

"You guys really do say jolly good a lot," Kevin said, when Barrington had clicked off.

"No I don't."

He thought for a second.

"Well, maybe I do."

"And?"

"Your suggestion seems to be working, London is following the diamond cases through their GPS signals. According to Mother, the thieves are about four miles from here and moving further south."

The plan to place a GPS tracking device in each case had been Bryan's, foreseeing the possibility of what had just happened. The cases themselves were constructed from titanium—designed to withstand the weight of a ten-ton truck—with the exteriors covered in black leather. The partitioned interiors had deep, honeycomb-shaped cells that held the individual velvet bags of diamonds, each bag holding similar shapes and weights. The handles, also leather-encased, were where the GPS units had been hidden. Experts said that it would take at least a half hour to open the cases; the electronic locks were designed to permanently secure if tampered with. Flame-cutting tools wouldn't penetrate; the only way in was to cut with a diamond-blade saw, which Kevin found somewhat poetic.

One of the Armani suits met them as Kevin and Barrington reached the gate.

"What's happening?" Barrington asked.

"They flew low and fast to an empty lot in an industrial park in Molenwatering. The helicopter was abandoned. Reports from office workers in the adjacent buildings say there were two identical white Mercedes sedans and a van waiting at the curb, when the copter landed. One of the suspects, and the cases, went in the van; the other three took the cars. Within seconds, they were gone. The N11 freeway parallels one side of the town; reports from the witnesses say that's where they headed."

"The helicopter?"

"It was reported missing this morning from a private air service at Rotterdam's airport."

"Thank you," Clive said, and turned to Kevin.

"They were good, very good."

"Thieves can be very inventive," Kevin agreed. "The safest place anyone can hijack a plane is in the middle of an airport, assuming that you can leapfrog over the police. Helicopter did that. They fly fast and low, and no one pays attention since helicopters are everywhere these days. Landing zone picked and staffed, quickly split up in identical cars going God knows where. They are in the wind."

"Except for the GPS."

"There's that, but for how long?"

"Hopefully long enough. You think the woman might be de la Vega?"

"Possible, but a long shot," Kevin said. "Since Sharon blew open her plantation operation, Vega's pulled out of any dealings with Cuba. She's in it for herself now. Yang said that the manager of the Cuban team, Cortez, also disappeared. Do you think he's the link between Vega and Altheimer?"

"With their history, it's probable. Altheimer's operation is based in Switzerland, but we're not sure where. Somewhere between Geneva and Bern. Heinz Altheimer has been tracked but still manages to shake any tails."

"You think that's where they'll go?"

Barrington stroked his mustache thoughtfully.

"Eventually, but there's six hundred kilometers between here and Switzerland. A lot can happen," he said.

"You know you have a mole or whatever you Brits call a spy in your operation. Only someone close to the top could have known all this, the timing and the change in plans."

"Yes, I knew that as soon as the helicopter flew over. It's

been annoying me since. They are also responsible for Sally's death and your kidnapping attempt. That's partly why I've kept you out of the loop on some things."

"Like most everything, Clive."

"Sorry about that, had to."

"I get it, but now what?"

"We believe in your bloody Silicon Valley technology."

"Shit, I thought you would say that."

Chapter 12

12a

Marta de la Vega pulled off her ski mask and dropped it on the deck of the helicopter. The two men on the facing seats kept their headgear on; each held an AK-47 vertically between his knees. They'd been on the helicopter when it picked her up in an open parking lot near the train station in Berkel, their masks already donned. De la Vega didn't care whether the hired accomplices saw her face, but she understood why they kept theirs hidden. Like her, they wore dark clothing and leather gloves. The only words she'd heard either man say were to the pilot. She understood their Spanish, even though the accent sounded Castilian. As the helicopter sped away from Schiphol, the two men stared blankly at her. They had done what they were hired for and in ten minutes they would be gone, their Swiss accounts just a little richer. Good men, as always, were hard to find. It seemed that Señor Cortez did know how to manage more than just ball games, she thought, not unappreciatively.

She watched the Dutch countryside pass by just five hundred feet below her; their flight would not last five minutes. It would take more time than that for the police to get someone up in the air to try and find them. The plan had been simple, the first two stages now done. The flight from Berkel in the stolen helicopter had taken less than fifteen minutes, then they'd simply waited on a small island in a lake south of the Schiphol airport for the call that said the plane was landing. Now the pilot was heading to the prearranged landing spot in an open parcel of land in an industrial park. He made one pass and Vega saw the two white Mercedes sedans waiting along with a small service van; no police activity was evident on the adjacent highway or anywhere within the industrial park. He set the helicopter down. The two men headed for one of the cars, got in, and as soon as the doors slammed, the car left. The pilot took the other Mercedes. Marta de la Vega carried the two leather briefcases and climbed into the van. In seconds, it followed the Mercedes sedans to the on-ramps of the motorway that paralleled the industrial park. The two Mercedes went north, the van turned south. In minutes, they were lost among the hundreds of trucks and other vehicles.

"It went well?" Jorge Cortez said, from the passenger seat of the van.

"Yes, exceptionally well. They were looking for something else. The helicopter completely surprised them. Now we need to open these cases and get rid of them. They probably have some type of tracking devices on them."

She inspected the cases, deciding quickly that there wasn't time to try the locks. She turned to the man sitting in the back compartment with her.

"Do you have the saw?"

"Si," the small man said, as he removed a powerful-looking battery-powered skill saw from its box.

"Place the first case here. It is probably very hard steel or titanium under the leather," he said to de la Vega, before clamping the case in a vise secured to the van's floor.

When he spun up the high-speed saw with its diamond-coated ceramic blade, the sound was a piercing whine.

"Stay back and wear this," the little man said, and handed Vega a clear faceplate.

He began to cut along the seam between the lid and the body of the case. Sparks flew, some landing on Vega's bare arm, where they burned hot on her skin.

The man looked up and grinned.

"Move back a little more, *chica*. And keep that fire extinguisher handy."

The smell of burning leather filled the van as the blade slowly cut its way through the titanium.

"Faster," Vega yelled, over the screaming of the blade.

"Can't. Patience, *chica*."

"You call me *chica* one more time, and I'll use that tool on you."

He stopped the saw and looked up at her. All they could hear now was road noise as the van thundered south.

"Marta, I suggest you let the man do his business," Cortez said. "Every second you waste is one more second they can track us."

"You say one more thing, old man, and I'll dump you on the side of the road."

"And then you will have no buyer, and my people will make it very difficult for you to sell these precious little stones anywhere in the world. Keep cutting, Pedro. Don't pay her any attention."

Pedro revved up the saw and the sparks began again. It took twenty minutes to cut open the first case. He immediately set the second case into the vise and started in again.

De la Vega carried the first case, still closed, up to the front of the van to Jorge.

"You can open it," he told her. "I don't think it will explode."

"You hope it won't explode," Vega answered.

She placed the case on the floor and with her gloved hands pulled the top off. Cortez played a flashlight over the interior. Nestled in each of the small honeycomb-like compartments lining the bottom was a small purple velvet bag.

Vega extracted one at random.

"Hold your hand out," she said to Cortez.

She undid the small tie at the top of the bag and turned the contents out onto the man's arthritic, gnarled hand. Forty diamonds tumbled into his palm, each the size of a hazelnut.

Cortez's hand began to shake.

"*Madre de Dios*, these are worth a million dollars each. They have to be eight or ten carats."

He put the diamonds back in the bag she held.

"Another," he whispered, barely audible over the whine of

the saw.

She did as told and from another bag poured dozens of exquisite round-cut diamonds into the manager's hand. Each stone was at least five carats.

"How many bags?" he asked.

Vega did a quick count.

"Forty."

"Are there any large stones?" Cortez asked.

De la Vega felt the bags with her fingers until she stopped at one and smiled. The bag felt heavier than the others. This time she placed the contents in her own hand: three stones, each the size of a quail's egg, one clear, one pink, and one yellow. Like Cortez, her hand began to tremble.

"My God, these are beautiful," she said.

"Yes, and they may be worth more than thirty million euros each." Cortez glanced at Pedro. "He's finished the second case, let's look at that."

As the van continued south toward Rotterdam, they rummaged through the second case. It too held more than forty small velvet bags, some containing diamonds in a mixture of colors from chocolate to almost blue. Vega had never seen such colors or even knew they existed.

"We need to dump these cases," Cortez said.

He told Marta to stow the velvet diamond bags in the larger baseball equipment bag they had with them.

"It's the next exit," he told the driver. "There, on the south corner."

The driver stopped at the petrol station Cortez had indicated. Signs for the city of Gouda pointed east.

"I will be leaving you here, Jordy. My work is finished," Pedro said, as he got out and then took the empty cases Vega handed to him out the side door. "I will dispose of these and wait to hear from you. Good luck to the two of you—you'll need it."

Vega watched the small man walk quickly to the backside of the service station and a trio of large grey-green receptacles with the international symbol for trash disposal stenciled on their sides. He opened the lid of the first dumpster and dropped the cases in.

"One second, my friend," Cortez yelled, through the open window.

He could just be heard over the traffic noise from the nearby freeway.

Standing by the trash receptacles, Pedro paused.

"Marta, please grab the bag."

Surprised when he spoke in English, she didn't have time to say anything before hearing the percussive report of a silenced pistol. Stunned, she looked at Cortez, then to the driver, whose blood was already splattered over the inside of the windshield and door. He jerked twice, then fell hard against the steering wheel, setting off the horn. Cortez pushed the man back, killing the sound. He opened the door on his side and then, holding the pistol tightly to his side, walked directly to where Pedro stood with a quizzical look on his face. The look turned to surprise, then fear, as Cortez raised the weapon and fired two rounds into the man's chest. The diamond case cutter was dead before he fell to the gravel.

Vega quickly reached over the driver's body and retrieved the small pistol she spied in his limp hand. She slid it into her waistband and pulled her black shirttail over the weapon.

Cortez turned back to the van and with his pistol directed Vega to get out. He bent down and removed a pistol from inside Pedro's coat, then pointed to a blue Volvo sedan parked at the rear of the station.

"Now, Marta, now," he demanded, again pointing the pistol at her. He put Pedro's pistol in his own pocket.

Five minutes later, as they headed back toward Amsterdam, a parade of police cars raced past them in the opposing lanes, lights flashing. Overhead, a police helicopter overtook the procession and quickly disappeared.

"That didn't take long. We were lucky. There had to be GPS devices in the cases," Marta said, from the driver's seat.

"Yes, it was to be expected. That is why we need to leave the

Netherlands as soon as we can."

"And how are we going to do that? They will be looking for us everywhere."

"Of course they will. You did well, but it will do us little good if we cannot get these baubles to my associates."

"Was all that necessary back there?" she asked him. "I had assumed that there would be no need to use such measures."

"The driver and Pedro were working together. They were going to steal the diamonds. While you were watching Pedro throw out the cases, the driver had started to remove his pistol, hidden in the door. He did not have time to point it when I shot him. Of course, Pedro was waiting for the shots, and when he hadn't heard them, I made sure to get him before he had a chance to pull his own weapon."

Cortez sighed. "I am very disappointed. He and I went a long way back. Pedro Silvera was quite the ballplayer when he was younger, good with his hands. I will miss him."

Jorge fell silent for a few moments, and Marta said nothing, wondering how much of what he said was true, or if he had plans for her as well. She felt the pistol pressing against her back—uncomfortable but comforting. Everything in Cuba was gone; the call from Acevedo was a shock. She hadn't expected that the rescue would work. Acevedo assured her he had everything under control. What a fool—he was only worth having around for access to the government's guns. Someday she would track him down and make him pay for his ineptitude. But now she had bigger problems, if Cortez didn't trust Silvera and the driver, would he trust her? Or would he put a bullet in her when he had the chance. She only had a few minutes to contrive some type of a plan. She would now have to find a way to rescue herself.

"Follow the signs to Apeldoorn," he told her as they came to an interchange. "There is a small airport on the east side and my associates will be waiting."

He smiled, more to himself than at her.

"Tonight, we will dine in Zürich," he said.

12b

Bryan and Barrington leapt from the police helicopter as it touched down in the middle of the street in front of the service station, where the last movement of the GPS devices had been detected. Barrington carried a pistol and Kevin a MP7 slung on a short leather shoulder strap. They could hear the sirens of the advancing police cars above the noise of the highway.

"Shit," was all that Barrington could say, after inspecting the carnage behind the station.

"Looks like a falling out," Kevin said. "The driver was killed where he sat. The other man was shot were he stood, we can only assume he was with the gang. No weapons visible, so maybe they were gunned down and their weapons taken. Money will do that."

Barrington looked into the waste containers. "The suitcases are here."

Kevin watched the crowd that was gathering.

"Can you have one of your men ask if anyone saw something?"

No one had seen what happened; it was their helicopter that brought the crowd. However, one of the Dutch policemen escorted a young girl to Barrington and introduced her.

"Do you speak English?" Barrington asked the girl.

"Yah, yah, I do. I work in London for two years before I came back to operate my father's petrol station—this is our business. We were very busy this morning, and it wasn't until your helicopter landed did I know anything about what happened."

She looked from the man on the ground to the van.

"Is he dead?" she asked Barrington.

"Yes, two murdered. Do you know something?"

"We have a CCTV up there."

She pointed to the top corner of the building, where a small box was installed."

"In the birdhouse?"

"Yes, every time we put up a camera, someone would steal

it. Now the camera's hidden inside. Everything is recorded on a hard drive in the office. You want to see it?"

She was correct in saying 'everything.' Bryan and Barrington watched as the crystal-clear high-def video played out. It was less like seeing an actual murder replayed than watching a television show, with each actor playing their part.

"I assume the woman is Marta de la Vega, but the man I'm not sure of," Barrington said.

"It could be Jordy Cortez, the missing manager of the Cuban baseball team," Kevin said. "But he has his hat down low and not once does he look toward the camera, like he knew."

They watched de la Vega carry a duffel bag across the parking lot and place it in the backseat of the Volvo. As the car left the station, they were also able to read the license plate.

"Have your guys look at the data and see if they can see who left the car," Kevin said.

Barrington passed the plate information and the time frame of the car drop to one of the Dutch policemen.

"The Dutch have an advanced system of license plate reading; it was set up to ticket speeders," Barrington told Kevin. "They are checking the database to see if the plate of the Volvo has been photographed."

In a few minutes, the officer reported back that the plate number had been verified on the motorway near Utrecht thirty minutes earlier; the car was heading east.

Back in the helicopter, Barrington told the pilot to head east with hope of intercepting the Volvo, if they could get ahead of it. Ten minutes later there was another update: the car had been spotted south of Apeldoorn five minutes ago.

Barrington relayed the new heading to the pilot and they gave chase.

"Do you think they are trying to get to Germany?" Bryan asked.

"Possibly. Cortez has a connection to Altheimer, who is in Switzerland. At least according to the latest reports, that's where Heinz Altheimer still is. But they also know that they can't get far unless they get off the motorway. Too many ways to track them."

"They can't fly commercial, and the train stations will be watched," Kevin said, as he looked at the thick traffic flowing below them on the motorway.

"What town is that?" he asked, pointing.

"Apeldoorn," the pilot responded,

"And what airport is that to the northeast?"

"Teuge Luchthaven. It's a small airport used by private planes and gliders. I've flown in and out of there a few times."

"Clive, what do you think?"

"I think you're thinking what I'm thinking. Call them and tell them we will be landing," Barrington told the pilot.

Kevin looked at his NATO-grade MP7 and chambered a round.

The pilot maneuvered in low and directly over the buildings grouped on the south side of the runway and taxiways, where at least a dozen small aircraft were parked along the taxiway, apron, and surrounding grass fields. Their pilot made one pass over the runway, then banked back toward the buildings. A tree-lined road extended from the airport to the motorway on the south end. To the mutual surprise of Bryan and Barrington, their quarry, the blue Volvo, popped out of the trees and quickly turned toward a group of hangers.

"The Cessna," Kevin said, pointing toward the small plane parked on the macadam, it's prop still turning.

"Set us down in front of it. I don't want them leaving," Clive said.

The pilot slowed the helicopter and let it hover over the airplane. The down draft made the grass adjacent to the taxiway glisten in the sun. A man standing outside the plane looked up at the helicopter, just as the Volvo wheeled in between the hangers and came up alongside the getaway plane. As the car pulled to a stop, someone inside the plane passed a rifle to the lookout on the runway.

"Shit, get us out of here," Kevin yelled, as he watched the

man shoulder the AK-47.

A split-second later, the shooter fired a burst at the helicopter. They felt the impact of the bullets to the copter's airframe; the window on Kevin's right cracked, where a bullet had punctured the glass. The engine coughed and sputtered.

"I've got to set it down. We've been hit. Are you two okay?" Kevin heard the pilot say through his headset.

"Yeah, we're okay," Kevin said, simultaneously realizing that Clive was clenching his left arm, blood dripped onto the seat and floor.

"Seems I've been fucking hit," Clive managed to say.

"Get us down, now," Kevin said over his headset.

"Roger that."

The pilot fought to control the helicopter that was becoming more like a brick than a flying machine. Smoke engulfed the interior, as he watched the oil pressure drop to almost zero.

"Hold tight," he said calmly.

He slammed the skids of the helicopter into the pasture; mercifully, it slid along the grass and did not flip up on its nose or dig a rotor blade into the turf. When they lurched to a stop, Kevin quickly climbed out and pulled Barrington away from the disabled copter. The pilot followed with a first aid kit and capably ripped open Clive's sleeve. His upper arm was a mess from the fractured bullet. He winced from the pressure as the pilot wrapped the wound tightly with gauze and tape.

"Not as bad as some of the shit I got in Iraq, but it still hurts like a son of a bitch," Barrington said, breathing hard. "What are they doing, Bryan?"

Kevin looked back toward the plane, now a few hundred yards away.

"Can't see much from here, but there are three or four people walking around. I assume they are going to fly out of here."

He studied the movement of the figures in the distance.

"Shit, is that gunfire?"

The sounds of multiple pistol and rifle reports echoed across the open field.

"Yes, but doesn't seem to be aimed at us—maybe another falling out?" Kevin said to Clive.

A minute passed, and then the Cessna that had been sitting on the taxiway began to roll out and head toward the runway. The two or three people left behind climbed into the Volvo and it sped away between the hangers. The Cessna angled across the grass that cut between two taxiways paralleling the runway, then pushed its way in front of two planes waiting to take off. The Cessna's engines roared as it rolled onto the runway and without hesitation accelerated down the two thousand feet of asphalt. Fifteen seconds later, it was in the air and banking north and away from the small airport.

Kevin looked back to the hangers and caught a glimpse of a dark-colored car between the trees as it escaped down the entry road.

"What the hell just happened?" Clive said.

He moved stiffly to stand next to Kevin.

"My guess, the age-old problem of a lack of trust. Clive, there's still no honor among thieves."

12c

"They are lucky," Cortez said, as he climbed out of the Volvo. "That helicopter could have flipped and torn itself apart. Yes, very lucky."

"But how could they have known we were coming here? How, Cortez?" Vega practically screamed at him.

The man who had fired on the helicopter now walked cautiously toward the pair. His eyes never left them and his finger never left the rifle's trigger. He was medium height, dark tan, and his thick steel-grey hair was combed back tight to his head. He smiled when he recognized Cortez.

"It is good to see you, my friend. I take it everything went well?" he said.

"Yes, very well. Marta, this is my friend, Heinz Altheimer.

He will take the diamonds now. Our part is done. He will drop us at a small airport in the south of Germany, and then continue on to his home. Appropriate deposits will be made."

"I did my part," Vega said. "I want my money now, not some promise. My share was one million dollars. I'll take it now."

"Do you know how big a package of money that would be?" Altheimer said, adjusting the rifle in his hands. "Too much to carry around. Far too much, and completely unnecessary. You will be paid."

"I said I want it now. If you don't have the money, maybe I'll take one or two of the purple bags. They may not be as liquid as dollar bills, but they will do."

"No, you will just have to trust me."

"I trust no one," Vega said.

She turned to the pilot, who was looking out the small open window of the cockpit.

"You," she yelled, over the growling of the plane's engine. "Get out now, or I will shoot your boss!"

It was then they noticed that she was pointing a small Beretta at Altheimer.

"There is no reason to do this, Marta, none," Cortez said. "Just put the pistol down, we can talk."

"This isn't one of your baseball teams, and I'm not one of your players. I want my money."

"Not going to happen," Altheimer said, and shifted the rifle.

A shot rang out. The pilot, who had tried to sneak out of the plane with a pistol, fell to the taxiway. Vega had fired one bullet, which hit the man high in the shoulder. Altheimer instantly raised his rifle, but she put a bullet in his upper chest; the impact spun him around to the ground. As he fell, the AK-47 let loose with a burst of eight or ten rounds on automatic. Vega turned to Cortez and aimed the pistol directly at his head.

"The pistol, give me your pistol."

There was nothing Cortez could do but slip the small automatic from the shoulder holster under his jacket and with two fingers gently place the weapon on the pavement near where

Altheimer lay.

"Jordy, put the gym bag in the plane."

She pointed to the Cessna.

"Think about what you are doing," he argued. "You can't sell them. They are useless to you, but it's not too late to stop this foolishness."

"Everything I built in Cuba is gone, so this is my only answer. I will contact you about the diamonds. You have resources, you will find a way, but you will pay dearly for them. Right now, I'm taking the stones and leaving."

They both saw Altheimer move.

"Or should I put a bullet in his head?"

Cortez put his hands out in a gesture that offered surrender.

"Go then, get out of here. You know where to find me."

He carried the duffel bag to the open door of the plane and tossed it onto the empty co-pilot's seat, then stood back as Vega collected the weapons littering the taxiway and then climbed into the Cessna. He watched as she piloted the plane down the taxiway, gaining speed before cutting across the grass in front of two planes holding at the end of the runway.

As Vega accelerated up the runway and lifted off, Altheimer rolled over and sat up.

"Does that fool know what's she's doing?" he said, climbing slowly to his feet. He slipped off his jacket and rubbed the area of his armored vest, where the bullet had ripped a hole in the covering fabric.

"I think I have a broken rib."

"You are lucky she didn't shoot you in the face."

"Yes, there's that too. Were you able to switch the bags?"

"Yes, she has just made her escape with my laundry from the last week. I will miss that yellow shirt, but I believe I can afford another."

"Many more, my friend, many more. Help me with Thaddeus; we need to leave now. They will have called for assistance and the sooner we are away from here the better."

Altheimer looked across the neatly clipped grass to the disabled helicopter a quarter mile away.

"They survived, and we need to leave. I assume that you have provided a replacement for this vehicle?"

"Of course, there is a BMW in the parking lot. Besides their efforts will now be on that plane. We will be a hundred kilometers from here before they can figure out what happened," Cortez replied.

He placed the bag with the stones in the BMW, while Altheimer administered to Thaddeus. The pilot was lucky; Vega's bullet had missed everything vital, leaving a clean entry and exit hole just below the clavicle. Altheimer gave him a shot of morphine as he lay in the backseat of the car, then loosened his own vest and swallowed a few aspirin as Cortez drove down the shaded entry drive and out onto the motorway.

Two police vehicles bounced across the grass toward the disabled helicopter, their overhead lights flashing.

"Is the radio working?" Kevin asked the pilot, who quickly reentered the helicopter and checked.

"No sir, power is gone, battery's probably shorted. Maybe one of the emergency vehicles has a radio.

"Clive, do you have your mobile?" Kevin asked.

"Damn it, of course."

For the next ten minutes Barrington was on the phone with Interpol, telling them everything that had happened and everything they knew. He asked the emergency people from the airport if the office had the number of the Cessna that had forced its way onto the runway and was pleased to hear that they had already done more than that; a complaint had been registered with the civil aeronautics board of the Netherlands, indicating the plane's type and tail number. Wherever it landed, the person or persons on board would be detained.

"The problem is, we don't know who is flying the plane or who escaped in the car," Kevin said. "We don't even know how many are in the plane or even the car. This has been one more serious fuck-up. These people are very good—well organized and thorough."

"And very greedy." Clive added.

Clive's phone rang; he looked at the screen and smiled.

"Bryan, it's your girlfriend."

Kevin accepted the proffered mobile and clicked on the speaker.

"Where are you?"

"And good morning to you. You seem a little stressed. Is that Englishman continuing to give you shit?"

"You don't know the half of it."

He spent a few minutes telling her what had happened. More police vehicles arrived, and in time they were surrounded.

"As I said, I can't leave you alone for one day without you getting into trouble. Are you okay?" O'Mara asked.

"Just my ego is bruised. Clive's nursing a bad wound in his arm. But any crash you can walk away from is good."

"That's bullshit. So Vega and maybe Cortez are behind all this?"

"We know she was involved in the ground operation and speculate that Cortez is also involved. We can only guess that it was Altheimer who flew in with the plane. But we don't know who left with the diamonds. The police are checking the area where the car met the plane. There's shell casings and some blood. They were in a blind spot for CCTVs, and no ground personnel or civilians saw anything. We know that the plane was registered to a rental service near Frankfort. They are chasing the paperwork, but we suspect that they will find it's all fake. With his money, Altheimer has access to a lot of options."

"We landed in Jamaica two hours ago. Kingston airport," O'Mara said, when Bryan asked where she was. "Toro Rodriquez and his agent are expected this evening. The family is very excited. Carlos, the son, is doing well but will spend a few days in the hospital here. It all went better than I expected."

"Better than you expected? You're lucky you and Gillis aren't spending the rest of your lives in a Cuban prison."

"Yeah, there's that, but all's well that ends well."

"Fuck, I wish we could say that," Clive said. "Someday, I want to meet you and find out what you really see in this man.

"Well, your wish is my command. There's a British Airways plane leaving tomorrow morning—I'm booked. I will be at the Savoy tomorrow night. They say I have a nice suite, and by now I can see that the two of you can't play well together. Someone has to take charge."

Chapter 13

13a

De la Vega leveled off the Cessna at eight thousand feet and headed northwest from Apeldoorn, Netherlands, not having a clue as to where she was going and what she would do when she got there. Civil defense and military planes certainly would be looking for her; she hoped that she would be lost, at least for precious minutes, in the clutter of commercial and private aircraft crisscrossing northern Europe. She checked the fuel gauge, half empty. She had to make a decision soon or find herself forced down; she was not going to make a suicidal decision lightly.

She banged a fist against the center of the control column, and let out a string of Cuban profanities. Her neat and comfortable empire was collapsing. She still didn't grasp exactly how it had all gone so wrong so quickly. Acevedo had been brief, but long enough to make it clear that Vega could never return to Cuba. An American red-headed woman, with help from a Mexican policeman whom Acevedo knew, showed up in Santiago de Cuba and wanted help recovering the relatives of one of the ballplayers who had defected to the United States. One Toribio Rodriquez, to be precise. Acevedo had hoped to trap them at the farm, but they had escaped with Toribio's family to the American naval base. Acevedo was now sure their gun dealing and smuggling would be known; he was trying to get off the island, hoping not to be shot for anti-Cuban behavior. As for Vega, she was now a woman without a country and sure of two things: the rules of the civilized world no longer applied to her, and she wished she had shot Jorge Cortez dead. On the other hand, she had a quarter of a billion euros in diamonds as her co-pilot. That would open any door in the world to her.

She looked around the cockpit of the Cessna TT, much nicer than her forty-year-old plane back in Cuba. Any other day, she would fly the plane as far as it had fuel. The airplane had an effective range of about twelve hundred miles. The half tank of fuel would translate into a little more than two hours flying time and roughly four hundred miles distance. She didn't delude herself; she would be found in less than a half hour by military or police aircraft. She needed an airport, something small, some services, maybe no tower or control. Then again, a deserted road would also do the job. She had maybe twenty minutes. She scanned the landscape in front of her. To the starboard, a small airport came into view. One runway, overall smaller than the airport from which she'd escaped at Apeldoorn. She was now in German airspace, her headset loud with German and Dutch; it would only be a matter of time before she was found. She lowered the Cessna to two thousand feet and made one pass over the airport, noted the wind direction, ignored the requests from the tower in German to respond, and deftly landed the plane. She taxied to the west end of the taxiway, as far from the small control tower as possible. Now came the fun part.

Flying over, she'd spotted three cars parked near two small hangers at the far end of runway. One was a taxi, with its obvious rectangular light on the roof. Her quickly formulating plan was to commandeer the cab and get to the village she had passed over to the west. She'd seen a train station on the western side of the town; from there she could move anywhere. Her short-term goal was Hamburg—why, she wasn't sure, but it just sounded right and in a big city she could more easily disappear. She slipped the small Beretta pistol again into her back waistband, deciding to put the other pistols into the bag with the diamonds. She hated to leave the AK-47, but it would be too difficult to hide. She opened the door, grabbed the duffel bag from the seat, and climbed down from the plane. She zipped the bag open, at the same time reaching for one of the pistols she meant to conceal. Turning back to the bag, she pulled it fully open and froze.

Yellow cloth, not purple velvet, filled the duffel bag. The cloth she pulled out of the bag was a man's shirt—the rest was underwear and socks. Cursing under her breath, she took a quick look down the taxiway toward the tower; two officials were headed her way. Instantly understanding what had happened to the diamonds, but with no time to spare, she placed the two pistols in the bag and hastily added the AK-47. Pissed hardly described how she felt, as she tossed the jackal Cortez's shirt over the weapons and slung the duffel over her shoulder. Quickly, she walked to the cab, where a man sat behind the steering wheel smoking a cigarette. When he saw Vega approaching, he quickly stood up beside the car and said, *"Haben Sie ein Taxi brauchen?"*

Her response was to point the Beretta at him. He threw up his hands. Vega waved him away from the taxi and pointed to the ground. He knelt, then laid flat on the pavement. She stashed the duffel in the backseat, slid behind the wheel, and before the men from the airport tower could reach her, she left the airport and headed west. Ten minutes later, off a side road deep in the forest, she cursed Jorge Cortez and what he had done to her. She didn't want the diamonds now as much as she wanted Cortez dead. In another ten minutes, she reached the train station and parked in a small lot between two large trucks, hoping that the taxi would be hidden at least for an hour. From there, she walked the one block to the station. With the bag full of weapons and Jordy's dirty laundry slung over her shoulder, she stopped at an automatic ticket machine and looked down the choices. All her identification, three passports, and two credit cards under different names were in a thin wallet that she kept on a chain around her neck, under her dark blouse. For all intents, she looked like a tourist. A station agent calmly asked her a question in German; she had no idea what he said. She gave the international shrug of 'I don't understand.'

"No comprende," she said.

The German pointed at the electronic schedule.

"Wo?"

"Hamburg."

"Kreditkarte?"

This she understood and unbuttoned the top of her blouse to the widened eyes of the attendant, who was quickly disappointed when she stopped at three buttons and extracted her small document holder. She handed him the card with a big smile. After the transaction was complete, she studied the ticket. Her train would arrive in twenty minutes.

"Comida?" she asked, making movement with her fingers to her mouth.

He pointed to the end of the station.

"Essen, gut."

"Gracias."

Later, she took a seat on the train and watched the German countryside click by as the sun sank to the west behind her. In two hours, she was in Hamburg, Germany, and found the hotel directly across the street from the train station acceptable. She didn't leave her room for two days. She spent the time figuring out how to get even with Jorge Cortez and Heinz Altheimer for what they had done to her.

The targets of Vega's thoughts climbed out of the BMW at the train station in Essen, Germany, around the same time Vega arrived in Hamburg. On the drive south from Apeldoorn, Cortez had checked the local train schedules.

"I can catch the five o'clock back to Rotterdam," he told Altheimer, in Spanish. "The championship game is at noon tomorrow."

"You and your baseball, my friend," Altheimer replied. "We, or should I say, you have done very well today. Why go back to those ungrateful young men? Let them all escape, be free."

"Like us? Free to do what we like? Looking over our shoulders every minute of the day."

"That's our choice. They are not old enough to make such choices."

"That's why I must go back," Cortez said. "I enjoy the competition. And besides, there is a certain very pretty blonde I have a dinner scheduled with tomorrow night after the game. I cannot disappoint her."

"My friend, my friend. Baseball and women, they will be the death of you."

"Most probably, but *they* are my choice."

Standing by the car, the two old friends gave each other a hug.

"Please be careful, my friend."

"And you too, Heinz. Interpol will be looking for you."

"I think they are more concerned right now about the plane. I have reported it stolen, and I'm sure the authorities are doing their best to find it. The people I rented it from in Frankfort are not happy, but then again, they are also looking for someone with the name Frederick Stolon. It was Freddie who rented it."

"Poor Freddie. A friend?"

Altheimer smiled.

"No, actually a banker from Geneva I am not entirely fond of. There will be questions."

"Questions that he will have no answers to."

"Surely. I will see you in two months."

Altheimer looked at his phone and ran his finger over the screen.

"The arrangements for the transfer of funds are complete, the money should be there this evening," he said to Jordy.

"Thank you, in two months. *Adios.*"

Cortez walked into the train station and never looked back, not even once. As the train pulled out from the station, rain left streaks on the window above his first-class seat.

Three hours later, he was walking from the Rotterdam train station to his hotel. It was almost eleven o'clock, and he was exhausted, but at least the rain had stopped just as the train arrived at the station. The streets and sidewalks glistened from the rain; the air smelled fresh, there was a touch of salt in the air from the North Sea, fifteen miles away to the north. The clouds, lit by the city's lights, scudded by above.

"Hey coach, missed you today," a voice said, as Cortez walked from the lobby to the elevators. He turned toward the sound of the familiar but unwanted Southern drawl.

"It's good to see you, Coach Yang. I had business in Antwerp today. Long day, very tired."

"That Cuban cop that watches your fellows, she gone?"

"What cop?"

"Come on, Jordy, everyone knows she's a government cop here to watch over the boys. Couple of my guys tell me they saw some of your players leaving the hotel with their bags. From the looks of the cars they got into, my guess is they're long gone."

He'd known this would happen, although Cortez had hoped that they could be in and out of the Amsterdam airport so fast that the damage would be minimized. But with Vega gone, there was no one to keep the boys that wanted out, in.

"Marta de la Vega? She's not here?" he said to Yang. "She told me that she would watch over the boys while I was gone. This is a disaster."

"Well, no one's seen her."

"I must try to reach her, find out what's going on. So, Señor Yang, I'm going to my room."

"Are you going to be ready tomorrow? My fellas said one of the players who hightailed it was that kid, Octavio. Not that I'd miss him, with that arm of his. But my guess is he's on his way to the good ol' U. S. of A. about now."

"We will be ready," Cortez said, hiding his impatience. "Besides, Octavio's arm was a little sore. I have a couple others."

"Not if they run out on you tonight, but that's your problem. They say this weather will blow through and the day will be great. By the way, did you get the e-mails from Major League Baseball?"

"What e-mails?"

Now Cortez was not only tired but getting extremely exasperated over Danny Yang not letting him get to bed.

"Yeah, the All-Star game is in San Francisco next week, and

they have invited both our teams to play an exhibition game the morning before the Home Run Hitting contest. All expenses paid. It works out real well for us; we're passing through San Fran on our way back to Taiwan, anyway. Will be a nice couple of days. The boys will love it."

"I'm not sure, Yang. Long way to go for a baseball game."

"Might make it easier for all your boys to defect."

Yang looked at Cortez and saw that he'd stepped over the line.

"That was just a joke, Señor Cortez. Just joking."

Jordy Cortez failed to see the humor in it, and when he finally got to his room and after pouring a large drink from the mini-bar, he opened the letter a hotel clerk had slipped under his door. It was from the Cuban consulate in The Hague: Cortez would agree to the request of Major League Baseball, and after his glorious win over Taiwan the next day, leave for San Francisco with his team and play for the honor of Cuba and the revolution. The note also said that the government was proud that he had graciously accepted and would inform Major League Baseball.

"Shit," was all that Jorge Cortez, baseball manager, diamonds thief, smuggler, and cold-blooded murderer could say as he poured another drink from the mini-bar. "Fucking shit."

13b

After yet another randy, pale Englishman had sidled up to her table to ask if the pretty lady would, "like another," O'Mara was tempted to punch the thin-lipped man in his ruddy nose.

"I'm fine, waiting for someone," she said.

He bent too close in his five-thousand-dollar suit, custom Pink brand shirt, Pink brand tie, and gold public school cufflinks.

"And that someone might be me?"

"Hardly. I have standards, and you are not even to midfield."

"Aren't we all, my dearie, aren't we all," the man said, and started to head back to his friends at the bar. He turned to take one more look at the gorgeous redhead in a striking grey business suit, sitting alone at the small table—a tumbler of scotch on the rocks sat on the table's reflective black surface. Five damp rings from the tumbler left their outlines on its top.

The Savoy suite was, well, wonderful. Sharon had stayed in every type of accommodation, from a tribal tent full of goats to Easy-On-Easy-Off motels, but having a suite with her own butler made the trip to London worth it. That and the long soak in the large bathtub helped to let all the troubles of the previous week just wash away. She had spent the morning acquiring a new wardrobe, from underwear to the suit she now wore. Three pairs of shoes, tops, a couple of blouses, slacks, a pair of jeans, even some socks. Everything she'd worn in Cuba was bundled in three paper bags that waited for Jeeves to remove and send to the trash.

The three days in Guantanamo were behind her; Colonel Jeb Simpson had smoothed things over with the base commander, even though it seemed that everyone in the American military was peeved at her, and also at Gillis. The commander had threatened to file a complaint with the Mexican government over the conduct of Detective Inspector Lopez, but after talking with Mrs. Rodriquez and the promise from Toribio of a signed autograph for the commander's son, it all seemed to be settled down. Despite the initial fear of blood loss, the overall damage to Carlos Rodriquez's shoulder was fairly minimal, and the surgeons said he'd heal quickly. The six of them had boarded a commercial flight from Guantanamo to Jamaica and stayed at a comfortable downtown hotel in the city of Kingston. The night they arrived from Cuba, Toro flew in from New York, accompanied by Eduardo Mendez.

Sharon sat off to the side in the lounge with Bobby; Lopez had taken the first scheduled plane back to Mexico he could find. She watched the reunion of the ballplayer and his family—for a man as big as Toribio, she was surprised by his tenderness. He openly cried when he saw his mother, gently held his wife, and when he saw his injured son, tenderly enclosed the boy with his big arms.

"Thank you, Miss O'Mara," Mendez said. "And Toribio thanks you. He asked me to express his sincere gratitude. There are really no words to say . . ."

Sharon raised her hand.

"That's all right, Eduardo, we understand. All things considered, we were lucky. These things never turn out the way you planned."

She pointed at the Rodriquez family.

"That's nice," she added.

Mendez looked and smiled his agreement. Toribio smiled back at the three people instrumental in retrieving his family, and mouthed a silent, "Thank you."

That had been two days ago. Now Sharon sat in the American Bar in the Savoy Hotel, nursing a Johnnie Walker Red on the rocks and fending off extravagantly dressed barflies. She did the math in her head and knew that the bill for her Cuban work would be steep; she considered cutting it a bit, then decided against it. She did have her standards, and besides, she had stopped the clock the moment she boarded the plane to London.

At precisely six-twenty, a disheveled Englishman walked into the bar, followed by Kevin Bryan. Kevin scanned the room, his eyes at first passing over her, then stopping and quickly retreating back to the redhead. Wearing a look of both surprise and recognition, in three strides he was at her side. She stood.

"Good God, it is good to see you in this heathen country. Can we go home, now?" was all he could say, as he hugged and kissed her.

"Kev, I just got here. Good Lord, you need a bath."

"Thanks, Mom, been on the run for the last couple of days. Can barely stand myself."

She looked past him at the distinguished, yet unkempt, older gentleman, whose arm was in a sling.

"Clive Barrington, I assume."

"At your service, ma'am."

"He's better looking than I thought from our conversations," Sharon said. "But with you it was probably that old Irish and English thing."

As they sat, the bartender dropped a Jameson and scotch neat on the table.

"And it seems you two have spent some time here recently."

She studied the Englishman more closely; he seemed familiar, but context eluded her.

Barrington also looked at Sharon, his mind doing flips. He knew this woman but couldn't place it. Somewhere in a grey fog, he and she were linked. As a wave of a memory swept over him, he shivered.

"You okay, Clive?" Kevin asked. "You looked whiter than normal."

"Thanks for that. Considering that both of us could be in a bag on a steel cart somewhere in Holland right now, I'll take white."

"To the Dutch!" Ken raised his glass.

"*Prost!*"

The three toasted. Clive looked again at Sharon and then knocked back the rest of the single malt, looked at the bartender, then back at Sharon.

"Taji, along the river. Taji," he said, and grabbed Sharon and hugged her.

It was then that it all flashed back for her as well: Taji, the Tigris River, the search for the British hostages, the ambush, the blood and gore of the dead.

"Sorry, I never made the connection," she said.

"Me neither. Last thing on my mind. I try to keep all of it buried. It was a very shitty afternoon, as I remember it. Then the after action was a cock-up, with the bodies of the contractors lost then found—all bloody fucked. It's good to finally meet you, Miss O'Mara."

"Well, I'll be damned," Bryan said. "After all this, you two know each other?"

"Yes, in a weird sort of way," Sharon said.

"Yeah, she and her team were a part of a joint operation I observed."

Clive raised his fresh glass to Sharon, who smiled back.

"Just doing my job," she said.

13c

Green Zone, Baghdad, Iraq, fall 2004

The pre-op preparation in HQ went through most of the night. The sun was just breaking over the city of Baghdad when Lieutenant O'Mara said, "mount up," to her squad after breakfast.

"What's up?" Gillis asked, as they loaded their gear in the first of the three Humvees.

"A rumor about those missing Brit hostages places them at a farm just outside Taji," O'Mara told him. We're meeting a patrol coming down from Taji; they'll be a mix of our boys and some Iraqi army. With all the kidnappings and suicides bombings during the last few months, none of this will go down easy."

Her orders from Major Simpson were to check the compound, extract anyone they found, and get their butts back to the Zone. He also said to watch the Iraqis, as there had been some uncomfortable actions against Coalition forces by some of the Iraqi regulars.

"Roger that," Gillis answered, when she'd finished filling him in. "I'm more concerned about the getting to than the getting back, especially with the Iraqi army."

"Understand that, Sergeant. Not my call."

The wreckage of the war lined Iraq's Highway 1, as their small convoy headed north out of the Green Zone to Taji. After crossing a large irrigation canal, one of many, they turned east toward the river. The road that paralleled the Tigris was affectionately called Route Cobra, a shit of a road that had a history of IEDs and ambushes. Nothing in Iraq is simple.

At the predetermined coordinates for the operation, O'Mara's squad had to wait for more than an hour in the 110-degree heat for the Taji patrol to arrive.

"I feel like Spam in a can in an oven," Gillis said to O'Mara. "Can't figure how anyone can live in this shit."

"Reminds you too much of home, Sergeant?" his lieutenant answered.

"Some, but at least in Bakersfield I'm not going to get blown up by some yahoo from Chechnya or some other nowhere place on a map."

"Very true, I guess."

A plantation of palm trees with a thick mixture of shrubs and tall grass lay to their left, the Tigris River and its low levee was to their right flank. Finally, the patrol from the north arrived, led by a Meerkat checking for mines and IEDs and two Bradley troop carriers. Niceties were exchanged that started with, "Where the fuck have you been?" and "I do not like to be a fucking target."

O'Mara was introduced to a dapper-looking British major attached to the Taji base. The name on his uniform was covered by his armor and much of his face was hidden behind his goggles and helmet. With the noise from the idling Meerkat and Bradleys she didn't hear his name, but from then on she called him "Major." The mustache, though, was quintessentially British.

Her squad began its sweep through the cluster of about twenty buildings, O'Mara's people on the left side, the Taji squad on the right. There's a sense a soldier gets when he walks an Iraqi dirt street and doesn't see anyone yet knows a hundred pairs of eyes are watching; every soldier carried that feeling. Two of O'Mara's Humvees drove down the center of the village with her people manning the 50-caliber machine guns. They swiveled the guns left and right, sweeping the rooftops and upper windows of the few buildings more than one story high. The patrols stopped at every building, bashed on doors, searched every room, found only women and children. The last building sat hard against the base of the levee; its upper floor looked out over the street and the river beyond it.

"Lieutenant, rooftop. Someone did a jack-in-box," a corporal said, in a low voice.

With two fingers, he pointed at his eyes, then the roof.

O'Mara nodded. She directed three men to cover the corporal. The four then quick-marched across the street and joined with the Taji patrol. O'Mara watched the men crash the door. Instantly, gunfire erupted from inside. More of her men took covering positions; the Taji squad split and worked their way down the sides of the concrete-block building to the rear and toward the levee and the river. More gunfire, this time from the roof, barked at them and the Humvees. The 50 cals pulverized the parapet of the building into a smog of dust and shattered concrete; the guns still kept popping up over the partially de-molished parapet, firing wildly down into the street. One insur-gent on the roof quickly stood, shouldered a RPG, and without taking too much time to aim, fired down on the first Humvee. Before he could duck below the building's edge, he was literally shredded by the 50-caliper machine gun. The ill aimed RPG flew over the Humvee and slammed into the building directly be-hind it, knocking the corner of the building into a million pieces. Screams from Iraqi civilians inside could be heard coming from the destroyed building.

More rounds continued from the building, but its intensi-ty was lessening. O'Mara could distinguish the sounds of her men and their M4s and the bursts from the AK-47s and AK-74s. Another insurgent stood on the parapet and tried to leap to the adjacent building; before he was halfway across, he was dead. Fragmentation grenades exploded inside the building, dust and debris blowing out of the upper windows.

Five minutes into the fight, it was over. Sergeant Gillis came out the street-side door and waved to his lieutenant.

O'Mara quickly crossed the street.

"How many?" she asked.

"I count nine dead insurgents," Gillis said. "It's not pretty though. We found two of the hostages; their throats had been cut. It looks like we caught them before they could remove the bodies."

"Was it us coming that made it happen?"

"Don't think so. They've been dead a while, maybe since last night. There's video equipment and a cell phone. We're gathering everything."

"Shit, any IDs?"

"We're looking. The British Major is checking the bodies against information he has. These poor guys were Brits, he says. They worked for a contractor building a new water treatment plant down the road."

"Great, try to do something nice and all you get is dead. It's all fucked."

The British major came out of the building carrying some papers, which he folded and slid into his vest pocket, along with a small camera. He looked at O'Mara and Gillis.

"Stupid way to die," he said.

"Is there a good way?" O'Mara said.

"Sometimes, but this wasn't one of them. I'll have the chaps remove the bodies, and we will take them back to the base."

The major planned to also collect the electronics, in the event anyone had been overlooked and might show up on the surveillance tapes.

"We'll match the dead to what we have on file," he said. "Looks like al-Qaeda. Two don't even look Iraqi, maybe Saudi. One looks like he could be Chechen—that would be a nasty, if that's the case."

He shook his head.

"It means a lot of bad guys from all around the Middle East are coming in."

"Like flies to shit," Gillis said.

"We've been seeing that for the last six months, sir," O'Mara said. "A lot of bad actors ready to die."

"Yeah, come to Iraq, strap on a vest, and blow yourself to paradise," Gillis said.

"That's not the part I mind," the major said. "It's where they do it. Too much collateral damage."

Ten minutes later, after loading the bodies into one of the Bradleys, they cautiously walked out the way they came in. As they reached the end of the street the afternoon wind picked up, making the heat feel even more like facing the open door of a blast furnace. Dust found its way inside every crevice and crack in their armor and gear. Two of O'Mara's men had tied camouflage cloths across their faces. The Iraqi army regulars had gathered off to the side of the road, smoking. They'd stayed back, out of the firefight. O'Mara wasn't sure why they were there, but she'd also been forced to take on Iraqi squads during some of her patrols, one of the unnecessary evils she'd learn to accept.

"Thanks, Lieutenant," the major said. "Sorry about the outcome."

"It's like that some days."

She pulled her glove off and extended her hand. The major did likewise, but as their fingers touched there was a crackling of gunfire from inside the palm grove across the street. Slugs stitched their way across the concrete block wall of the building behind the major, shattered concrete tore in every direction. O'Mara instinctively drove her shoulder into the chest of the British major. The major spun backward, his body slammed down into the dust, O'Mara directly on top. Twenty American automatic weapons shredded the palm grove in response; overhead, rapid concussions from the 50 cals rained hell down on whoever thought that shrubs and grass could hide them. Even some of the Iraqi regulars joined in.

O'Mara rolled aside and off the major. The major gasped for air from her NFL-like tackle. She saw his upper right shoulder was turning bloody; he was still conscious. The slug had caught him in the shoulder; it looked busted as well, but luckily his vest had taken the second round two inches above his heart. Along with the hole in his shoulder he'd have a good bruise.

"Are you hit anywhere else?" O'Mara yelled.

"Bloody fucking hell, you ever play rugby? That fucking hurt."

"If not, you would be dancing in paradise right now."

Fifteen seconds later, anything taller than an Iraqi rat would be dead from the onslaught of weapons. Gillis signaled everyone to hold. Only the wind echoing through the palms overhead broke the silence.

"Take three men and check out what's out there, Sergeant," O'Mara told Gillis. "I don't want potshots."

"Roger that," Gillis said, and pointed at two others to join him.

As the trio slowly advanced into the grove, every eye in the two patrols watched for any movement in the grove or from any of the nearby buildings. Any civilians taking cover inside had learned not to move until the Americans had left. Later, three dead Iraqis were found in the palm grove; all died where they stood firing on the Americans.

The medic O'Mara summoned wrapped the major's shoulder wound in a HemCon pack and secured the coagulating pad tightly.

"How are you doing, Major?" Lieutenant O'Mara asked.

"This fucking hurts all to bloody hell. I've fought in the Falklands and Iraq twice, and this is the first fucking wound I've received. And I was supposed to be at one of your American barbeques this afternoon, not out here in the bush getting shot. Bloody hell."

"Glad to see that your humor hasn't left you," she answered.

The major stood upright and while wobbly managed to take the hand of O'Mara. "Thanks lass, I owe you."

Two hours later, they rolled back into the Green Zone, cleaned up the Humvees, and stowed their weapons. After a shower, O'Mara found some of her men standing on the levee above the Tigris. The air was a haze of burnt dust.

Gillis passed her a beer.

"Fucking day, but none of the good guys died," Gillis said.

"A good day."

"Yes, a good day."

"I never got the name of that Brit. Any of you guys catch the major's name?" she asked.

"You know us, all majors look the same," a corporal piped up.

"True, but still I hope he'll be okay," O'Mara said. "He seemed like a nice chap, as they say."

"Here's to the major," Gillis said, raising his bottle. "A bloody nice chap."

"Bloody nice chap," was the response from the soldiers and their lieutenant, as they looked across the river to the disaster that was Baghdad.

Chapter 14

"Well, I'll be damned," Kevin said, after his drink had been replaced twice.

"Yes, quite a day," Barrington said. "I have to admit, Ms. O'Mara, you look a lot nicer in civvies than in camo and armor."

"Thanks. And your shoulder?"

"It mended well. I have a nasty scar, but all in all, it could have been worse. Now I have this mess in my other arm. A bloody matching pair."

Bryan looked at the two former soldiers; he understood camaraderie from his years on a police force. But never having been a soldier, especially one in a war, he knew he could not completely appreciate the bond between men and women who'd fought side-by-side in combat. There were times he wished he'd been a part of it.

"Okay, boys, now what?" Sharon asked. "You lose a quarter of a billion in diamonds and the thieves as well—there's got to be a lot of very pissed-off people asking questions."

"There are," Clive said. "I'm also certain that it was Altheimer and his people."

"Altheimer? Who the hell is he?" Sharon asked.

"An international jewel thief, Swiss based. He is also the man behind the gunrunning from Cuba to Africa. He's mixed up with that woman, and maybe the Cuban baseball manager."

"The Rodriquez family, they okay?" Kevin asked Sharon.

"Yes, surprisingly well. Toro is thrilled to be with his family again. You should have been there. The big fella was a blubbering father with his son; his mother just put her hand on his cheek and kissed him. And after everything he put his family through for his baseball, his wife never left his side the whole time I was with them. She will be a force in his life going forward, I can tell you that."

"Never did understand athletes," Kevin said. "Away from home so much and it demands so much from their families. A tough life."

"At least the opponents don't try to kill you," Sharon said.

"Sports have always been similar to war and battle," Clive responded. "It seems that as we reduce the reasons for armies, we increase the need to do something with our warrior clans, so we create sports, hard contact sports. Your American football, our rugby comes to mind. Both are tough physical sports that appeal to a warrior mentality. I've known some coaches who read *The Art of War* to better understand competition. Seems we humans just have to compete with each other, and the tougher the contests the better."

"I wouldn't equate sport and war that closely," Kevin said.

"You should watch Australian Rules football, that will change your mind."

Clive's mobile began to ring. He looked at the screen and excused himself to take the call.

They watched him leave the bar, his mobile tight to his ear.

"You okay?" Sharon asked. "You look tired."

"I'm exhausted. This whole trip has been one screw-up after another, from landing here in England to returning this morning from Amsterdam. Reminds me of one of our adventures."

"Him?"

"Clive grows on you, though I still don't think he's been too straight with me. Not the trusting sort. And the woman we found dead at the apartment was close to him, his goddaughter. All this is very personal. I think it's clouded his thinking."

"Any idea who else beyond this Altheimer character was involved in the diamond heist?"

"From the interviews with the pilot and the attendant, they said there were two men and a woman. Cameras weren't much help; it happened too far away. But from the descriptions, the woman was Spanish or Latin American, at least that's the accent that the attendant heard. Never saw her's or the men's faces. They all wore gloves. There were no prints anywhere on the plane that couldn't be placed, and nothing on the stolen helicopter we found five minutes south of the airport. The two dead men at the gas station were known to Interpol though. Both were Spanish, with long records for theft and robberies, and some ties to Cuban gangs."

"Do you think they were killed to keep them quiet?"

"Or they decided to try and steal the diamonds for themselves. Obviously, that didn't work out for them. They didn't match the physiques of the two men at the plane. Both were smaller, and one was at least sixty. Name of Pedro Guerra, with ties to the Spanish mob."

"The Spanish have mobs?"

"Yes, and Clive tells me they enjoy using very long folding knives. The other dead guy was a kid called Ochoa. Barrington thinks that both Ochoa and Guerra may have had connections to Basque separatists. There were reports that some of their weapons came from Cuba. So this is all over the map of the world."

Kevin drummed his fingertips on the table.

"What?" O'Mara asked.

"I keep coming back to the baseball thing. Your woman and her prison camp and her connection to the Cuban baseball team. She's in Rotterdam and Holland at the same time as the hijacking, and now she's missing from the team. Clive says that Interpol interviewed the coach, a man named Jorge Cortez. Apparently, Cortez also was absent the day of the heist but returned to the team late that night. Coincidence? Interpol's not sure. Neither am I."

"So you think that this Marta de la Vega may be connected?"

"She's certainly a person of interest. Interpol has her on one of their lists. With her Cuban government connections, she could easily be passing as someone else. Passports are a dime a dozen, Clive tells me."

Sharon laughed.

"Maybe we should get a few while we're over here. You never know when we might need a backup or two."

"Yeah, instead of looking like an Irish terrorist, you could pass yourself off as a Scottish baroness."

"Funny, very funny, but I like the thought."

Clive sat back down at the table. Another single malt magically appeared.

"The wonders of technology just make my head spin"—Barrington was smiling broadly—"we caught him."

"Who, what," Sharon and Kevin said together.

"Seems that in their haste to put as much distance between themselves and us, they neglected to sort through all the bags of gems. One of the techs in South Africa, one of *my* boys, I'm proud to say, placed a transmitter into a very large, dark acrylic diamond. We were able to pick up its GPS signature. Kind of like the GPS in your phone, we hoped the fake would be overlooked among all the other bags of diamonds. Took a while to track its signal, because they were moving around, but when they finally settled down, we found them at a small airport outside Frankfort."

"I thought the only locators were in the handles of the briefcases." Kevin said.

"Always a good idea to have a backup plan," Clive said, ignoring the look Bryan and O'Mara exchanged.

"The ones in the case handles were more powerful, so it took a little longer to locate this one. They made the arrests an hour ago at the Mainz-Finthen airport," he said.

"So who was it?" Sharon asked.

"Just who I thought—Heinz Altheimer. He had all the jewels with him, but it was only he and a driver, waiting for Altheimer's plane to arrive from Switzerland, all nice and easy. It also turns out he rented a plane at the Frankfort airport, and it turned up at a small airport in northern Germany. A lone woman left the plane, then hijacked a taxi and disappeared."

"Someone stole Altheimer's plane?" Kevin said.

"Yes, it was that Cessna we saw just before we crashed. Altheimer may have intended otherwise, but it was used by one of the individuals to escape, so we assume."

"I thought I saw more than just three people when we flew in," Kevin said.

"So did I, but we can only account for two of them: Altheimer and his driver. One woman left with the plane, and at least one other person went with Altheimer, and now they've disappeared. And Mr. Altheimer is not being very cooperative."

"I'm shocked." Sharon said, as she raised her finger toward the bartender. "Shocked."

14b

Marta de la Vega scanned the morning Madrid newspaper she had purchased at a shop in the hotel lobby while acquiring some toiletries; it was more comfortable reading in Spanish than the English papers. *Robo Del Diamante Enorme En Holande,* screamed the headlines.

She glanced over at Cortez's gym bag.

"*Bastardo!*" she said out loud.

She turned on the television and clicked through the channels until she found the news. It was in German, but the photo in the upper corner was unmistakable. It was the son of a bitch she'd shot at the airport. But there he was, sandwiched between two men in suits, as he was escorted to a large Mercedes sedan. His hands were manacled. The crawler at the bottom read: *Heinz Altheimer—Zwei Verhaftet, Diamanten gewonnen.* Her German was weak, but she knew it meant arrested, two arrested; *diamanten* could only mean diamonds. One of the arresting officers held the bag up for the press to see, the same bag she'd put in the car after the heist and the duplicate to the one now on her bed.

"Serves the son of a bitch right," she muttered. "*Bueno.*"

She watched closely for others in the images but she only saw the two people, Altheimer and the man who had piloted the plane she'd stolen. No Cortez, no fucking Jorge Cortez. Her heart was racing. He hadn't gotten away with the diamonds, but it also meant that Cortez had escaped. She tossed the paper on the bed. If there were one thing she would do now, it would be to find that asshole and put a bullet in his head.

From the small, high-end woman's shop in the lobby, she bought slacks and a loose-fitting top, rather like an elegant sweatshirt. After a relaxing shower, she slipped on the new outfit and rolled all her old clothes in a tight bundle and placed them in one of the shopping bags. Later she would drop them in a trash bin.

The paper strewn on the bed lay open to what might have been the sports page in other countries. All it said was *Noticias de Fútbol* across the header in inch-high letters, and beneath were columns of text describing the latest on the teams across Europe; culturally soccer was to Europe like baseball was to Cuba. The columns rehashed the past season, trades, and team managers and owners' quotes. As she toweled her hair, she noticed the words Cuba de béisbol toward the bottom of the page. The short article had a Rotterdam dateline. She quickly read the piece.

The Cuban national team was going to the United States to play against the Taiwan team that had handily beat them 6–2 in the final of the Dutch Port Tournament. A "friendly," as the paper called it, mixing a soccer term with baseball, the game would be to help celebrate the American All-Star game to be played in San Francisco the following week. The article concluded with a quote from the manager of the Cuban national team, Jorge Cortez.

Vega was now livid. He'd escaped, no one knew his part in the heist, and now he was going to the United States. And even though, as the quote said, Cortez had lost some players to the predations of the American capitalistic system's love for money, he knew his players would put on a good game for the American fans of true baseball.

Still fuming, Vega walked into the small travel agency next to the sundries shop in the lobby and asked if anyone spoke Spanish. A demure woman, dark with Castilian features and raven-colored hair, smiled.

"*Si, puedo ser de ayuda?*" she said.

"Thank God," Vega replied in Spanish. "I am desperate for help. I have been traveling here in Germany and I just found out that my mother has become frightfully ill. She lives near Madrid, and I must get a plane ticket. Can you help?"

"Of course, my dear, of course. Please sit."

The woman turned her screen toward Vega and began. Twenty minutes later, using the name on her Spanish passport, Maria Hernandez had a business-class seat on the late Lufthansa flight out of Flughafen, Hamburg, to Madrid. The fare was charged to Vega's Hernandez credit card, the same card that she had used to pay for the train and the room. She also booked a hair appointment in the salon and shocked the stylist by asking that her hair be trimmed close, something in vogue, with highlights. Her boyfriend had suggested it, she said, winking when she offered that bit of gossip. The hairdresser saw it as a challenge. In two hours, Marta de la Vega became Maria Hernandez; she also looked ten years younger.

Later she called down to the desk and asked if they had a hotel in Madrid. She would have to leave in a couple of hours, a change in business plans.

"Yes we do, a fine hotel in the heart of the city — the Germans, so polite, so official — would you like us to make reservations? We are sorry to see you go."

In ten minutes, the desk clerk called back to advise that the room and a late arrival had been confirmed. Maria Hernandez took a taxi to the Hamburg airport, a small carry-on her only luggage. Five hours later, in Madrid's international airport, she stopped at the American Airlines desk and made arrangements for a flight the next day to Los Angeles.

"Is this your first time going to Los Angeles?" the gentleman manning the information counter asked, in Spanish.

"Yes, it is," Vega/Hernandez replied. "I'm going to visit my sister, who is teaching at the university they call UCLA. She's said so many nice things about the city."

"It does have an ocean, but I'm not too partial to it."

She gave him a bright smile.

"I'm always looking for an adventure. This is my first trip to California. It's exciting for a single woman, like me."

"Your accent, it's hard to place," the Spaniard said, as he completed the transaction and handed back her passport.

"I worked in a hotel for a few years in Cuba. People tell me it rubbed off. I can't tell."

"It's nice," the man said.

He handed her a boarding pass.

"All taken care of, confirmed as well. You'll clear customs in Dallas. Have a nice flight, Señorita Hernandez."

She smiled again.

"Thank you, I will."

She had purposefully purchased a ticket routed through Dallas, thinking it better to go through customs there with her Spanish, rather than New York or Chicago. The reason for Los Angeles, instead of a direct flight to San Francisco, was simple. There was a man, a Cuban, who lived in Los Angeles and who would sell her a weapon and ammunition. She would also rent a car and go north to San Francisco, find Cortez, and kill him.

14c

The next day Clive's driver picked them up at the Savoy. The car was a Jaguar sedan.

"Very nice," Kevin said, admiring the black limousine. "A lot newer than yours."

"No cracks about my car, I am not in the mood," Sharon replied, as she watched the butler hand over her new bags to the valet who neatly placed them in the boot.

"You own a Jaguar?" Clive asked.

"Yes, a sedan a few years older than this one."

"More than a few," Kevin said.

"Stop with the trashing my car, Kevin Bryan."

"A history?" Clive said.

"More than you want to know. I will tell you someday."

On the way to Heathrow Airport—Kevin took the roomy front seat, Sharon sat with Barrington in the back—he asked again if they didn't want to stay another night or two.

"I have more than enough room in my place in Tunbridge Wells," he said.

"Is it true it has forty rooms?" Sharon asked.

"Who told you that?" Clive responded.

"One of the girls in the office, when we stopped by yesterday. She was all nice about it, said it was beautiful and had gardens surrounding it. Even a moat."

"A moat?" Kevin put in.

"Yes, a moat," Clive said. "Built in the fourteenth century to keep out the French or some other invading foreigner. And to be precise, it has forty-three rooms, so you two wouldn't be a bother."

"He said we wouldn't be a bother, Sharon. Now I know we're going home."

"He is a handful isn't he, Ms. O'Mara?"

"Yes, but I love him all the same. But yes, Clive, we need to get back. I miss my pup; he'll think I've abandoned him. Mexico, Cuba, England—now I know how the jet set feel."

"Been a couple of weeks, but it's more like how international crime fighters feel," Kevin added.

"It was good to finally meet you after all these years," Clive told O'Mara. "Too much has passed since that afternoon south of Taji. I'm glad that I now have better memories than what I've been carrying. I always wondered what happened to that redhead on that dirt road."

"Closure's a good thing, Clive. I hope that you can find the killer of your goddaughter."

"I'll find them if I have to put Altheimer's nuts in a vice."

"That's my boy," Sharon said. "Let me know when, I'll bring the scotch."

"Deal," Clive said.

He pulled the car up to the British Airways drop-off at Terminal 5. They said their good-byes, then O'Mara and Bryan checked their luggage and headed straight to the Business Lounge—one of the perks that Sharon had carried forward after her time with her past client and dear friend, Alain Dumont.

"Travel in style, or don't travel at all," Dumont had said. "There's nothing sadder than a traveler too tired to enjoy the trip."

Thirty minutes prior to departure, they relocated to the departure lounge. Their business-class tickets allowed them a little separation from the hoi polloi, but Kevin had to admit he was feeling the envy of the other patrons.

"They don't really give a damn," Sharon said. "What they're really hoping for is an open seat next to them and no crying baby within ten rows."

As if cued, a wailing began in the back of the lounge.

"I'll be damned," Kevin said.

"Now what?" Sharon said.

"I'll be right back."

He wound his way through the bags and carry-ons that littered the floor of the lounge. When he tapped a man on the back, Danny Yang turned around.

"Son of a gun, you are the last person I'd think to see here. Did your trip go well?" Yang said.

"It did. But I never found out how the game went."

"We beat them, 6–2."

"Good for you. Heading home?"

Yang told him about the exhibition game with the Cubans at AT&T Park.

"All expenses paid," he said.

"I see the guys look as tired as I feel."

Bryan waved his arm to indicate the players sprawled in chairs with headphones and computers open, getting one last shot of e-mails in before they had to board.

"They are exhausted," Yang agreed. "The rain out put them out of their routine, but they played well. I'm proud of them."

"I understand that the Cuban coach eventually showed up," Kevin said.

"Yes, the morning after I saw you. Lucky son of a bitch, the rainout probably saved his ass. He tried to hold his team together considering he'd lost maybe five guys to the scouts, but in the end we beat them fair and square. Nice feather in my cap, if I don't say. There's a rumor that I might get a bonus, but only a rumor."

Bryan learned from Yang that the Cuban players were traveling on the same plane, since the charter they'd arrived on from Cuba wasn't authorized to fly in U.S. airspace.

Danny scanned the crowded lounge.

"I saw them a few minutes ago," he said. "Cortez was somewhere over there."

When Kevin turned to look, he saw a more somber group sitting in the corner of the lounge. Not one had earphones on. A few were reading comic books.

Over the loudspeakers came the boarding announcement for British Airways Flight 287. Kevin turned and looked around for Sharon, as "now boarding all first-class and business-class passengers" blared overhead; the perplexed look on her face told him everything.

Danny followed his gaze toward Sharon.

"Girlfriend?"

"No, just a good friend."

"She's too good looking to be just a friend, Kevin."

"You have my card," Kevin said. "When you're in San Francisco, call me and we'll have dinner. There's someone I want you to meet. He's a client of my good friend."

"Who was that?" Sharon asked, when Kevin had made his way back through the crowd to where she stood in line.

"Danny Yang, he's the manager of the Taiwan baseball team. They were playing a tournament in Rotterdam, and they beat the

Cubans. The two teams have been invited to San Francisco to be part of the All-Star game festivities."

"Not the same Cuban team that Marta de la Vega ran security for?"

"The same. In fact, the Cubans are also on this plane, along with their manager, Jorge Cortez."

"I'll be damned. Small world."

She asked if he'd seen Cortez.

"No, but Yang says they're on the plane."

Kevin thought for a moment, then asked if she thought they should call Barrington.

"My guess, he already knows. But what's he going to do? I, for one, want to go home and not sit in the lounge until the Bobbies and Scotland Yard come and arrest him, and for what? He's a public person. I'm sure he was flagged the minute they landed in England. We need to get out of here—send Clive an e-mail from the plane. And besides, once we are in the air, Clive and the authorities will have ten hours to figure out what to do. We can keep an eye on him if need be."

Kevin's police gut said that Cortez was involved in what had happened in Holland, but there was nothing he had to prove. In fact, he'd brought up Cortez that morning in Barrington's office, but there was nothing they could now do about it. Someone on Barrington's team had suggested there could be diplomatic immunity attached to Cortez's position in the Cuban hierarchy. "For a baseball manger?" Kevin had said, skeptical. At the moment, Barrington had let it pass. But now, Cortez was on their plane, and Kevin found it hard to ignore the inconvenience.

Flying west didn't faze Sharon as much as traveling east. How many times had she made the eastern trip to Europe and Iraq? She'd lost count at twenty. Going west felt like racing with the sun, just a little behind, but still moving in the same direction. Maybe it was only having to adjust her watch by three or four hours. The two previous weeks caught up with her—as well as the two drinks in the lounge and the glass of champagne served as they were seated. Kevin had the same reaction. Shortly after dinner, reheated grilled chicken with couscous served as they flew over Greenland, they both fell asleep in their seats.

Sharon woke feeling barely rested. She glanced over at Kevin, who was still asleep, wearing an eye mask supplied by the airline. Two hours until arrival. She shook off the dream of the fire fight on the bus as they'd raced from de la Vega's prison—the flashbulb-like muzzle flashes, the loud pinging of bullets hitting the overhead liner of the bus. Her shoulder still felt sore from the kick of the rifle she'd handled.

They were the first off the plane and quickly made their way into the miasma that one might call immigration, customs and passport control at San Francisco airport. Any of the perks of flying business class were not shared in immigration. Here they were the hoi polloi; as they approached the immigration station via a large corridor, all they saw were hundreds of heads ahead of them.

"Great," Sharon said.

"Well, at least we got some sleep. When I called Gina, she said that as long we got in on time she'd pick us up. If the plane was late she'd send a limo."

As if signaled, his phone beeped. *Out front waiting, love Gina,* the text message read.

"Good, at least we can save a few bucks," he said.

"We just blew almost fifteen grand flying from England, and you are worrying about saving limo fare. That's why I love you."

"What? What did I say?"

Gina Cavelli was waiting as they finally burst through the doors of customs, their bags piled on a shopping cart–like contraption. Kevin was pleased; it was free.

"Right on time," Gina said, as she hugged her friends. "Car's in the lot. You want me to go get it, or do you want to go with me?"

"We'll go with you. How's Basil?" Sharon asked.

"Pissed. When I picked him up at the farm, he knew you were coming home, but I could tell there will be hell to pay. He checked every room looking for you, then just sat down and looked at me. So be prepared."

As the three friends stood talking, a disturbance at the other end of the concourse began with raised voices and some pushing and shoving. In seconds, police appeared.

"Give me a second," Kevin said, when he spotted Danny Yang talking with a trio of officers. He quickly walked over to where they stood.

"Hi, Sergeant, what's going on?" he asked.

The San Francisco police officer turned at the sound of Kevin's voice.

"Damn, Detective Bryan, what are you doing here?"

Bryan explained that he was arriving home from business abroad, and that he'd been on the same flight as Yang and the team.

"Seems some of the Cuban boys were a little high from one too many cocktails and got into it with the Taiwanese. Mr. Yang was trying to control his people, and Mr. Cortez was doing the same with his. All quiet now. Would be a bit embarrassing if this got out of hand."

Kevin turned and saw Jorge Cortez a few yards away, demonstrably telling his ballplayers to behave. The players stood awkwardly; the studious attention they paid to his scolding gave away their inebriated state. As Bryan watched Cortez, the man turned and stared back at him. For a few long seconds, the two men looked at each other, before slowly turning away, Cortez to his team, and Bryan to go back to his friends. Unbeknownst to Bryan, Jordy Cortez turned back and took another long look at the receding back of the man whose face he'd last seen looking out of the helicopter window, just before Altheimer's pilot had shot it down.

Gina had a hundred questions for each of them. Why were they in Europe? She thought Sharon had been in Mexico with that charming policeman. How did they both end up in London?

"You look tired, Kevin," she said. "I guess you are just not cut out for insurance."

It went on like that until they drove into the Caldecott Tunnel, slicing through the Oakland hills, where the echo of traffic noise in the tunnel drowned out any chance of conversation in Gina's Mini-Cooper.

Kevin, folded up like a Swiss Army knife in the front seat, kept quiet. He was still processing what had gone on in Holland as well as seeing Cortez at the airport. He had already formed a number of questions for Barrington; he'd call in the morning.

Sharon just let all Gina's questions roll over her like unwanted noise. Where the hell was Marta de la Vega? Was she part of all this? At least Interpol could take care of finding Vega, *not my problem.*

They dropped Kevin off at his cottage in the lower hills of Lafayette. He pushed open his door to find mailed piled up behind it. He waved back at O'Mara and Gina as he went inside.

"You okay?" Gina asked Sharon, as they rejoined the late-evening commute heading to Walnut Creek.

"Yeah, just a lot of unanswered questions."

"Outside of the obvious, you never told me why you and Bobby Gillis went to Mexico. Señor Lopez is okay, but you could do a lot better."

Gina grinned.

"Mother knows these things, you know."

"Well, Mom, I didn't go to Mexico to see Xavier. Bobby and I were on a job."

"A job, what job?"

"I was hired to go into Cuba and help a family escape from the clutches of one evil bitch—and we did that."

"No fucking way," Gina said.

She swerved the car, nearly hitting the shoulder.

"Cuba? Who the hell hired you?" she asked, unperturbed by the near miss.

"A ballplayer."

"Not Toro, with the Giants?"

"How did you know that?"

"It's been all over the news during the last week. There was a big press conference. When it came out that his family had escaped Cuba and was now safe in Jamaica, there was quite a stir on the news and sports stations. I can't believe you were the ones who got them out."

"It wasn't easy. In fact, there was a little bit of shooting as well."

"You okay? I remember Venice like it was yesterday, and it still scares the hell out of me. What you can do? Bobby and Xavier okay?"

Sharon promised to tell her more later. She asked Gina if the news had mentioned her name or any details of the escape.

"No, no name and nothing about what happened. It was quite mysterious, if you ask me."

"For once, they may have been telling the truth," Sharon told her.

Gina pulled to the curb in front of Sharon's house and helped her with the bags.

Sharon opened the door, Basil was all over her. In a second, dog and human were both on the floor, roughhousing. Basil outweighed her by maybe thirty pounds, and in seconds he had her pinned to the floor. She playfully begged to let her up; he wouldn't give.

Gina was beside herself with laughter.

"Shows you what I know. I thought he would ignore you."

Sharon pushed Basil off and got to her feet, using the dog as support.

"Oh, he'll make me pay, I can assure you. You hungry or something? I've got some things in the freezer I can thaw, some of your spaghetti or raviolis. Not sure what else."

"Love to, but can't. Geno's awaits. The Giants are on to-night."

Gina checked her phone.

"Damn, they will already be on when I get there. Playing St. Louis. Toro's been back for a couple of days, killing the ball and destroying pitchers like he'd had a weight lifted. Now I know why."

"They still in first?" Sharon asked.

She went to throw her suitcases on the bed, and returned to the hallway.

"Yes, two games out," Gina called to her. "But the Rockies are hot. After tonight, two games with the Cards then the break. It's hard to believe that the Giants have four players on the All-Star National League squad. And your friend Rodriquez has a chance at the Triple Crown. Still a lot of ball left, but he's great. Did you meet him?"

"I thought you had to leave."

"I do, but please tell me everything."

"We shared a pizza right here in this room, and between Toro, Eddie Mendez, and Kevin, there wasn't much room left for little ol' me."

"Bryan was there? That SOB, he could have said something."

"To one of the most indiscreet women in the county?"

Gina laughed.

"Oh, the stories I want to hear, and repeat. How did his trip go?"

"Outside of the jewel heist and the helicopter crash, I guess it went well."

"What the fuck?"

"You have to ask him. Now get out of here."

Sharon pushed her friend down the hall and out onto the porch.

"Out!" she said, when Gina turned to ask another question.

"No more, we'll talk later," Sharon promised her. "Tomor-row night, okay?"

She closed the door and scratched the top of Basil's huge

head.

"I suppose you're hungry? And Mom needs a drink. Show me the way."

Basil quick-stepped down the oak floor of the hallway, his nails laying out a nice beat.

After a dinner of thawed raviolis, and two glasses of scotch, Sharon took a shower, admired the bruising to her right shoulder, brushed her teeth, and collapsed in bed.

Chapter 15

"One out, in the bottom of the ninth," the play-by-play announcer said. "Two on and down a run, six to five. Perfect for Toro, don't you agree, partner?"

"What's not to like? He's three for four this year against this closer. My book calls that ownage. I think I see his knees shaking," the color guy said.

"Hard to see that. This pitcher has ice water in his veins. He was selected for the All-Star game by his own manager."

"That figures. When you win the pennant, you usually get the All-Star manager gig. But he now has eighteen saves, and there's a lot of games left."

"Good point, but he's already walked one and didn't get much help from his infield with the throwing error. Bad luck around. Men on first and third, one out."

Toro knocked the weighted donut off the bat and slowly walked to home plate, as the announcer made the introduction. A chorus of boos followed him as well as a smattering of applause by the loyal Giants fans that sat in amongst the St. Louis Cardinal fans.

"Is it me, or does Rodriquez look a little taller than earlier in the season?" the announcer said.

"I think we all are little taller, partner. Now that's quite a story. There are some good players in both leagues from Cuba, and the road they took to get to America was different for each of them. But the story of Rodriquez's family being held captive all this time has to be one of the best-kept secrets."

"Strike one, low but just caught a corner. This guy won't give Toro anything to hit. He'd be crazy to be anywhere near the plate."

"I totally agree, but pitchers have egos too. He won't load the bases if he can help it."

"Ball, inside, tight. Toro spun away from that one."

"This pitcher has twelve years in the big leagues, the last four as the closer with the Cardinals. His reputation is never to give in to the hitter, never."

"Rodriquez has faced this pitcher every year since joining the Giants," color guy said. "First with Houston, then the Cubs, and now with the Cards. The numbers are impressive. He's also struck out Rodriquez twenty-two times over the years."

"Yeah, good point, but Rodriquez has hit fifteen of his five hundred and thirty home runs against this guy, and twelve triples too."

"I still say the guy's knees are shaking."

"Swing and a miss. Strike two."

"He's got him where he wants him, with a chance to tie the game or even go ahead. Lot of pressure."

The St. Louis crowd was on its feet; a double play would move them into a tie with Milwaukee—tied for first would be a nice way to go into the All-Star break. Even the Giants fans were drowned out by the cheering of the hometown Cardinal fans.

"Ball two, low and outside. That one almost got away from the catcher, but then again, he's not a gold-glover for nothing."

"Rodriquez still hasn't left the batter's box, just like his hero, Barry Bonds. There are so many parallels between the two—it's amazing."

"Yeah, other than he plays right field and not left, and bats right, and is maybe four inches taller."

"Details, partner, details. The man never fails to entertain. Even Bonds says Rodriquez is the best playing the game today."

"That's a lot to carry. There's a throw to first to keep the runner tight."

"I wouldn't do that. One mistake, and the man's on second

and the game would be tied. Bad move, the out he needs is at home plate."

"Agree, but a single would tie the game. It's two and two to Rodriquez."

The third home park for the Cardinals and their storied past, the ballpark in downtown St. Louis is called by some New Busch Stadium. Unlike the previous incarnations, the current Busch Stadium wasn't named after Gussie Busch of the Budweiser beer family. Now, like every other baseball park in America, it was tagged with a corporate name, after the one St. Louis–based Anheuser-Busch Company. The company still made beer but now it was owned by AB InBev, a Belgian-Brazilian brewing company that included Budweiser, Corona, Stella Artois, and more than a dozen other international brands. Beer, like baseball, was as international as most any sport played around the world.

Whatever its current moniker, the 43,975 fans had come there to root on their team as well as see the power and grace of one of the premier ballplayers of their age, even if he played for their historic rivals, the San Francisco Giants. The stadium's right field foul post stood 335 feet from home plate, the center field wall was 400 feet away, and the left field post stood 336 feet away. With the count 2–2, Toro Rodriquez slammed an inside pitch fifteen rows above the right center field wall, giving his Giants an 8–6 lead.

"I just felt it in my shoes, partner. Just felt it. Rodriquez will not be denied."

"My hand is still shaking as I mark my scorecard. That home run cleared the bullpen by at least seven rows, easily four hundred-twenty feet. Prodigious blast, incredible!"

"I think he's ready for the All-Star break. I know I am."

The one station that Marta de la Vega could get on the car radio, as she drove north from Los Angeles on Sunday afternoon, was a local Fresno affiliate for the Giants. And all the better, since the broadcast was in Spanish. She wanted Rodriquez to strike out, and the home run only made her more pissed at Cortez as well as that Puerto Rican, Eddie Mendez. Cortez, because it was his laxness a decade earlier that had allowed Rodriquez to defect, not to mention that he'd just screwed her out of millions in diamonds—and Lord only knew what else the man had been involved with behind her back and that of the Cuban government. Vega had no problem with her own covert activities, including her gunrunning; everyone she knew in government took a taste. They all knew the régime would fail someday, just like the Soviets had more than twenty years earlier. But her own little empire had just collapsed, specifically due to Jorge Cortez, Toribio Rodriquez, and Eduardo Mendez—she knew Toro's agent had to have been involved in the freeing of Rodriquez's family. If he'd only been patient, she might have found a way for him to pay her for their release. Now, aside from what she had stashed in Swiss bank accounts—that would need to be liquidated very shortly—everything she'd worked so hard to acquire was gone. Vega's boundless fury targeted the three men she held responsible, mainly Cortez.

The California Central Valley extends for more than three hundred miles north from the Tehachapi Mountains that surround Los Angeles. Hundreds of thousands of acres of cotton, almonds, walnuts, and row crops parallel the two major spines of Highway 99 and Interstate 5. On a good day, the four hundred–mile drive up I-5 from Los Angeles to San Francisco might take six hours, but Vega drove conservatively. She was in no rush and did not want to encourage the California Highway Patrol. She had already passed three cars pulled to the side of the highway for speeding. As long as she was in San Francisco before eight o'clock that evening, she would have time to put her plans into action. With the help of the hotel concierge in Los Angeles, she'd booked a room at the iconic Hyatt Regency on San Francisco's Embarcadero. The walk from the hotel to AT&T Park was short; she was told when she called the Hyatt to confirm a late arrival. She'd already checked the schedule—conveniently published in the *Los Angeles Times*—for the activities surrounding the Tuesday night All-Star game. The international game between Cuba and Taiwan would be played the day before, at ten o'clock Monday morning, with the home run contest starting late that afternoon. Vega had never understood the need to have these annual events, contests, exhibition games, and what else just to sell beer and cars. The game itself was becoming secondary to all the craziness. She might have said, 'capitalistic atavism inherent in American media,' but she had, in fact, grown quite fond of the American dollar and all that it could do. She might also have said, 'just play the game and get on with the season,' except that in this case, the circus of events was going to work in her favor.

Her plan was simple: go to the Monday morning international game, locate Cortez, follow him, and at an appropriate time when they could be alone, shoot the bastard. She would then drop off the car she was driving at the Oakland Airport, use a different car rental and secure a car under another name, and leave San Francisco. Maybe try for Vancouver and Canada. Any connections left in Europe would be days behind her. In time they would connect the dots, but she planned to stay just far enough ahead of Interpol and the American police to permanently escape.

15b

On Sunday afternoon, at the ancient bar inside Geno's, O'Mara and Bryan sat nursing beers. After landing back in the States with their internal clocks out of sync, the following day—meaning yesterday—had been a blur for both of them. To Sharon, who professed some immunity to jet lag, it was shocking. She passed it off to being in Cuba, then England, then California, all in less than four days.

"Or you're just getting old," Kevin said.

"Don't say that too loud," Gina said to him. "She's been

known to tear the arms off of lesser men."

"I have not, and you stop saying things like that," Sharon admonished. "It hurts my image. Besides, he's right. After this last week, I hurt in places I thought I'd never hurt. It's too much like Iraq, where every day brought some new pain to some new part of the body."

"See, even she agrees," Kevin said, looking at Gina.

"You both are getting old, and I'm tired of your bitching. And she says your helicopter crashed, and there was that diamond heist, the one on the TV. Was that you? I want to know!"

For the next hour Kevin related his European adventures, from the death of Sally Montgomery to the capture of Heinz Altheimer in Germany.

"Holy shit, all that and not a scratch," Gina said. "Kev, you are one lucky SOB. The next round is on me."

The crowd in Geno's let out a collective shout, and all three at the bar turned to look at the largest of the ten flat screens mounted high on the walls. Rodriquez had just hit a triple to the right field corner in St. Louis.

"And to think, I'm this far away from meeting him," Gina added, as she watched the big Cuban stand on third and point to the stands. "Six degrees of separation, hell, I know people who know that man."

"Feeling better?" Sharon asked Kevin, when Gina went to serve patrons at the far end of the bar.

"Much better. Two good nights' sleep in a row did the trick."

"Me too, and Basil's even talking to me. Hey, I got a surprise."

She reached into her handbag and extracted an envelope; Kevin couldn't help but notice the handle of her Beretta, snug in its holster in the large green bag. He said nothing.

"Gina, come down here," Sharon said.

Gina glided back their way, running a towel over the bar's smooth mahogany surface as she did so.

"What do you need, Red?"

Sharon said, "Seems that Señors Mendez and Rodriquez

have given us four tickets to both the Home Run Derby and the All-Star game. They are in a luxury box over the first base side. Either of you interested?"

Kevin was the first to answer.

"Absolutely. A little money in the bank and some free tickets—why not? I'd probably stay home and watch the game anyway."

"What, you wouldn't be here?" Gina said, a pretend pout on her face.

As he fumbled for an answer, she cut him off.

"I would absolutely love to come too, but I can't. It's a big night here, both Monday and Tuesday, and a full house will more than make the month. But you promise me that at some time in the future you will get that Toro fellow out here. You must introduce me to him. Deal?"

"Deal. Are you going to the international game tomorrow morning—Taiwan and Cuba?" she asked Kevin.

He was scheduled to meet with the insurance company on California Street that morning, but he'd be done in plenty of time to make it to the Home Run Derby—"let's meet at the Hyatt Regency at the bar, and then we can walk down," he suggested.

"Works for me. See you there about three," Sharon answered.

As she stood, Kevin heard the weight in her handbag hit the bar with a solid tap.

"You won't be able to bring that with you tomorrow. Don't forget to put it in the safe."

"Yes, Kevin, always taking care of me."

The Cubans got even for the loss in the Netherlands; they beat the Taiwanese team 9–3. Even Jorge Cortez was surprised, considering the team that he could field with players missing. Even more rewarding was having four major league All-Star players from Cuba come by to say hello. Two were infielders, one a left fielder, and one a pitcher. The Cuban All-Stars wanted to meet Cortez's team and hear the latest from Havana and the rest of Cuba. But Cortez was disappointed that Toribio Rodriquez didn't show; Cortez had been proud of the man so many years earlier, but he also understood. He'd heard about the recovery of the Rodriquez family and knew that if Marta de la Vega were here she would be totally out of control. He was glad she was five thousand miles away.

After the game, he and Danny Yang were interviewed on National television and then ESPN, big hugs and handshakes to show international sportsmanship. He put on a good face, but all Cortez wanted was to be as far away from San Francisco as possible, and as fast as possible. He'd heard the news reports about the arrests in the diamond heist and was surprised that it disappeared as quickly from the news reports as it had arrived. All the better as far as he was concerned, and the sooner he could leave America, the sooner he too could then disappear. He would miss Heinz Altheimer though, but the transfer had been completed before he left Europe, and sadly this was just one of the unwanted consequences of being an international diamond thief. Standing in the press's camera lights, he mopped his forehead, surprised at how dizzy he felt. The pressure and hectic pace of the past few weeks was catching up with him.

"Yeah, grew up in Atlanta," Cortez heard Danny Yang say to the reporter, a quite good-looking brunette with what might be called a Southern Accent.

"Never made the big leagues, but I was a bullpen catcher for the Braves about ten years ago, so it was natural to move into managing," Yang went on. "Didn't hurt that I learned Chinese from my grandmother as I grew up. It's been quite a ride, I'll say."

No wonder Yang got the job, Cortez thought. He had to admit that the man did manage his team well, and even today if it hadn't been for their three home runs, the Cubans might have lost. His pitcher had just been less tired.

Cortez scanned the field. He still loved American stadiums.

They were more like cathedrals than ball fields, and he'd seen his fair share during his forty odd years in the game. The ballpark was a bustle of activity as the network prepared for the Home Run Derby. Cables were snaked over the infield and there was bustle to set up tables and booths for the celebrity announcers. In a few minutes he would be dismissed, his part in the festivities now over. He decided to try and leverage his status into a seat on the field during the Derby. He watched his boys walk through the left field gate to the bus that would take them back to the hotel. Two buses, one for each team. Cortez told his assistant coach he would be along later, he had some things to do with the major league officials. The coach was duly impressed and said he would see Cortez at dinner.

"Yes, if I can, I will see you then," Cortez assured the coach.

Fat chance. He took a deep breath to slow his racing heart. He was going to stay for the Derby, and he wanted to talk with Toro. Maybe it would be a way for him to make some amends for the Cuban government's treatment of the young ballplayer before Toro had defected. The man would probably not give him the time of day, but he wanted to give it a try.

For the next few hours, when approached by security, Cortez waved his credentials in the plastic envelope hung around his neck. It was good for the day, and he would make the best of it.

15c

Sharon O'Mara climbed the north side stairs that led to Market Street out of the Embarcadero BART station at exactly 2:48 p.m., crossed through the California Street cable car turnaround near the hotel's valet station, and then rode up the interior escalator leading into the vast cavernous space of the Hyatt Regency. Around its unique interior space, the hotel floors were stacked like the inside of a hollow layer cake, with each level climbing to the sun-filled glass windows at the top. Music from a single piano greeted each new arrival, the soft sound blending perfectly with the two fountains that separated the main level into walkways, reception areas, lounges, and bar.

Kevin waved from where he sat waiting in the bar.

"Kind of early, don't you think," Sharon said, looking at the tumbler holding what she assumed to be Jameson and ice.

"Still on London time," he quipped.

She groaned and ordered a club soda.

"How did it go?" she asked, after a frowning bartender had retrieved a bottle from under the counter, filled a matching tumbler with ice, and poured.

"Better than I thought. Barrington Skyped in to the meeting. He's very happy now that everything turned out as well as it did."

"How about that insurance friend of yours. He okay?"

"Yeah, he even offered me a more permanent position, international troubleshooter."

"As I said, insurance companies will suck your soul dry."

"Yeah, but their checks don't bounce."

"You watch yourself, Kevin Bryan. I know these people."

"Clive also said to tell you hello, and he extended an invitation to his place in Tunbridge Wells the next time we're in England."

"That would be nice, landed gentry and all that. We know the nicest people. Tell him thanks, and yes, next time."

Barrington had found the mole inside his department; a woman in International Investigations who had been leaking information to Altheimer and a few other bad guys, including some Bulgarians the department had been after for contract killings in London. In return, the woman had collected more than a million pounds that Barrington knew of.

"Altheimer has a reputation of not forgiving anyone for slights," Clive told Kevin. "There was a rumor he had his own brother killed for some indiscretion."

"Jesus," Sharon said, when Kevin relayed this.

"Altheimer's the one who targeted Clive's goddaughter and had the Bulgarians kill her," Kevin said. "My arrival was just coincidental, but he was also the one who had me kidnapped."

According to Barrington's intel, the kidnappers had been told that Bryan was worth millions and that if they delivered him to some people in the West End, they would each get five hundred pounds.

"Now they just get jail time," Kevin said. "This Altheimer is quite something."

"Yeah, just a fun and games sort of guy who plays poker with people's lives—like it was diamonds for death. I'm glad he's sitting in a German prison."

"Have you heard from Bobby or Xavier?" Kevin asked.

"E-mails from both. Bobby's home in Bakersfield, no problems returning. He went through Miami, then directly into Los Angeles and drove home. Xavier, on the other hand, says he's under a lot of scrutiny over our little adventure, even when he said he was investigating the transportation of illegal Soviet weapons from Cuba to Mexico. Do you think that Clive might be able to throw in a word or two about the guns going to Africa?"

"I'll ask," Kevin promised. "It shouldn't be a problem, and besides he owes me some favors for being a little too closed up about the goings on."

Kevin's phone was sitting on the bar and began to vibrate. He looked at the screen and pointed to the name as he looked at Sharon.

"Speak of the devil . . . Clive, a little late isn't it? . . . Sure, I'm here with her now, but it's too public to put you on speaker. Tell me, and I'll tell her afterward."

Kevin motioned for something to write on, and Sharon handed him a small pad and pen from her bag. He began to write quick, short notes, interspersed with an occasional, "Got it, no shit, you are kidding," then "wow."

Sharon couldn't decipher what he was writing, so instead she motioned to the bartender, pointed at Kevin's glass, and held up two fingers.

Kevin smiled his thanks.

"Got it, good God. Great work, Clive. I will keep a lookout," he said. "You are sending the FBI? . . . He must be at the ballpark.

We are on our way there now."

After ending the call, Kevin took a deep breath and then a sip from his refreshed tumbler.

"Here's how it went down with Altheimer's arrest," he plunged in. "They managed to get ahead of him by putting out a BOLO on the man; it was sent to all transportation terminals and hubs in northern Europe. Altheimer and his driver went to a small airport west of Frankfort to wait for Altheimer's plane to arrive from Switzerland. He didn't know the plane had already been put under surveillance at an airport near Bern, so Interpol was alerted when it took off. Seems the small Frankfort airport was managed by a retired German air force major. He got the BOLO and the e-mail with Altheimer's photo. When Altheimer and his pilot showed up, he recognized them and offered the airport's very comfortable lounge—he then called the police, served the men coffee, then locked them in. The German police in full SWAT gear took Mr. Altheimer down, as we like to say."

"The diamonds?"

"Sitting next to him in the lobby. Quite something, Clive says. He said for as smart as the man is, criminals often just plain fuck up. I can attest to that. Apparently, Altheimer was slightly injured during the arrest but hasn't said a word. His driver, on the other hand, has been very cooperative as well as requiring medical care. The driver says that when they landed in Holland, they met two other people at the airport—the ones Clive and I saw just before we crashed. He thinks they were Spanish or Latin, and he never heard the woman's name, but the other was called Jorge, or something like that. He thinks this Jorge and the woman are the ones who robbed the plane at the Schiphol Airport."

"Jorge?" Sharon said.

Kevin nodded.

"No shit, as in Jorge Cortez, the manager of the Cuban national baseball team," he said. "When a picture of Cortez was shown to the driver, he picked him out of the photo lineup."

"No kidding!"

"And here's the really interesting stuff. Seems the woman

tried to steal the diamonds from Altheimer, but ended up with an identical gym bag full of the Jorge's dirty laundry. The driver says Altheimer and Jorge got quite a kick out of it. She's the one who stole their plane."

"I'll bet she was surprised when she opened the bag, and probably murderously pissed."

"Gets better. Seems that this woman landed at a small airport in Germany, stole a taxi, then went into the nearby town and asked a policeman for help buying a train ticket with a credit card to Hamburg. They also got her picture from a CCTV camera on the platform. They canvassed the hotels around the Hamburg station and flashed her picture; someone at a nearby Hyatt ID'd her. She was traveling under the name and passport of Maria Hernandez, a Spaniard. They missed her by one day. She'd bought a ticket for Madrid from the agency in the hotel and left that night. She also changed her appearance with a haircut and makeup."

"Seems that she'd done this before," O'Mara mused. "No panic, very professional."

"Yep, and in Madrid she booked another flight, this one to the United States—Los Angeles, specifically. Went through customs in Dallas as Alicia Gomez, also Spanish. This woman had more passports than a CIA spook. They lost her in Los Angeles."

"Do they know who she really is?"

"You will love this. She was positively identified as your favorite Cuban prison farm coffee grower and warden."

"You have got to be kidding. Marta de la Vega is here in California?"

"FBI and Homeland checked airport cameras and spotted her. She also rented a car. She's in the wind."

"My guess, that wind's blown her here," Sharon said. "She's either after Jorge Cortez or yours truly."

Kevin's phone buzzed again, this time with a text message from Barrington forwarding a picture of de la Vega. He opened the image and showed it to Sharon.

"So that's what the face of evil looks like. She could be my high school Spanish teacher," O'Mara said.

Kevin happened to place his phone back on the bar, just as the bartender walked past.

As all good bartenders do—it's a survival thing—this one watched everything and could grasp more in a second than many can in five minutes.

"She a friend?" he asked Kevin, after merely glancing at the face on the small screen.

"No, why do you ask?" Kevin said.

"She was sitting here last night until about eleven, when I closed. Nice woman, pleasant. Said she was from Madrid, out here looking at the wine country. As I said, very pleasant."

"She's staying here?"

"Yeah, I put the drinks on her room. Why?"

"It's a police matter. Can you check your computer and see what room?"

"I'll need some ID on that request, sorry."

Kevin extracted his Lafayette police identification card and flashed it past the bartender.

"Good enough?"

"Yeah, we're good."

The man went to his terminal and tapped some numbers on the screen.

"I thought they took all your identification from you when they made you retire?" Sharon said, speaking quietly, but with a big smile on her face.

"A spare—you never know, it might get washed in the laundry or something. No gold shield though, just the paper."

The bartender came back and handed Kevin a printout: *Alicia Gomez, room 612.*

"You are not going to try to do this yourself," Sharon said.

"Absolutely not, she's settled in and could be prepared. I'll call Clive, and then I'll call the FBI. They can take it from here. You and me are going to the ballpark. I've never seen an All-Star Home Run Derby, and since our good friend Toro Rodriquez will be the star, I want front-row seats."

"It's a luxury box."

"Whatever."

Chapter 16

16a

The Home Run Derby is a totally made-for-TV event. Select a special few players known for hitting prodigious home runs, set up a series of at bats where fat pitches are thrown, and count the big flies into the stands. The seats in the bleachers were almost more favored than seats behind the plate. If a fan caught a home run ball, it was theirs.

Sharon and Kevin took their seats in the luxury box, directly above the announcers. TVs hung on the walls, a counter was piled high with ballpark food, and an accommodating bartender filled their glasses.

"It's going to be hard to sit in the cheap seats after this."

For once Sharon couldn't argue; it was great. Eddie Mendez sat in the front row and filled them in on the latest gossip and dirt about the players. A half-hour before the start, Toribio Rodriquez stopped in to say hello and sign autographs. Mendez had a dozen balls ready for the people in the lounge. Toro disappeared as quickly as he'd arrived, and ten minutes later Sharon saw him on the field being interviewed. She turned toward the door, when two large security men walked in, followed by Toro's wife and son.

Sharon stood and quickly walked to them.

"It is so good to see you," she said, in halting Spanish. "I'm so glad you could make it."

Elena put her arms around Sharon and gave her a kiss on the cheek. Carlos, his arm in a sling, stared out into the great space that was the ballpark, mesmerized.

"*Magnifico*," was all he could say.

"How is your arm?" Sharon asked.

"Still sore but good. It is a pleasure to see you again, Ms. O'Mara."

His mother looked at him and nodded her head.

"Thank you, it was something very special you did for our family. Thank you," the boy said.

"It was my honor to help," Sharon answered.

She introduced Elena and Carlos to Kevin, and asked after Toro's mother.

"Angela decided to stay at Toribio's home, I mean our home," Elena answered. "She needed a little peace. The last week has been, how you say, crazy."

"I can agree with that."

The announcer came on over the speakers and began to introduce the players. When Toro's name was announced, the fans went wild. 'TORO, TORO, TORO,' filled the ballpark.

"I didn't realize how much the people loved him," Elena said.

"He's a hero to a lot of people here, especially the kids. He works with the schools here to set up all kinds of after-school sports, and he gives lessons to the students on hitting and fielding," Sharon told her.

"I have missed him," Elena said.

She looked out on the field.

"I wished I could have been with him."

"You are here now. That's what matters."

Sharon turned and looked at Kevin; he had his phone to his ear. He tilted his head to the door at her questioning look.

"Make yourselves comfortable," Sharon said quickly to Elena. "Señor Mendez will tell you what's happening. I will be right back."

She followed Kevin out into the quiet hallway.

"Clive has been coordinating with the FBI. Her room was empty, even her clothes were gone. They had agents at the ballpark entries but didn't spot Vega," Kevin explained. "So either she's not here or is already in the park. There are security guards at the entries to this corridor; they have her picture. The San Francisco police are also watching, but they have their hands full with forty thousand fans. Luck is going to have to play a big part in catching her."

For the next two hours, the fans went nuts over the number and length of home runs hit. Eventually, as the odds makers would have made it, Toribio Rodriquez and the Venezuelan center fielder for the Yankees were the last men standing. Each hit five home runs in a row, then each made the requisite three outs, each a fly ball landing at the base of the center field fence. Eventually, because of exhaustion or sportsmanship, the pair stunned the crowd by shaking hands. A tie was declared.

"Well, I never," Kevin said. "Wow, good job. Only way it could have ended."

"They must be going crazy in Cuba and Venezuela. Weird, don't you think?" Sharon said.

"Yes, very weird."

Kevin had moved to the railing that ran across the open window of the box and was looking down at the crowd.

"Do you see who that is?"

Sharon looked down and saw Jorge Cortez, standing next to some ballplayers. She recognized one of the men, a Cuban defector who played with Miami.

"Old friends?" she asked.

"Yeah, probably. I wonder why the FBI hasn't picked him up. I'm going to go down and talk with him. You coming?"

"Right behind you."

Sharon said good-bye to the Rodriquez family, and she and Kevin took the elevator down to the promenade level and then walked down the steps of the now empty lower box seat section above first base. When they reached the field, Cortez was nowhere in sight. She asked one of the security guards where the man who had been talking with the players had gone.

"Who?" the guard answered.

"Great, now he's disappeared too," Sharon said.

The crowd in the stands had thinned to just a few hundred people dotted around the stadium. Television crews were clearing up their gear and getting ready for the big event the next night.

Cortez had told the Cuban professional players, before they left, that he was proud of them. Now he stood alone, looking up at the expanse of stadium seats. He had to admit, this was one of the nicest ballparks in the world. What a place to play this game he loved so much. He was pleased to have been able to manage a game, a winning game, in this baseball park.

Looking partway down the lower right field stands, his gaze rested on a lone figure sitting in the shadows of the overhanging club level. For a moment, he wasn't sure why the figure had caught his attention. There was a familiarity about her, he was sure it was a woman, but a large hat shaded her face. He continued to stare as she rose to her feet, tilting the hat forward over her face as she stood. As she turned and began climbing the steps, the familiarity continued to grow. There was something about that woman. At the top of the steps, she turned and took off the hat and her sunglasses and looked directly at Jorge Cortez. His heart froze. He felt himself gasping for breath, then as if he suddenly couldn't breathe at all. Then his frozen heart began to race.

Standing at the top of the stairs stood a smiling Marta de la Vega. She slowly raised her right hand and pointed at him, as if holding a gun. She mouthed a single word.

Bang.

Then she disappeared onto the concourse.

The morning walk along the San Francisco waterfront from the Hyatt Regency hotel to the ballpark had taken just twenty minutes. It was the first time Vega had ever been in the City by the Bay. She now understood its attraction. She'd watched small sailboats and powerboats heading toward the cove immediately outside the right field wall of the Giants' home stadium, hoping to find a mooring. Their goal was to be part of the game's atmosphere; there was even a chance to retrieve a home run ball that might land in McCovey Cove. Compared to Cuba, everything was clean, orderly, bright, and rich. Vega felt like a stranger from another planet. The game between Cuba and Taiwan had been mildly interesting. She even felt a little pride when the young man she'd set eyes on in Cuba hit a two run home run to take the lead, a lead the Cuban team never gave up.

She spent much of the morning walking the halls of the stadium, looking for a particular room. She knew they would clear the stadium when the Cuban game was over, and she needed a way to hide until they reopened the gates. The door she sought was conveniently labeled in English and Spanish: SERVICE-SERVICIO. Ducking through the door, she quickly found what she was looking for: bright green employee jackets stacked in orderly rows. She slipped one on, and placed her own jacket and large hat inside a plastic trash bag that she took with her. Returning to the concourse, she bought a Giants' cap at one of the souvenir stands. For the rest of the morning, after the ball game and throughout the afternoon, she carried the bag around the stadium, playing the part of one of the hundreds of custodial staff that busied themselves throughout the park. No one gave her a second glance. When there were enough fans again filling the corridors, she slipped into a bathroom stall and got rid of the green coat and cap. Strolling back onto the concourse, aside from the pistol skillfully secured in the small of her back, Marta de la Vega was now just another fan, wandering among the food and souvenir stands waiting for the Derby to start.

She moved from seat to seat watching the home run contest, never staying more than ten minutes; only once was she asked to show her ticket. She apologized in Spanish and quickly left. The entire time, her eyes never left Jorge Cortez. Only when the Derby ended, did she relax somewhat and take a seat in the stands. It was then that Cortez had spotted her.

Good, she thought. The son of a bitch knew she was here.

Let him stew. The asshole deserved it.

She quickly retraced her steps through the food prome-nade that circled the main level of AT&T Park, keeping a watch on Cortez as she navigated the length of the concourse. She watched him leave the cluster of ballplayers and look about for a way off the infield. He stopped and said something to one of the grounds crew, who were beginning their preparations for the next day. The man pointed to a gate at the far left field cor-ner, where men were entering, carrying rakes and hoses. Cortez walked quickly toward the gate, the same gate his players had walked through almost eight hours earlier. Vega watched it all from above; she saw the open gate, turned, and paralleled Cor-tez. She would catch him there, just as he was leaving. The pistol rubbed her back; it comforted her.

As Vega watched, Cortez reached the opening, just as two people who were not groundskeepers entered through the gate. Vega didn't recognize the tall man or the woman with red hair. When they spoke to Cortez, he stopped, seemed to wave his hands, then turned and began running back toward the in-field. The man and the woman chased after him. Vega watched her quarry cross the left field grass, but at the edge of the re-cently raked infield directly behind second base, he stopped and turned back to the pair behind him. The only footprints in the dirt were his. Cortez reeled, his head rolled backward. He clutched awkwardly at his upper left arm, then his chest. He lurched toward second base, staggered a few steps, then fell to his knees and then onto his face, his body over second base. De la Vega watched in abject fascination, as the redheaded woman waved and seemed to yell for a doctor. The man knelt beside Cortez. When the man rolled him over and began to press heavi-ly on the manager's chest, all Vega could do was smile. It served the son of a bitch right. Cortez would die on the field of the game he loved so much.

Vega watched the scene for some moments more, then calmly walked down the stairway and out into the after-game crowd gathered along the street. The fresh air felt good. When she reached a small park on the San Francisco waterfront, Vega stopped and considered what had happened. Jorge Cortez was no longer an issue. Yes, she would have liked to have put a bullet in the man's brain, but this was cleaner, neater, and with no involvement on her part. Her best and most logical choice now would be to get out of the United States and head to Canada or Mexico. There she could blend in and hide. She had her accounts, her passports, and her contacts there and in Switzerland.

But the woman on the field — Vega stared absently toward the San Francisco–Oakland Bay Bridge, with its digital light show — the red hair nagged at her. Acevedo had said the woman who took the Rodriquez family had been a redhead and good looking. Vega didn't believe in coincidences.

16b

"Damn it all to hell," Sharon said.

Jorge Guadalupe Cortez, manager of the Cuban national baseball team, was dead. All the signs pointed to a heart attack. The paramedics, still on scene after the game, more due to the chance of snagging an autograph than any professional duties, tried for thirty minutes to restore life to Cortez's busted heart but to no avail. It was after eleven o'clock that evening when they rolled Jordy Cortez off the field to the waiting ambulance.

"This close," Kevin said. "How he knew who we were, I can't figure out. But he was scared, scared to death."

"Cute, gallows humor," Sharon said. "But I agree, he wasn't running because of us. Did you see him look up toward the concourse — a couple times while he was headed for the gate. There was someone up there. He was running from someone he feared more than us."

"Marta de la Vega?"

"Probably. He would be the only one to recognize her."

Two men came up out of the Giants dugout and walked to the group standing on the infield grass.

"If those guys aren't FBI, I'll be shocked," Sharon said.

"Kevin Bryan?" the taller of the two asked.

"That's me."

They shook hands around as introductions were made. Agents Hirschfeld and Fong worked out of the FBI's San Francisco office.

Hirschfeld, the tall one, said they'd been on the way to arrest Cortez. The paperwork had been completed; they'd tried his hotel first and learned that he may still be at the ballpark. They were not up to date on Cortez's current location—an ambulance headed to the morgue.

Kevin explained what had happened on the field.

"He was to be extradited to the Netherlands," Fong said. "Seems he is wanted as an accessory to a jewel heist and for two counts of murder.

"This will save you a lot of paperwork," Kevin said.

"Anything about Marta de la Vega?" Sharon asked.

"We have a warrant for her arrest as well. Her picture was e-mailed to us from Hamburg."

"Same as this one?" Bryan said, holding up his phone.

"Yes, how did you get that?" Fong asked.

"I was there when the heist went down. That woman ran the team that did the job."

"Well, the word is out, but we're stretched thin," Hirschfeld replied. "Our hope is that she'll use one of her passports or credit cards. The Hyatt is staked out, of course."

"She may have other aliases," Sharon added.

"Possibly, but we can only go with what we have."

"We think she was here when Cortez had his attack," Sharon said. "Do you think you have a little pull with the SFPD? Maybe there are security tapes of the concourse. We know the time, should be easy."

Easy? Nothing was easy. The Giants' ownership, while upset over the death of the Mr. Cortez, was far more concerned about the All-Star game, less than eighteen hours away. But with a little push from the FBI—especially when the words 'possible international terrorist' and 'extreme security for the game may be required' were thrown in—the management's mood and assistance improved dramatically. The security center of the ballpark held the latest technology; the room rivaled the radio and television broadcast center behind the game announcers on the club level.

The security technician, whom they caught as he was locking up, ran through the digital catalog of the dozens and dozens of cameras that were placed throughout the ballpark.

"All HD," the man said. "Almost as good a quality as HDTV."

"Start on the food concourse level," O'Mara told him. "She's medium height. Most of the fans had left the park by then, so it may be easier to find her."

The tech queued up the files and began running through them, often at four or eight times speed. The time stamps rolled quickly past on a string of numbers racing across the bottom of the image. Twice Kevin asked the tech to stop to check a figure, but then went on.

Coffee was brought in by one of the team's assistants.

"Stop, there, the woman with the large hat," Sharon said, when they'd been at it a while.

Standing in front of the peanut vending wagon on the concourse level was the woman they believed to be de la Vega; she was looking intently down on the field. The camera's angle, high and toward the length of the concourse, showed a portion of the left field as well, where could be seen three people.

"That's us, just as we stopped Cortez," Kevin said to the agents. "That's why he was running, from us and from her as well."

On the screen, the woman with the hat turned and followed Cortez as he disappeared out of the image, blocked by the seats in the stadium. Her profile flashed by for just a moment.

"Marta de la Vega," Sharon said. "It's her."

Vega continued to stand there, unmoving for the next ten minutes.

"She watched him die," Kevin said.

They followed Vega as she walked down the concourse toward the exit.

"That's the stairs to the street. She's gone now," Sharon said. "That was almost two hours ago. She could be anywhere."

"She didn't go to the hotel, and they said she didn't have a car when she checked in," Agent Murray said. "She'd be a fool to go back there."

"I know she has a car. That's the only way she could have come up from LA undetected," Sharon said. "She must have parked it somewhere near the hotel. She would need it to escape from the city."

Kevin said, "We could get lucky, but my guess is she came to take care of Cortez. Now that that's done, she's trying to get out of town."

"She can't take a plane or a train, or even a bus," Hirschfeld added. "The FBI has all her known alias passports in the system, so Marta de la Vega, or Maria Hernandez, or Alicia Gomez won't be taking public transportation."

"She could be an hour to Mexico or Canada by now," Sharon said. "I'm going home, Kev. BART stops running in an hour. If I miss the train, it's an expensive cab ride home."

"I drove, tightwad," Kevin said. "My car's at the garage on Harrison. So don't worry, I always have your back."

"Good luck finding her, and be careful. She is one bitch of a woman," Sharon said, as they left the agents.

Sharon and Kevin walked along the waterfront. Now only a few huddled homeless people, hidden under layers of blankets and cardboard, populated the walkway. The Embarcadero, even this late in the evening, was still busy with traffic. Ahead, lit like the campanile in Venice, stood the Ferry Building and its clock tower, the hands showing 1:45. They crossed over the streetcar tracks to the garage. Five more human-sized bundles of rags and blankets were wedged in along the base of a chain link fence that enclosed a triangle of land full of construction equipment.

Kevin had parked on the fifth level.

"I'll wait while you get the car," Sharon told him.

She held up a cigarette she intended to smoke.

"Take your time," she said. "And don't forget to pay."

She lit up as he headed toward the elevator after paying at the machine. Standing at the exit to the garage, she looked up and down Harrison Street. If it weren't for the homeless, there would be no one on the streets. She took a drag and watched a large container ship pass between the city and Yerba Buena island. *What a strange way to make a living I've chosen. Now Cortez was dead, de la Vega was in the wind, but Toro and his family were finally together. There was that.*

Hearing the low thud of a car thumping over a speed bump on the down ramp, Sharon took one last drag, then snubbed out her cigarette. From where she stood, the approaching headlights momentarily blinded her; she reflexively took a quick step back onto the sidewalk. As she waited, the car pulled through the pay gate and then stopped directly in front of her.

Mildly confused, Sharon bent down and looked into the passenger-side window as it lowered. What car was this that Kevin was driving? The woman driver turned to face Sharon. It took a second for Sharon to realize that she was looking right at Marta de la Vega, and another second to register the automatic pistol Vega held in her right hand.

Kevin took his time climbing into his ancient Mazda. For a man of his size, the car surprisingly fit him—he secured his seatbelt. He wound his way down the garage ramps, pulled up to the exit gate, and stuck his ticket in the machine. The cross arm rose, but another car was directly ahead of him, blocking the last few yards of the exit way. In the light of his headlamps he could see Sharon, bent forward looking into the passenger-side window of the vehicle. Then driver's side door opened, and a woman stepped out. The pistol in her hand flashed unmistakably in Kevin's headlights, as the woman raised it and pointed it at Sharon.

Sharon looked at Kevin. The woman also turned toward the

Mazda, blinking into the headlights. Kevin pushed hard on the hub of the steering wheel; the car's horn blared loud and sharply into the night. Sharon dived to the ground, as Vega swung and fired the pistol at the Mazda.

As the muzzle flashed, Kevin floored the accelerator and tried to smash into the rear of the car but only caught its left corner. But it was enough force to push the car out through the passageway and onto the sidewalk.

Vega fired again. The bullet punched a clean hole through the windshield, passing a scant three inches from Kevin's right ear. Still blinded by his headlights, Vega continued firing wildly toward Kevin's car. He bent over, pulled out the ignition key, and fumbled with the lock on the glove box as yet another bullet tore through the interior. Finally the small door dropped open, and he reached for his Glock. More bullets ripped through the car and out through the plastic rear window. Kevin felt a sting in his left shoulder, like he'd been stung by a giant bee.

"Fuck," was all he could say. Even with his gun, how the hell was he going to shoot? He'd have to sit upright, making a perfect target.

More shots, one after another, rang out in the cavernous garage. They echoed above and behind him. But none hit the car. He took a chance and sat up, swinging the pistol upward. But no one was standing next to the car. Instead, on the ground two figures rolled and punched each other like it was an Ultimate Fighting Championship battle to the death.

Sharon had gone in low and knocked the gun out of Vega's hand, even as it fired its rounds into the ceiling of the garage. It flared for a second in Bryan's headlights before sliding under the car. Sharon jumped quickly back to her feet. Vega swung out her leg and kicked hard at Sharon's upper thigh. O'Mara stumbled, but quickly recovered, and responded with a kick herself that brought Vega within the range of her fists. She lashed out with hard punches to both Vega's arms, as the other threw them up to protect her face; she then lowered her target to Vega's belly and groin. Vega responded with a vicious right that raked Sharon's jaw. Sharon backed away momentarily but came back with a left that clipped Vega's angular cheek, splitting the skin. The intense exchanging of blows traveled with the fighters out of the garage and into the street.

Kevin pushed open his car door and rolled out onto the concrete paving. In a second, he was up and running toward his friend and Vega. They were standing in the street, warily eying each other, breathing heavily in the beams of light thrown by Vega's rental car. Both were bloodied from the fight.

Marta slid her hand into her pocket and extracted a knife; a small gift from the man who'd sold her the pistol. She snapped the knife open and then quickly moved to her left, swinging the tip of the blade toward Sharon in a large arc; she missed. Vega lunged again, screaming something in Spanish.

Another explosion ripped through the air. Vega stopped mid-lunge and spun toward Kevin. She stumbled, looking surprised in the glow of the headlights as the knife fell from her hand and clattered to the street. She put one hand to her chest; her white blouse was turning red. She faltered for another second, then collapsed in the street.

His pistol in this hand, Kevin's eyes never left Vega, even when Sharon kicked away the knife.

"You okay?" he said.

"Yes, fine. She punched like a girl—I could have taken her."

"Maybe, but she would have cut you like a man."

The flurry of gunshots had alerted the police, and sirens could be heard approaching through the narrow alleys between the high-rises that filled the blocks of lower San Francisco.

Kevin found a couple bottles of water and some napkins in the truck of his car. He opened one of the bottles and handed it to Sharon. He used the other to soak the napkins, then wiped the blood from Sharon's split lip and dabbed at the scrapes on her cheek and forehead.

They stood under the lights of the garage as they waited for the cavalry.

"Going to be black and blue tomorrow," Kevin offered.

"Better than being dead today. Thanks, again. You know, we really need to stop doing this."

"What? My saving you . . . again?"

"Yeah, that. Thanks."

"What is this, the fifth time? Means you only have four lives left."

"Who's counting?"

16c

For the next two weeks, a seemingly endless parade of Homeland Security investigators, FBI agents, and even Interpol officers flown in from Europe questioned everyone involved. They focused on Sharon and Kevin, and even the military kicked in with a few follow-up questions about Guantanamo. It turned into a feeding frenzy. From London, reports were leaked about Vega's connections to gunrunning. From Cuba to Africa, she was becoming one very important international criminal. Marta de la Vega was also very lucky; Kevin's bullet had pierced her right lung and not killed her. The damage was severe, and she was touch-and-go for more than a week, secured in a guarded room in the county hospital. The paperwork had already begun for her extradition to the Netherlands, where she was accused of the same crimes for which Cortez had been wanted. Two deaths during the commission of a felony was more than enough to send her away for a long time. One newscaster joked that by the time Vega got out of prison, there might finally be a regime change in Cuba. The Cuban government denied any involvement or knowledge of Vega's misdeed; they were most probably telling the truth, but that would be hard to verify. Nothing was said in the Cuban news about Acevedo.

By mid-August, the baseball season was heading toward the make-or-break-it month of September, when careers would be made or lost. The Giants were still one game up on the Los Angeles Dodgers and three up on the Colorado Rockies. Since the All-Star break, Toribio Rodriquez had found another gear and was heading toward setting many new Giants' season records for home runs, steals, and runs batted in. His average had dropped but still was a respectable .328. Only one man, another Cuban defector, was ahead of him in hitting average and that was by a slim seven-hundredths of a point.

The demands placed on Sharon and Kevin by the FBI and other officials had prevented their attending the All-Star game that had been allowed to proceed on the day after Cortez's death and Vega's shooting. Now, two months later, Sharon and Kevin sat comfortably in the same luxury box they'd shared during the Home Run Derby, albeit still miffed over missing the earlier celebrity game. To their right sat Elena and Carlos Rodriquez; this time Toro's mother had come along too. Eddie Mendez was there as well, pointing out to Carlos the Bay Bridge and the big ships he could see from where he sat. And standing in the rear of the box was Clive Barrington, in town to assist in the extradition of Marta de la Vega.

Barrington swirled a glass of single malt scotch in his glass and walked down the steps to where Sharon and Kevin sat.

Clive said, as he settled into a seat directly behind the two, "Thanks again for picking me up at the airport. I didn't think the first thing I'd be doing in San Francisco would be attending a baseball match."

"It's called a game, a baseball game," Sharon said.

"See, that's the difference. We have matches, you Yanks play games. It makes a big deal when it comes to perception."

"Yes, and we don't call it a pitch, whatever that is," Kevin added. "It's the ball field, and there are three bases and a home plate, not two where you run back and forth, back and forth—doesn't it get hard to keep count? And why do they have to carry the bat with them? And what are those little pegs set on top of the posts?"

"They're called wickets."

"My point exactly, and they call the fella who's pitching a bowler?"

"Yes, he throws it to the batsman."

"I like batter better."

"You would."

"And the whole team gets to bat."

"Only ten players of the eleven, unless they decide to play a specified number of overs—"

"That's enough from you two. Stop it," Sharon admonished. "We are here to watch the game, not discuss the merits or faults of cricket and baseball, got it?"

"She always this bossy?" Clive said, nodding his head toward Sharon.

"Actually, worse sometimes."

Kevin gestured toward the bar.

"Refill?"

He and Clive stood near the bartender and watched the game below. The Giants were up 3–1 in the fifth.

Carlos came up to ask the bartender for a Coke.

"You okay?" Kevin asked.

"Yes, but your Spanish is terrible," Carlos said.

"And your English isn't too hot, either. How's school?"

"Excellent, but the teachers are a little too easy. My teachers in Cuba were tough."

"Then you can study harder. It's a lot to take in over such a short time."

"I never thought I would ever see my father again, but every day that he is home, we do things together. I didn't realize how big a hero he is to many Latinos and Cubans until I went to school. It's nice to be Toribio's son."

"Don't let to go to your head," Kevin said.

"We talk about it all the time. How to act, what to say, how to avoid trouble."

"How is your grandmother taking the change from Cuba?"

Carlos thought for a moment.

"It is hard to tell. She was always very quiet, and never talked to the men who watched us. She would hum little songs and talk about Father like he was just away for a few weeks. When he is home, they spend hours together talking about Grandfather and the country before Castro. My grandfather disappeared many years ago; it was when my father was very young. Grandmother raised him by herself. It was she who told him to go to America and play ball, because it would allow him to do many things he couldn't if he stayed in Cuba. I see that now. I was very mad at him for many years. Now things are changing."

"That's good, Carlos," Eddie Mendez said, as he walked up to the bar and pointed at a beer. "He needs you and your mother. He missed you very much."

"I am beginning to see that, but I'm not like mother, who instantly forgave him."

"Mothers and wives can do that. Sons have other things going on with their fathers," Mendez said. "You will, in time, work it out. I am sure of that."

A thunderous roar came from the crowd. Carlos turned and watched as his father, Toribio Rodriquez, crossed third base and completed the last ninety feet of his forty-second home run of the year. As he crossed the plate, he looked up at the box and pointed to his mother and then to his son.

Yes, it would be an excellent season of baseball.

The End

A Note from the Author
The Flyer

I have tried to pare these stories into a manageable length that you can read in less than eight hours. At about 60–75,000 words, the idea is that you can read about half the book on a four-hour flight and the rest on the way home. I call them *Flyers*. But if you aren't flying, settle back, pour a good drink, and enjoy.

Gregory C. Randall was born in Traverse City, Michigan. He grew up in Chicago. Greg has never forgotten his roots. Mr. Randall makes his home in California.

Mr. Randall is the author of fiction and nonfiction works available through Amazon.com.

For more information about the other Sharon O'Mara Chronicles, and planned sequels, please visit and connect with Greg online:

www.gregorycrandall.info

See his blogs:
http://www.writing4death.blogspot.com

Other books by Mr. Randall:
Fiction
The Cherry Pickers

The Sharon O'Mara Chronicles
Land Swap For Death
Containers For Death
Toulouse For Death
12th Man For Death

Diamonds For Death
Limerick For Death

The Alex Polonia Thrillers
Venice Black
Saigon Red
St. Petersburg White

The Tony Alfano Thrillers
Chicago Swing
Chicago Jazz
Chicago Fix
Chicago Boogie Woogie

Max Adler OSS WWII
This Face of Evil
Pawns in an Ancient Game

Science Fiction and Slipstream
Sector 73
Seven Hours to Barstow

Nonfiction
America's Original GI Town, Park Forest, Illinois

Additional copies can be purchased through Amazon.coms.